# BLOOD

## SO

# BLACK

DARKEST HEART: BOOK 1

# BLOOD SO BLACK

# G. N. SOLOMON

Copyright © 2021 Gwyneth Solomon
All rights reserved.

eBook ISBN: 978-1-7377717-0-8
Paperback ISBN: 978-1-7377717-1-5

*Moon Tower Publishing*

To the people I love (and cannot stand) most in the world—
My family.

Thank you.

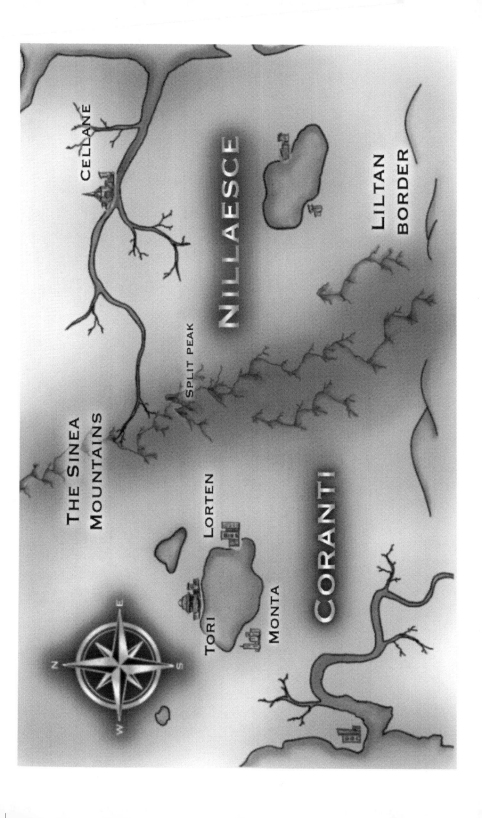

# PART ONE:

## THE MAGICIAN

# I

*"Soul so silver and blood so black,*

*Two dead witches lying in a stack.*

*His mind so twisted and his heart so dark,*

*Killing witches is a walk in the park."*

—*Modification of an old Corantian children's rhyme, adapted to fit the recent resurgence in Darkheart killings. The number of dead witches in the second line increases each time the rhyme is repeated.*

op hat securely on my head, a few tricks up my sleeves, and bitterness in my heart, I was ready for a day of work. It was a gorgeous afternoon, sunny and bright, and just a little too hot for the cusp of fall in central Coranti. Little beads of sweat slipped down my forehead from beneath the uncomfortable and utterly absurd top hat, and I fidgeted with the rough cloth of the cheap costume magician's jacket, trying to bite back the grimace lurking in the corners of my mouth.

Today was not a good day.

Swallowing my pride, I pulled the hat from my head, now damp with sweat, and waved it with abandon at any passersby on the crowded city street who showed the slightest inkling of interest.

"Magic trick? Just a coin, ma'am, sir, for the greatest show of your life!"

The coins I'd sewn in the lining of the hat rattled as it shook, the two Coran clinking sadly.

A young boy, dressed in a tank top and shorts far more appropriate for the current weather than my itchy "uniform," stopped in front of me, staring at the hat. He fidgeted in his pockets for a coin as a woman tugged on his arm.

"Hector, come on," she said, barely sparing me a passing glance. Honestly, just plain insulting. I wasn't wearing a black polyester jacket with shiny "gold" buttons and an egregiously tall hat only to be ignored, that was for certain.

The boy pulled a single Coran from his pocket, grinning triumphantly at the gleaming coin. "I'm gonna see a magic trick."

The woman—his mother, I assumed—rolled her eyes. "We don't have time for this, hun."

Hector shrugged, tossing the coin at my hat as his mother pulled him off into the crowd. He missed the hat completely, sending the coin clinking away on the asphalt. Being the desperate fool I was, I skittered after it, plucking it up and tucking it in my hat.

I could only imagine the state I'd be in if I relied on only such measly, legal methods of income. It was no wonder I was just about the only street magician in Monta. Of course, the slim earnings weren't the only deterrent, in a time where, despite the new queen's best efforts, magic was borderline taboo. Minnie may hate my pickpocketing tendencies, but she needed to face that it was, frankly, the only thing keeping me fed.

My next patrons were a gaggle of teenage girls, probably a couple of years younger than me. They waited, cell phones in hand, ready to record my show.

"Do you take bank credit?"

I blinked, at first thinking she was accusing me of stealing. After a few seconds, however, I noticed the thin plastic card in her hand and I realized she was trying to *pay* me. With bank credit.

These girls had credit cards? That meant money. They probably had something worth stealing on them…

There. A gleaming bracelet on the girl's wrist, the one trying to pay a street magician with a credit card. That would do nicely.

"No, I don't. I'll take Coran bills or a bank check, though."

The girls started to turn away, disappointed, and I stepped forward. "Wait!"

They blinked at me, and I forced a smile, trying not to show how much I wanted to take that bracelet and pawn it off.

"For you lovely young ladies, I'll do a trick for free!"

I pulled my deck of cards from one of my pants pockets—not the nice ones from my father, those were safely hidden away in my duffel bag. These were my work cards.

I splayed them out expertly and offered them to the girl with the bracelet. "Pick a card, any card."

She deliberated for a second, examining the deck, before gingerly plucking out a card from near the middle. She showed it to her friends, who all craned their necks to get a look, obviously familiar with the basic premise of most simple card tricks.

This was nothing special—a classic. She inserted her card back into the deck, and I shuffled the cards several times, all the while subtly keeping my finger on the card she'd chosen.

"Are you sure you remember which card you chose?" They nodded. "Really, really, sure?"

Making sure the chosen card was on top, I held the deck out before me as if pondering. Then, I slid the four top cards to my left hand, counting them out loud. But with the third card, I slid two in its place, resulting in five cards sitting in my hand where they saw four. The first card, the card they'd chosen, I slid up my sleeve under the guise of shifting the cards. They were watching me like hawks. I transferred the stack of four to my left hand, sticking the rest of the deck back in my pocket.

"This isn't your card." I flipped over the top card in my little stack of four. The two of spades. They shook their heads, and I palmed the card in my left hand, sliding the sleeved card underneath it as I reached to flip another card.

The witch of knives, the three of songs, and the knight of flame all got added to the stack in my left hand in a similar procession.

"That's all four." Bracelet girl had been counting. "You're a horrible magician."

"Four, you say? Don't you mean"—I fanned the mini-deck out, revealing the five cards—"five?"

Two of the cronies gasped. I smirked.

I flipped over the new top card, the knight of songs, presenting it to my audience. "This wouldn't happen to be your card, would it?"

The girls all confirmed with each other, some awed and a few frowning, trying to figure out the simple trick.

At that moment, I fell over, spilling cards all over the pavement. This was precisely the reason I didn't bring my nice deck to work. My tumble tripped the credit card girl, and she fell with me, my arm gripping her wrist for "support" as my fingers deftly popped open the latch of her bracelet.

I stayed on the ground, gathering my scattered cards, as the girl's friends righted her and they stalked off. I slipped the cards back into the pocket with the rest of the deck, the bracelet neatly tucked in a secure pocket on my pants, near my calf.

Grinning like the Devil herself, I stood and gathered my hat. I slipped through back alleys, walking for several minutes to distance myself from the scene of the crime before setting up shop again on the next busy street. At least there wasn't much competition—in terms of street magicians, that was. Even after eight years of witch-run government, there was a tension in the air where magic was involved—even just the kind executed with fancy tricks and sleights of hand. And for good reason—riots were becoming more and more common these days. Wouldn't that be ironic, if a revolution supporting the old government rose up to tear down the government established by the last group of revolutionaries?

The next hour earned me some nasty looks, a single Coran, and a gum wrapper. No, wait, on a second inspection, that wasn't a Coran at all, but a very melted chocolate coin.

Goodie.

The plastic coin I was pretending to levitate swayed in a gentle breeze, perhaps signaling a cool night to come. It was a cheap trick— just a plastic trinket and some fishing line—so you could imagine my surprise at the reaction it got.

"Dirty witch!"

I blinked at the sweaty, red-eared buffoon looming before me. In a country quite literally run by witches, you would think there wouldn't be many dunces stupid enough to so vehemently oppose witchcraft. And yet, the evidence was right before me, jamming an accusatory finger in my face. Intriguing, truly. A few passersby on the busy street had stopped to stare at the commotion, a few choice individuals of which seemed to even *agree* with this moron.

I stepped carefully away from the oaf, daring a glance at his shirt pocket, which bulged with a wallet he wasn't so much as attempting to hide.

"Not a witch," I answered sweetly, wearing my most antagonizing smile.

"You're a girl doin' magic. Sounds like a witch to me."

"Not magic," I corrected him again.

I slid away from the sweaty lump of a man, holding my "magic" before me. I twanged the fishing line with my fingers, confirming the utter lack of anything supernatural happening here. Whoever said a magician never revealed her secrets clearly had never been faced with a brewing mob who thought they were centuries in the past. Well, a decade in the past, at the very least. Still, they looked just about ready to burn me at the stake.

"You and your demon magic needa get the hell out of my country, you foul, vile—"

I cut him off before he could think of any more one-syllable insults. It was just embarrassing. For him, of course.

"That's not how real magic works, my good friend," I said, grinning patronizingly up at him. He was the type of person still stuck in a democracy—still utterly unadjusted to life since the revolution. These days, you couldn't just bellow your crude hatred into the void to have it validated as a "political opinion."

"It's magic, plain and simple," he snarled. "You're a filthy witch, corrupted with evil black magic. The science confirms as much."

The science confirmed no such thing.

I was starting to get angry. "If you hate witches so much, why don't you go to Nillaesce? Join an anti-*nornei* riot?"

"I'm no Nillaesce pig! I'm Corantian, through and through. And this was our country before you witches, *nornei*, whatever you call yourselves, took over."

I frowned, adopting a look of mock pensiveness. "You know, I think they prefer the term *supernaturally gifted* these days." I didn't have time to argue politics—or basic common sense, for that matter—with this fool. The crowd was getting restless, and I made the stunningly brilliant deduction that it was, in fact, time to get myself out of here.

My fun, sunshine-and-rainbows new friend was far beyond reason. He lunged for me, and I regretted nothing as I used the opportunity to slip his wallet from his shirt pocket before I made my escape.

The queen's forces were stretched so tight with the war, they'd hardly send anyone to stop a harmless little mob outside the capital anymore. But more and more unrest had been blossoming throughout the country since the revolution, and between the war outside and the riots at home, the government seemed just about ready to fall apart.

Which, really, was too bad for them. I had other problems.

I dodged a mass of flailing arms, barely avoiding a slosh of beer as someone lost control of their bottle. I tore the tell-tale black hat from my head, flattening it into a disk as I stashed the wallet in my pants pocket with the bracelet.

I barely made it to an alley, but from there I could cut across more roads until I was several blocks away. Only then did I stop to breathe, and realized it was probably time to take off this ridiculous jacket too.

I fumbled for far too long with the cheap plastic buttons before remembering they were fake, and the cursed costume was fastened with little plastic clasps. With a snarl, I ripped off the jacket and wadded it up in my left fist with the hat, relaxing against the rough bricks and enjoying the wisp of an afternoon breeze on my bare arms. Beneath the jacket, I wore my favorite shirt—black, sleeveless, and high collared. I owned about five shirts exactly like this. Minnie mocked me about it incessantly, but you couldn't go wrong with a classic, right?

"Bad time?" I nearly jumped out of my skin at the voice. Still near the heart of the city, it was loud even in a derelict side alley, and I hadn't heard her approach.

I straightened as she moved closer, feeling defensive. She looked... dangerous. Taller than me by a good several inches, very muscular, and definitely at least a decade my senior, she wore a full military uniform despite the warm air, complete with shiny medals galore. Over her heart, a white patch read *Akins*. A visit from a member of the military right after having taken possession of a few things that may or may not legally belong to me? That sure boded well.

"Miss Akins, what can I do for you today?" I bowed my head to her deferentially, trying oh-so-hard to keep my natural tendencies towards all things sarcastic and charmingly witty at bay.

"It's Captain Mila Akins, Supernatural Ground Division of the New Coranti Army," she corrected, looking down her nose at me. Or maybe she was just looking at me. I wasn't short, not really, especially not compared to Minnie, but this lady must've been nearly six feet tall. Her nose was all crooked, and it made me uncomfortable just looking at it. I couldn't help but wonder how many times she had broken that.

"Captain Akins, how may I be of service?" I said, as docile as was possibly possible for me.

She looked me over, eyes lingering on the black cloth in my hand. "I don't suppose you have supernatural gifts?"

"No, ma'am." Lying to authority figures was always a fun way to go. Luckily for me, she didn't seem to be carrying any sort of blood test.

"Hmph. Well, that's not the kind of magic I'm interested in at the moment."

I raised my eyebrows. "Ma'am?"

Akins nodded at my bunched-up costume and hat. "You don't see a lot of people doing magic tricks and such these days, but you do that sort of thing, right?"

I nodded, unease still curling in my stomach.

"Wonderful." She pulled a ripped piece of lined paper and a pen from her pocket and began scribbling furiously. "I'm hosting a party, a real classy shindig, all sorts of top-notch military folks are going to be there." She handed me the paper, upon which was scrawled an address, a date, and the name Captain Mila Akins. "You're hired."

I stared at the paper dumbly. "Excuse me?"

"Two-hundred Coran to work the event, do tricks, the like, but you can probably get a good amount more from tips. Like I said, it's a real fancy party. Lots of rich and powerful witches."

"I—alright." I took the paper. "Ma'am."

She turned on her very shiny black boot heels, apparently done with the conversation, before hesitating and rounding on me again. "Oh, and get a nicer costume, would you? That piece of junk looks like a five-year-old's dress-up outfit."

And she was gone.

# 2

*"Magic is a dangerous and vile poison, which complicates even the most simple extermination of a* nornei. *When one of their kind is killed, their magic seeps back out into the earth, all the way down to the dwellings of the Devil, who redistributes it to more* nornei, *and even curses that which slew the* nornei *with a morsel of this cursed poison. And it is here any just and holy soul must tread carefully, for to simply kill a* nornei *will taint your blood in the most dark and twisted way. The only ways to truly erase a* nornei's *unholy magic from this earth are to drown her in holy water, pierce her heart with a blessed blade, or burn her alive."*

—*A Study in the Modern Science of the* Nornei, *second edition, written by Sir Edrecio Motarn and published by the order of the Leitoi.*

I had to knock three times before Minnie opened the window, all the while perched uncomfortably on the tree I'd used to climb to the second floor. The branch bobbed ominously beneath my weight in a way that made me doubt whether this was still an entirely safe method of entry.

I was grateful when Minnie finally unlatched the window and helped me clamber inside. The room wasn't too small, with space for three bunk beds and a shared dresser. Dusting my hands off on my pants, I went to toss my costume on what used to be my bunk before seeing the neatly folded sheets. Right. That was someone else's bed now.

"Welcome back, Isla. It's been weird not seeing you for so long at a time," Minnie said somewhat sarcastically, though her usual bite was gone from the words.

I smiled, but there was no happiness behind it. "I've missed you too, Minnie."

"Ugh, this place is so boring without you."

"Then leave." I knew as soon as the words left my lips that it was the wrong thing to say, especially now. That wound still hadn't quite recovered after two weeks, though she seemed to understand why I left.

"Maybe I will."

That took me by surprise. She'd never told me about considering leaving before. It had never seemed like an option for her. I smiled.

Eight years of memories flitted across my eyes like half my life through time-lapse. Minnie teaching me the ropes, Minnie standing up for me, Minnie and I whispering late into the night when everyone else had fallen asleep.

Plopping down on Minnie's bed, I looked around the familiar space. The cot in the corner was new. I raised my eyebrows at Minnie.

"Seven girls? We never had more than five in this room when I was here."

Minnie rubbed the spot between her eyes, squinting at the ceiling. "Yeah. New wave of war orphans." She collapsed onto the bed beside me, eyes closed momentarily and her arm flopping onto the pillow beside her.

"And yet, you mock me for avoiding the war?" It was supposed to be a joke, but at the same time, it wasn't.

"I don't mock you. I just..." Minnie sighed. "You have power, you know? You might actually be able to do something, to change something—"

"Power's no good if I don't know how to use it."

"Then learn, you bleep!"

"So I can be shipped off to the front lines and get shot from a distance because I have no fighting skills whatsoever and magic only works close-range? No thanks, I'd rather live." I turned my lip up in a snarl, noticing but choosing to ignore that I was taking out all my recent frustrations on some petty argument. "And honestly, Minnie, if you're going to curse, would you please just say the Omili-forsaken word? The whole 'bleep' thing is driving me out of my mind."

We stewed in the tense silence of friends who'd spent years rehearsing the same sad argument, letting it boil down to the barest bones until, frankly, there wasn't much left to say.

After only a few moments, Minnie bolted upright, turning so she could drag me from my seat. "I didn't sneak you back in here to argue, dummy. Go take your shower. You stink."

"Right, right, I'm going."

I'd technically left the orphanage two weeks ago, but Minnie and I had arranged a system to sneak me back in to shower every now and then. I wouldn't have moved out for another two years, until the orphanage kicked me out, if it weren't for the draft.

Minnie had cleared both the room and the hallway outside of nosy children, and we made our way to the communal girls' bathroom without incident.

Minnie hesitated at the door. "Oh—I hope you brought your own conditioner."

"You've got to be kidding me, Minnie. I'm practically homeless."

Her eyes lit up. "Practically? Does that mean you found a place?"

"We have *so* much we need to catch up on. I'll fill you in later." My smile fell. "What happened to the conditioner?"

"Bryson and Tom used it all, the little bleeps."

I gaped. "What in Omili's name were Byson and Tom doing in our shower?"

"Oh, right, you probably didn't hear about that. The boys' shower broke yesterday, so they've been using ours."

"And of course they already managed to use all our conditioner." I groaned. "You know, I really wouldn't have pegged the two of them to be the ones most invested in coiffure."

Minnie giggled. "Tom's hair always does seem to be in a perpetual state of disarray, doesn't it?"

"Yep." I ran a hand through my ponytail, greasy and knotted, and sighed. "Guess I'll have to go without conditioner this time."

After a brief shower, luxurious all the same, I changed into a fresh pair of cargo pants and a shirt almost identical to the one I'd worn before. I retrieved the bracelet and wallet from my old pants and replaced them safely in a pocket. I'd have to visit a pawn shop at some point for the bracelet and check through the wallet for valuables. Tomorrow.

In the same pocket as my stolen goods was the torn piece of notebook paper. I'd almost completely forgotten about my run-in with Captain Mila Akins. I didn't recognize the street on the address, but I figured it was somewhere nice. The date was five days from today, the time twenty-one hundred hours. Sighing, I folded the paper and tucked it in my duffel bag for safekeeping.

Hefting the bag onto my shoulder, I left the girl's bathroom. I'd left all of my stuff here, in this bag, tucked beneath Minnie's bed. Five black sleeveless shirts, all pretty much identical, a navy jacket for when it got colder, which at this rate it never would, some leggings and some cargo pants. My cards were in there too, the deck from my father, all inky black and gorgeous, wrapped up in a little black bag, and a little wallet crammed with bills and coins, all the Coran to my name.

"You think I can get away with using the home's laundry machine? I don't feel like splurging on a laundromat and I've already worn everything I own like three times." I wrinkled my nose. "My duffel bag is starting to get a bit gross."

Minnie snorted half-heartedly, fiddling with her necklace. She did that when she was worried. I went to sit beside her on her bed, hands folded in my lap. My question about the laundry machine hadn't been rhetorical—I really did want to know her thoughts on the plausibility of such an endeavor—but even I knew when to shut up.

"What's up, Minnie?"

She stared off into space, her eyes like a black abyss. Since I was on her right, I couldn't really take her hand without draping mine awkwardly across her, so I rested my hand on her right shoulder instead, just above her stump.

"I…" With a sigh, Minnie released the pendant of her necklace and straightened the chain, making sure the clasp was resting on the back of her neck. She forced a laugh. "So, spill!"

"What?" I was taken aback by the sudden cheeriness, but she clearly didn't want to talk about it.

"You found a place?"

Right, that. "Um, pretty much." A wry smile tugged at my lips. "It's a funny story, actually. So, the other day I was poking around some warehouse-type buildings about a mile away, near the water, hoping one of them would be, I don't know, abandoned, and I could squat there."

"That's illegal!" Minnie said, though of course she didn't sound surprised.

I laughed. "Are you kidding me? Pickpocketing and avoiding conscription, much?"

"Right, right," she grumbled jovially.

"But don't worry. It worked out being perfectly legal. Well, kinda."

"Kinda?"

"Just shut it and let me finish the story, all right?"

"Fine."

"So, I'm poking around these buildings, right? And they're all locked up and stuff, and I'm thinking about giving up, but then I stumble across an unlocked back door with a big 'Do Not Enter' sign taped up."

"You totally went inside, didn't you?"

"Seriously, with the interruptions?"

"Sorry, go on."

"Yeah, of course I went in. And you'll never guess what I found inside." Minnie looked about ready to guess anyway, but I cut her off, just about laughing at this point. "An old, fat guy running a drug den!"

"Wait, what does this have to do with you finding a place to stay?"

"Hush, I'm getting there. So I tell this guy, 'hey, I could totally report you to authorities right now but guess what, you can buy my silence!' Thankfully, he doesn't call my bluff, because obviously no way am I reporting anything to the authorities, and he asks me to name my price. I say that I won't say a peep as long as he lets me stay in a little side room of the warehouse, and he agrees!"

"Yay?" She frowned. "I don't know, Isla. You're telling me that you're essentially living surrounded by illegal narcotics and dangerous criminals? That doesn't seem too safe."

"Safer than dying a bloody death on a battlefield. Don't worry, he just stores the drugs there, and per our conditions, he won't tell anybody I'm living there. Really, it's perfect. No paperwork, no payment, a place to stay indefinitely where I'm not legally registered but am not constantly in fear because the person who owns the place actually knows I'm there. I mean, it's only six feet by ten feet and is pretty much just one giant puddle, but the door locks and I think once I figure out how to fix the leaky pipe, maybe get a rug in there, it'll be pretty homey!"

"That's great. I'm happy for you, I really am. It's just—" Minnie paused, something new apparently occurring to her.

"What?"

"What happens if the den gets raided?"

That sobered me up real quick. "Well, then I'm screwed. But it's fine, I only found it by accident, and I made sure to tell Big U to keep the back door locked from now on." I pulled my new "house" key from one of my pockets and jiggled it in front of her.

"Big U?"

I rolled my eyes. "That's my new landlord."

"The bleeping drug dealer?"

"The very same."

"Dare I ask about the name?"

"His name is Ulysses, but apparently that wasn't 'gangsta' enough. He's a big softy, I swear."

That made Minnie laugh, and I smiled.

"So, how's school?" I asked, more to be polite than out of actual interest. I hated school. We never learned anything important; it was just busywork, war propaganda, and stupid teachers. With the truant officer being the moron he was, I used to skip more often than not, and I'd stopped going altogether when I left the orphanage. Still, school was the only topic of small talk I could think of. Mentioning the weather was just trite, whereas bringing up something like the recent riots would only launch Minnie into a political rampage.

"Alright. We have mid-season exams coming up, so that's fun."

"Ew, exams."

"My thoughts exactly."

I stood, pushing my dropped duffel bag under the bed with my foot. "Where's our nail polish stash these days?"

Minnie stood too, way more gracefully than I could ever hope for, even with two arms. Her balance amazed me every time.

"Same place."

I nodded, clambering onto my old bed, the bunk above Minnie's. I pushed aside the ceiling tiles, coughing in the dust that followed. My groping fingers tapped against a plastic bin, which I gingerly pulled out, taking Minnie's chocolate stash with it. She gave me a sheepish look and I tossed the plastic bag at her head. I left the ceiling tile resting on the bed, reminding myself to clean off the poor girl's bunk when I replaced it.

Sitting cross-legged on the floor, I examined the selection. The six little bottles were all different brands and shapes. Three different shades of light green (Minnie's favorite color), one navy blue (my favorite color), plain black, and blood-red, from a phase we went through a couple of years ago.

"We're low on remover," I remarked, shaking the clear bottle.

"And Minty Fresh."

"A true shame. Was that the one you wanted?"

Minnie extended her hand, the green paint on her fingernails chipped in places and completely gone in others. "That's what I'm wearing now."

"Alright." I pulled out the polish remover and a couple of cotton pads. "Want me to take it off?"

She shook her head. Her opinion on letting me paint her nails changed by the day. Minnie was a proud, confident person, something I greatly admired, and she didn't like having to rely on other people to do things for her.

She ripped off her socks and wiggled her toes at me as I scrunched my face up in disgust. "I think I'll just paint my toenails." She pondered the colors before her. "What do you think, Ageless Sage or Limeade?"

"The lime one is so bright I think you can see it from space, so—"

15

"Limeade it is." Minnie reached for the bottle, then hesitated with her hand hovering over the paints. "Actually, I'm feeling bold today. I think I'll go with Cherry Kiss."

"What?"

"The red one." She nodded to the red nail polish and the color name on the lid. Cherry Kiss.

I passed it to her. "Knock yourself out." I hesitated, seeing how her long curls kept falling in her face and getting dangerously close to her toes when she was hunched over like this. I knew she had trouble tying back her hair herself with one arm, and that she hated to ask. "Want me to pull your hair back for you?"

"Sure," she said off-handedly like the thought hadn't even occurred to her, though it undoubtedly had.

I'd completely forgotten about my hair, still damp from the shower, and cursed. It was probably super frizzy and gross by now. I stood, grabbing Minnie's brush from the dresser and using it to brush out my hair in front of the mirror. I always wore an extra hairband on my wrist, and since I'd used one for Minnie, I used the other to painstakingly pull my hair into a high ponytail, using the brush to straighten any lumps as I went. When I was finished, I pulled the front two strands from the tail so they framed my face in light brown. Minnie mocked me for dressing like a cartoon character with pretty much the same clothes and hair every day, but really, it was a lot simpler than changing it up all the time.

I returned to sit by Minnie, pulling the black polish from the bin and painting my bare fingernails. Minnie had already finished her first coat and was just sitting there, letting her toes dry.

"I might be able to grab some nail polish remover from the drugstore tomorrow," I said.

"I thought you were saving up for a sleeping bag."

"That's not as big a deal now that I have a place to sleep. A blanket will do." I paused, trying to remember what I was going to say. "Oh! I got a job!"

Minnie raised her eyebrows, smiling. "Really? Like, a real, legal job?"

"I mean, not a steady source of work or anything, but I got hired to do magic tricks at some fancy military gala in a couple of days."

"That's great, Isla!" She was beaming ear to ear.

"But I need a new magician costume by then. Something snazzy-looking that didn't cost me ten Coran at a discount party store."

"Sounds possible."

"Yeah, I can use that money I was saving for a sleeping bag, plus I got a pretty good haul today, so that will go towards it too."

Her expression soured, and I groaned inwardly. We'd had this argument a thousand times. "Any chance your 'haul' today was as legitimate as your job?"

"Yes, Minnie, the single Coran I made from doing party tricks today was a real jackpot."

"I really think—"

"I know what you think!" I didn't mean to explode at her, but I was bone-tired of this. "I know you think I'm horrible, and dirty, and a no-good scum-bag. But guess what I think? I think that I'm good at this, I think this is the only thing keeping me afloat, I think the spoiled little princess whose bracelet I stole didn't even need it anyway, and—"

"What if it was the last thing her parents gave her before they died?" Minnie said coldly, lips pressed into a thin line.

"I don't care! If I saw you walking down the street and I had the chance to steal that precious necklace of yours, I'd steal it too! It's just stuff!"

"Is that so? What if someone stole your daddy's deck of cards, huh? Stuff matters sometimes, Isla."

"Don't you dare bring my dad into this." I bit back.

Minnie was on her feet in an instance. "Then don't bring my moms into this!'

I deflated, dropping my head and rubbing at my neck. Minnie was the sort of person to argue in a circle until her opponent gave in, and I didn't have the energy for that today.

"I'm so sorry, Minnie. I didn't mean it. I... I would never steal your necklace. I know how much it means to you."

She ignored me and stood simmering a couple of feet away until a timid knock at the door reminded us both where we were. Our eyes met, wide with panic, and Minnie scrambled to shove the nail polish under her bed as I climbed up to replace the ceiling tile as quietly as I could without smudging my still-wet nail polish.

"Minnie?" A young girl's voice.

"What is it, Ruby?" Minnie asked.

Grimacing at the ceiling dust on my replacement's bedsheets, I hopped off the bed and pulled the covers off, shaking them out a couple of times.

"I want to come inside. Why is the door locked?"

"Uh…" Minnie looked around, scrambling for a reason to stall her. "I'm naked!"

If the atmosphere wasn't still so tense from our little spat, I might have laughed.

I replaced the blankets on the bed, groaning slightly as the black paint on my index finger smeared all over the corner of the blanket. Goodie.

"Why are you naked, Minnie?" This girl sounded older, probably thirteen or fourteen. How much of an audience did we have?

"I'm changing. I'm almost done, give me one second." She gestured frantically at one of the other bunk beds, this one with fewer things tucked under it than ours—than hers.

Without wasting a second, I dove under the bed, rearranging a few things to hide me better and praying the little urchins didn't think to look down here, just as Minnie unlatched the door and swung it open.

# 3

*"To be deemed fit for duty in the Coranti Military, a willful recruit must pass tests for: physical fitness, mental stability, and genetic conditions."*

—*So, You've Enlisted in the Coranti Military? Here's Your Helpful Guide To All the Relevant Handbook Rules, compiled by Andrew Wilkins.*

••  ━━━━━━━  ••●••  ━━━━━━━  ••

The door had barely opened when a series of harsh, loud knocks sounded from downstairs. The Monta city orphanage wasn't a small building—two floors, with the girls' and boys' bedrooms on the second floor, across the foyer from each other. The hallways outside the rooms looked down on the entryway like an indoor balcony, and the girls had fled to look as soon as they heard the knock.

In the silence that followed, heavy with expectation, I could clearly hear the front door squeal open on rusty hinges.

"Who is it?" asked Director Bryce, the head of the orphanage. She was a nice lady, short and round and pasty skinned. I was itching to crawl out from under the bed and watch what was going on with everyone else as heavy, booted footsteps followed her question and the door slammed closed again.

"We're here for one of your orphans. Records say you have an untested sixteen-year-old girl." Omili above, I recognized that voice. "She should have had her blood checked and the results sent to us on her birthday fifteen days ago. We're here to follow up."

"Of course, ma'am," said Bryce. "What's the name?"

Captain Mila Akins cleared her throat, and the rustle of papers followed. "Isla Byrne?"

And of course, she pronounced the 'S'. Honestly, the number of people who did that was astounding. Had they never heard of an island before? Cursing under my breath, I slid slowly out from the bed, straining to hear the not-so-quiet conversation going on below.

"Isla? I'm so sorry, ma'am, but she isn't with us at the moment."

"Isn't with you?" This was a second voice, also female, and unfamiliar. "What does that mean?"

"She... she ran away, ma'am."

I crossed to the doorway and peered out, still unable to see anything going on down there over the heads of the other girls watching the show. But I could see clearly as Minnie left her position at the railing and headed towards the stairs, tugging on her shoes as she went. What was she doing?

Captain Akins cursed. "Ran away."

It wasn't a question, but Bryce answered anyway. "Yes, ma'am."

"Excuse me, Captain?" It was Minnie.

I pushed past two of the girls at the railing, not even caring if they recognized me, but they ignored me, riveted.

"What are you doing here, girl? Go back to your room." I could see the speaker now, a woman, probably barely taller than Minnie's five feet and two inches. The name on her uniform, which was significantly less glittery with medals and stars than her counterparts, wasn't legible from here, but her short red bob and pale skin stood in contrast to Akins' darker complexion and braids.

"I'd like to enlist."

The soldiers blinked, clearly taken aback. I felt like I was going to be sick. This couldn't be happening.

"How old are you?" Asked Akins' sidekick.

"Minerva Aberle, seventeen years old." And two months. Minnie's voice didn't waver, but my white-knuckled fingers had the railing in a stranglehold. I cursed under my breath and the seven-year-old standing next to me gave me a dirty look. I ignored her. Minnie's back was turned to me, hiding her face.

Captain Akins frowned. "You're not a witch, I assume?"

"I'm a witch." Technically, though not a very powerful one.

This caught our visitors off guard.

"You can do a blood test if you want." I followed Minnie's inclined head to the plastic bag in Akins' fist.

"No need." The shorter soldier gestured for Akins to read something on the portable tablet she held. "We have you on record."

"So why—" I could see the exact moment the Captain looked at Minnie, really looked at her, and noticed the way the right sleeve of her baggy green sweater hung limply where her arm ended halfway to the elbow. She sighed, running a hand down her face.

"Kid, I... You don't pass the health requirements. You can take it up with the officials at the enlistment center if you want, but there isn't much I can do about it."

"I've already tried that." News to me. "Look, I'm a good fighter, very athletic, a decent shot with a pistol, though I'm sure I could pick up a rifle easily enough, and I'm a competent witch."

Redhead looked like she wanted to say something, but Minnie wasn't finished. "If it wasn't for my arm, I'd have been conscripted over a year ago, no matter what my abilities. I'd be willing to bet I'm better than most of the recruits you get from the draft, so just let me enlist."

"Just leave it, girl," said the other soldier. Selne? Suina? I squinted at her uniform again, but I still couldn't see it clearly.

"One second, Sergeant. The kid's got a point." Akins squinted at Minnie. "You're a good fighter, huh? How about this: You do a little hand-to-hand with Sergeant Salma here, and if you can hold your own, I'll put in a good word with my superiors. Sound good?"

Minnie bounced a little on her heels, and I could practically see her giddy face in my mind, but a knot of worry was sinking in my chest. A fistfight with a trained soldier who actually had two fists? I'd known Minnie had been teaching herself some self-defense on the internet, but I realized now I wasn't sure to what extent. It was becoming increasingly clear what a horrible best friend I was.

"Yes, ma'am." Without wasting an instant, Minnie pulled off her sweater, revealing a black tank top and the stump of her right arm. She immediately started stretching.

"Excuse me, Captain, but this is ridiculous. I'm not fighting a cripple."

Without ceremony, Minnie stepped forward and sucker-punched Salma in the jaw, sending her tumbling to the ground. I sucked in a harsh breath. Attacking a soldier could get you killed, but Akins just laughed.

"Looks like the cripple will fight you whether you want to or not, *Sergeant*." The Captain placed emphasis on the last word. I was no expert on military rankings, but she was clearly pulling rank.

Salma grimaced, pulling herself to her feet. "You are *so* going to pay for that, little girl."

Minnie looked short next to most people, especially Akins, but she and Salma seemed pretty evenly matched in the height department. I leaned forward, the edge of the railing digging into my ribs, and watched as Akins and Bryce cleared the area and the combatants began circling each other.

Salma looked downright murderous, the red flush of a bruise already beginning to form on her jaw, and when I could finally see Minnie's face again, she was a mask of determined composure.

I so desperately wanted Minnie to be okay, but even more than that, I wanted her to lose. That was probably selfish of me. No, it was definitely selfish of me, but I didn't care. I couldn't lose another person to this war.

Salma threw the first punch this time, and Minnie dodged it easily, light on her toes. I relaxed slightly, letting myself breathe a bit even as my stomach churned in worry. She was the strongest, most capable person I knew. She would do fine. Hopefully not any better than fine, but fine.

Minnie darted forward, leaning heavily right as she landed a blow to Salma's midsection, then ducked under her arm and pivoted, kicking Salma in the ribs as the soldier tried to turn. Salma grunted, but grabbed Minnie's leg, twisted, and pushed. I winced as Minnie fell hard on her right side, without a hand to catch her. She hopped right back up to her feet, though, and I supposed it was lucky she hadn't fallen on her left side. The instinct to stop her fall might have sprained her wrist or worse. She'd been born without most of her right arm, so she'd never had to learn and unlearn its instincts, unlike amputees.

The pair were circling each other again, like venomous sharks, ready to bite. Minnie didn't look much worse for the wear, but Salma was bent ever so slightly around what was probably a bruised rib. I grinned. All Minnie had to do was hit her in the same spot a couple of times, and it would be game over. At least, that was my best assumption based on those horrible action movies Minnie loved. The few fights I'd actually been in had ended quickly, neither party anywhere near the skill of these two.

"You can do it, Minnie!" Maria Thompson bellowed from nearby, and I jumped a little. I remembered Maria—her parents died pretty recently, I thought. Not a war orphan, though we'd seen plenty of those lately. Her parents died in a car crash. Minnie didn't let herself get distracted, but I could've sworn she smiled as more orphans, from both sides of the foyer, took up the call, and dear Director Bryce finally realized all her charges were spectating.

"Minnie!"

"Minnie!"

She was pretty beloved. I was hit suddenly with a pang of jealousy, which I immediately felt guilty for. Minnie was my best friend. She deserved my support, not my petty jealousy. But... she seemed to be so perfect at everything, all the time. I knew she wasn't perfect. I knew that better than anyone. She was always interrupting me when I tried to tell stories, she did crunches like a girl possessed, she had a horrible sugar tooth, and she was too proud to admit when she needed help. But she was also strong. And brave. And kind.

And I wasn't ready to lose her.

Minnie's long, dark curls were still in the loose ponytail at the back of her neck from when she was painting her nails, and strands were starting to fall out now. But even if she could have tightened it herself, I wasn't sure she would have. She and the sergeant were locked in a deadly dance, weaving around each other with a blunt grace.

Minnie hit Salma in the ribs again, and Salma managed to land a punch to Minnie's unprotected right side.

From the balcony, I couldn't tell if they were sweating or breathing heavily by now, but if they weren't, they would be soon. Minnie's lips moved, whatever she said was inaudible at this distance, drowned out beneath the uproar. Salma sure heard, however, and she didn't seem to like it much. She growled and charged Minnie, fists raised. Minnie kicked her shins, hard, and Salma lunged forward, pulling Minnie to the ground with her. The soldier pinned Minnie's arm beneath her and began raining down punches, anywhere she could reach. I saw a brief flash of red as Minnie's lip broke.

Then, with the core strength that came from what one might call borderline-obsessive exercises, she lurched upwards and clonked Salma on the ear with what right arm she had. Hard.

That gave Minnie enough leeway to shove her opponent off her and press her knee to Salma's throat as the roars of her little crowd, me included, rose to a feverish pitch.

"Surrender," Minnie gasped, barely audible above the shrieks of surprise and joy. But she wasn't talking to us.

Salma gurgled something that might have been a surrender, obviously struggling to breathe, and Minnie rolled off her, fighting her way to her feet.

I let myself wallow for a few moments in a bittersweet combination of relief and dread until I realized that the distraction was over. The orphans were beginning to turn to each other and chatter amongst themselves, splitting into packs based on age and relationships and whatever other petty things they used to define their social groups these days. Which meant, more relevantly, that they were beginning to notice me.

"Wait, didn't you leave?" Some little prepubescent girl I vaguely remembered was staring at me.

"I'd love to tell you about it sometime, really I would, but I need to be going now." I began to slide backwards towards the door before Maria Thompson, the little brat, grabbed my arm.

"Hey, you're Isla Byrne. You're the one the soldiers were looking for, aren't you?"

I fumbled in my pocket and pulled the melted chocolate coin out, pressing it into Maria's hand. "Run along dear, go skip rope or whatever. I've got to dash."

Maria said a vulgar word under her breath, staring down in disgust at the gooey brown foil in her palm. "I'm thirteen years old, you can't bribe me with gross candy," she shouted at my back as I got away from there as fast as I could.

I didn't go far. Just outside the bedroom window, I waited for nearly an hour beneath the tree, until the sunset and the lights inside clicked off one by one. I wasn't eager to walk all the way back to my super safe new neighborhood under the cover of darkness, but I had to talk to Minnie.

When the coast finally seemed clear, I made my way back up the tree and rested my palms on the windowsill. The window was locked.

I tapped lightly on the pane to the chorus of Minnie's favorite song, humming quietly under my breath as the song lyrics rang through my mind. *Oh please don't you leave me, darling, I can't bear to say goodbye, maybe you could hold me tight, and I would never leave your side.* It was a love song, and yet was beginning to feel startlingly relevant at the moment.

No reaction. I tried again, slightly louder this time. On the third repeat of the chorus (I didn't know anything else), the latch clicked and the window slid upwards. Minnie poked her head out, glowering. She didn't offer for me to come inside.

"What do you want?" She hissed. All the different apologies and pleas I'd rehearsed in the last hour left me.

"Are you really still mad about—"

"Does it matter?"

"Minnie, please, what are you doing?"

"I'm doing what I've known I should for a long time now."

I stared at her, lit softly by the streetlight, hair still partially pulled back. Maintaining eye contact with me, she ripped the hair tie from her hair and offered it to me, several dark curly hairs still knotted up in the band.

"Here's your hair tie back. I'm leaving for the enlistment office at seven tomorrow morning. You can come by before then to get your things. No use keeping them here when I'm gone." Her tone was brisk, cold.

I stared at her dumbly, taking the hair tie and tucking it in my pocket. "Minnie—"

She slammed the window shut, nearly catching my fingers, and the window was a pool of black once again.

I kicked every rock and can within reach of my feet on the walk back, and even a lamppost, which might not have been the brightest idea. I didn't care.

I only had one more chance to convince Minnie not to go, and I couldn't waste it.

I racked my brain for something to do or say that could possibly change her mind, but she was so stubborn.

She was going to get herself killed.

The warehouses were silent this time at night, and the chill off the lake made me wish for my jacket. I wrapped my arms around my bare shoulders, shivering, as I lowered myself to sit on one of the massive, industrial-sized loading docks. My feet dangled off the edge, just above the water, and I stared out at the glossy black of the lake. Across the lake, the glimmering lights of Tori, the capital city of Coranti, reflected beautifully off the mirror-like water, looking like a sky full of stars to match the reflection of the nearly full moon.

"Everything's falling apart," I whispered to the water.

I'd thought that maybe, just maybe, things were starting to go my way. I had a place to sleep, a job, and, most notably, I wasn't dying horrifically at the hands of a Nillaesce soldier. I shuddered, both from the cold and the gruesome image of Minnie bleeding to death from a bullet wound, or worse, captured and burned at the stake. Or whatever gross death those religious freaks had planned for those who dared to be born into magic.

I thought I could get it all together, keep me and Minnie safe, maybe even live my life? But now Minnie was leaving, and she was angry at me, and I wasn't quite sure what to feel.

I'd lost sight of the moon by the time I finally pushed myself to my feet, joints creaking.

I fumbled in my pockets for the key, fingers shaky. Had I really been sweating from the heat earlier today? The back door creaked open and I stifled a yawn. It must be nearly midnight.

But the lights were already on in the warehouse, and I blinked in the sudden brightness.

Inside, Big U was talking with a tall, skinny man in, of all things, a black trench coat. They both looked up when I entered, and trench coat guy's hand flew to the gun on his belt. I raised my hands placatingly.

"Don't mind me, just passing through," I said, forcing a chuckle into my voice. Big U, the old softie, scowled and gestured to his buddy that I wasn't important. They turned back to inspect a big box of something that was probably illegal in the city of Monta as I turned the key in the lock of my new home and slipped inside.

It was gross. I'd placed a bucket under the leaky pipe, a temporary fix, and scrubbed as best I could at the mold growing on the floor. Like I'd told Minnie, all it needed was a rug and a little bit of love. And probably a bath in anti-bacterial cleaning fluid.

I didn't have anything to change into, seeing as just about everything I owned was still under Minnie's bed. I didn't even bother taking off my boots before I wrapped myself in my thin blanket and laid down on the rough, slightly damp floor, squeezing my eyes shut and waiting for sleep to take me.

# 4

*"We're losing."*

—*Ex-General Adam Docks of the Old Coranti Military, military strategist, in a recorded interview for the Tori Daily.*

•• ——————— ••●•• ——————— ••

I woke not only to the screech of a cheap alarm clock but also to the bellow of Big U from across the warehouse.

"Turn that thing off!"

I cursed loudly, flopping over to whack the shut-off button with my palm. My eyes were sticky with sleep, ironic considering I'd barely slept. I groaned as I sat up, my muscles sore from sleeping curled up on an uneven floor for countless nights in a row. I missed beds. It took me a second to remember why I was awake at five in the morning. But when I did, my stomach twisted in a knot.

My best friend was about to go running headfirst to her death.

"What are you doing here this early, Big U?" I asked, locking my room door behind me.

He was sitting cross-legged on a crate, glaring at me beneath bushy grey eyebrows. "I come here to meditate. Because it's *quiet.*"

"Sorry, sorry, I'll get out of your hair."

It was just over a mile walk to the Monta City Orphanage from the lake, and I planned to arrive with plenty of time before Minnie left to convince her not to go. I trudged along in the pre-dawn dimness, scuffed shoes barely leaving the pavement, mind twirling and twisting in circles.

What could I possibly say to Minnie to get her to stay?

I passed a propaganda poster for the war, encouraging healthy citizens to enlist. *We need you to fight for equality!* Typical crap. They were overselling the equality thing—the majority of the population weren't witches and weren't ready to go to war to prevent a massacre. Maybe the queen's advertisers should highlight the fact that if the Nillaesce won the war, they would be perfectly content killing thousands of innocent civilians on their way to murder the government.

Only two blocks away from the orphanage, I got suddenly nervous that somehow, I'd misjudged the time. What if I was too late? What if Minnie was already gone forever?

It was times like these I really wished I'd splurged on a new watch. I still wore my broken watch from when I was six—navy blue band and a face sprinkled with stars. It may not tell time anymore, but it was full of memories, and it held my father's last message to me tucked to my skin.

"Hey! You!" I ambushed a jogger, some crazy woman who had decided that going for an early morning run was somehow a good idea. She seemed fit. Why hadn't she been conscripted already?

Sighing, she pulled out her earbuds. "What is it?"

"What's the time?"

She glanced briefly down at her watch, then met my eyes again. "Six thirty-four."

Swallowing my fear, I nodded. "Thanks."

No lights shone through the orphanage windows, probably because all sane people were currently nice and toasty in bed.

I crossed the street to the orphanage, hands tucked nervously in my pockets. I only knew one thing: Minnie couldn't leave. If she died, I would lose my only family left in the world. I reached the tree outside the second-floor window, ready to climb, but my gaze caught on something near the wall.

Oh, no. Oh, no, no, no, no, no.

Sitting on my duffel bag beside a small bottle of jet-black nail polish there was a little note in Minnie's tight, curly script.

*Sorry, Isla. I didn't want to argue with you again before I left, so I might have fudged the time a bit. Here are your things. Hope they don't get stolen.*

*Love you forever,*
*Minnie.*

I crumpled the paper in my fist, cursing loudly. This had to be some sick joke.

I slumped against the wall and watched the sunrise, knowing it was too late. Minnie was gone. I would never see her again unless by some miracle the war ended before she died. Or… unless I joined the military.

Would I really throw away my life along with Minnie's? Would she want that? Honestly, she probably would, but that was only because she didn't fully grasp how futile this war was. She'd wanted me to join the military so I could make a difference, fight for witch rights, blah de blah—and then she'd gone and fought for it herself.

And she would die. She was going to die, and there was nothing I could do. My life already felt so empty without her—but I supposed I would have to get used to that.

It took the bright glint of early morning sunlight off a window to jolt me from my moping. I couldn't be sure how long I spent leaning against the orphanage wall, but it was long enough for my back to ache with the print of the bricks on my back.

I couldn't do this forever. I had to resume my life, as hard as it was.

After only a couple minutes of walking, I stood before the small, run-down pawnshop nearest to the orphanage. There were five reliable pawn shops in Monta, as far as I knew, and I tried to alternate between them with my stolen goods to avoid suspicion. I'd even had Minnie go in for me a couple of times. She hated the whole experience and was a horrible negotiator, so that arrangement didn't last long.

The air was heavy and stale in the pawnshop, and I coughed at the dust my entrance swirled into the air. I wasn't exceedingly fond of this particular pawn shop, but it was the closest and probably the only one open at this hour. A young man was working the desk, fulfilling the early hours advertised on the front door. To say he was working might have been a tad generous—he laid with his head on the desk, snoring softly. I couldn't blame him. Only weirdos and workaholics were up at this hour. And, apparently, girls who failed to save their best friend from certain death.

I poked at the guy's head, my finger disappearing in a greasy black mop of hair. I recoiled, wiping off my hand on my pants, and grabbed a bejeweled cane—quite the stylish accessory—off a nearby shelf and jabbed it at his shoulder gently. His snores snuffled to a halt, and he bolted upright, blinking bleary eyes at me. Poor guy. I yawned in sympathy, replacing the cane on the shelf.

"I've got some old family heirlooms to cash in," I said, nice and loud.

He grumbled in reply, beckoning me to the desk. I withdrew the bracelet from my pocket and set it gingerly on the table before him, along with a small gold earring I'd procured the other day. He ran his fingers over them, consulting a chart with squinted eyes that told me he still wasn't very lucid. Good.

"I'll give you fifty Coran," he grumbled, reaching for the bracelet and earring.

"No."

His hand stilled. "We don't negotiate here."

I grabbed the jewelry and shoved it in my pocket, turning to the door. "Fine. I'll get a better deal from your competitors anyway." I fiddled with my bag on my way out the door, praying he would call my bluff. Thankfully, he did.

"Fine. Seventy-five."

I turned back around slowly and deliberately, one hand going to my pocket.

"That earring is pure gold." I had no clue if it was gold or not. "And the bracelet? Inlaid with real diamonds. My grandmother got it after the Sinea Diamond Rush," I lied through my teeth, crossing my arms over my chest. "And you're trying to cheat me with seventy-five Coran? I should tell my friends that this establishment tries to swindle its customers."

The boy's eyes were wide with panic. A review like that would get him fired, easily.

"Alright, alright, one hundred it is."

"I'll accept no less than one hundred and fifty. Final offer."

He hesitated, glancing down at his sheet. "I'll need to inspect the jewelry again."

As it turned out, my luck held. The earring was actually gold after all, and the guy didn't bother testing the 'diamond' bracelet after my first claim proved true. Honestly, if he worked for me, he'd be fired in a heartbeat. But as a beneficiary of his laziness, I honestly couldn't care less.

In a way, I wished I cared more about his ineptitude, so I could get my mind off the loss of Minnie. Something to think about besides my own self-hate for failing to save Minnie would be nice.

I tried to force a pained smile onto my features as I approached the obnoxious purple awning of Billie's department store, the classic gold and purple emblem glaring at me from both of the glass doors.

"Excuse me?" Inside, I hailed a middle-aged woman wearing a purple uniform, seemingly the only employee here this early. "Where might I be able to find a magician's costume?"

She furrowed her brow. "A... magician's costume?"

"Yeah, you know. Black, kind of a suit jacket type thing, maybe a cape? Don't worry, I already have the hat taken care of." I hoisted my duffel bag, which had my old costume, hat included, wrapped up with my clothes and money.

"We might have something like that."

There it was. The perfect costume. It was meant for men, because the sad truth was that all the women's costumes were a little more... revealing than I was comfortable with. The employee let me try it on, and I twirled before a full mirror, cape flying behind me. The exterior of the coat and cape was black and silky, the inside lined in a gorgeous, iridescent deep blue that glimmered like a still lake at midnight, speckled with glittering "stars." If I pulled in the waist a little, it would fit like a dream.

The problem was the price. I could technically afford it, but it would cost nearly half the Coran I'd been saving up for that sleeping bag, including the money from my recent sale. Not like I really needed a sleeping bag anymore. Still, that money could go towards so many things in my new lodgings—a rug, for starters, food, probably lots of stuff more useful than a flashy new costume.

Maybe it was the grief talking, maybe it was how futile the whole situation felt without Minnie. But who was I kidding? I was totally going to buy the costume.

On my way to pay, my eyes caught on a bookshelf near the door. A classic murder mystery novel, *Tomorrow's Last Mystery* by Roberta Tinn, was on sale for only four Coran. I couldn't resist. And as I waited to pay, the current song ended and a familiar soft, haunting melody piped out over the speakers. *No, darling, I can't bear another goodbye. Please won't you say you love me, even if I know it's just a lie.* Minnie had played that song on repeat for days when it was first released a couple of months ago, and I was completely baffled by her ability to still listen to it without bashing her brains out.

When both the sale cost and the insane wartime taxes were paid, I was left with barely a third of my meager savings. *That party better pay well.*

I finally left the department store behind, not sad to be away from the obnoxious purple theme. And that song… that would be stuck in my head for days. It really didn't help that it only served to remind me of Minnie.

My feet carried me to a small cafe, staffed only by a single bleary-eyed waitress, ready to serve coffee to the early risers of Monta. I slipped into a hard plastic seat at a small, round table in the corner. My duffel bag filled the seat across from me, and I reached over to pull my new book from the bag. I shared the cafe with only one other person, so I had time before the cafe was busy. Then, the waitress would realize I had no interest in paying ten Coran for lukewarm coffee and kick me out for taking up a seat. Until then, I could enjoy the quiet and smother my sorrows away, hiding behind Detective Fetz.

The book was actually amazing, and I devoured the pages, so wrapped up in the suspicions and intrigue that I actually jumped when the waitress came to take my order.

"Can I get a menu?" I asked, stalling for time. A few patrons popped in for coffee, busy-looking types who didn't bother sitting down. I sighed, setting down the book and pulling my duffel bag towards me. I rifled through it, finding the small interior pocket that held my most valuable possessions. I pushed past my rather sad-looking wallet to reach the small black bag that held my father's cards. I slid the deck out of its protective velvet sheath, fingers running over the smooth black cards almost reverently. In an almost mindless motion, I shuffled the cards multiple times, glad to have a motion to occupy anxious fingers. When the cards were thoroughly shuffled and my fingers were properly warmed up, I began rehearsing a new trick, running over the movements again and again until the motions looked effortless and the cards slipped between my fingers like water.

I lifted my eyes, a proud smile still lingering on my lips, at the sound of a chair being pulled out. An old woman, face creased like the crumpled napkin I used in one of my tricks, settled herself into the seat across from me that my duffel bag had vacated.

"D'you play with those cards, or just move them 'round?" I recognized her as the only other dine-in visitor to the establishment.

I grinned. "Name the game."

"Y'know Wild Knight?"

"Does the queen wear a crown?"

"Never met 'er, but I suppose that's a yes."

I dealt the cards quickly and efficiently, and we began playing. After examining my hand and indicating that she should play first, I nodded at her wrist.

"What's the time?"

She didn't spare a glance for her watch, eyes locked on her hand. "Dunno. This watch has been broken for years."

I raised my eyebrows. "But you still wear it?"

"So do you." She met my eyes, and we both looked at my watch, forever fixed on the time eight fifty-three.

"Checkmate."

She slapped down a pair of cards, and we played in silence for a few minutes. She was good. I examined my remaining cards, chewing my lip thoughtfully. If I played this right, I could win. I played three of my cards, a triple, hoping I'd made the right choice, and sure enough, she played a two of witches. That could only mean she had no better cards to play.

Feeling victorious and struggling to keep a bluff face, I slammed down the rest of my cards in one final play.

And she won.

I gaped at the winning hand before chuckling. "Good game."

"You're a lil' cocky, y'know that?"

I grunted. "I may have been told that before."

"I'd learn to fix that if I were you. Makes you easy to trick. Easy to play," she remarked as the waitress swooped down on us to take our order. She'd never brought me a menu, but I wasn't about to call that to her attention now.

"I want a biscuit and a large coffee," the woman said with a yawn.

The waitress turned to me next, eyebrows raised.

"Oh, I won't be having anything, thank you."

"Nonsense," my new friend said, waving a hand at me. "My treat."

I grinned. Free food. "Well, in that case, a biscuit sounds heavenly. I'd like two, in fact.

The waitress nodded and left, and I dealt a new round.

"So, who are you grieving?"

I raised my eyes from my cards to meet hers. "What?"

"I could practically smell your dejection from 'cross the room, girl. Figured you needed a shoulder to talk to." She frowned. "I think I'm getting my sayings mixed up."

"I… Thank you, but I don't really feel up to talking." I stared down at my hands again.

She hmphed. "I'm here if you need to, though."

Two hands later, the words began to spill out of me unbidden

"My mother died in childbirth," I said, matter-of-factly. "I never knew her."

The woman paused in the middle of setting down a card. "Oh."

"My father raised me until I was eight, then he died too. He's the one who taught me Wild Knight."

I played another card, eyes still locked on the game so I could ignore the tingling of tears brewing.

"But it was alright. I recovered. I made friends. I found someone that filled his spot, in a way. Someone who made me feel whole again, you know?" I noticed, as if from outside my body, that I was gripping my cards too tight. I loosened my stranglehold, not wanting to crinkle my father's cards.

"And this morning—" My voice broke, and I cleared my throat futilely. "This morning, she left to enlist in the military. She's going to die, and I-I can't save her."

I looked up, tears brimming in my eyes, unsure how the woman would react.

"You love her." Her tone left no room for argument.

My voice was soft, broken, and the words were barely audible. "Yeah." I started shuffling the deck again, giving my fingers something to do. "But not romantically, or anything," I amended. "She's like a sister to me. She's the only family I have left."

"And the family you choose? That's the strongest love of all."

I met the woman's eyes, shining with a memory, and I wondered who she'd loved and lost.

As if to punctuate the moment, a familiar melancholy rhythm poured out of the overhead speakers and I groaned. "Seriously? This song again?"

I blinked unshed tears out of my eyes as my new friend chuckled. "I know, right? It's all o'er the place. 'Parently it's number one on the charts again."

*I won't give you up, no I'll never say goodbye, when I see you again, I can't bear to ask you why, but darling why... I swear I'll fight to keep you at my side...*

I swallowed, setting my cards down on the table.

*...I'm nothing without you, so please don't say goodbye, I can't bear this lonely life.*

"You know what you have to do?" She asked, voice hushed, as crinkles formed around her eyes.

"Yeah. I'm going after Minnie."

# 5

*"Witches curse, and witches scheme,*

*Witches dance in a fever dream*

*Witches kill, witches break,*

*Witches burn at the holy stake."*

——*Popular nursery rhyme adapted from an old Nillaesce war chant. Currently banned in Coranti by order of the queen.*

I spent half an hour outside the recruitment office, eating my biscuits, which I'd taken to go in a paper napkin, and waiting for the doors to open at a quarter to nine. In hindsight, it might have been a bit premature to rush over here to enlist immediately. Based on the closed-ness of the office, I assumed Minnie hadn't gone here. She'd probably taken a ferry straight to the capital. Should I have done that first and enlisted at an office there? I didn't have money for the fare, but I supposed I could always steal some.

"Lookie, Nicole, we've got an eager beaver. Trying to avoid the line, huh, kid?"

I stretched, standing up to face a man and a woman in uniform, both fairly young, probably in their late twenties or early thirties, holding open the door.

"What line?" The woman, Nicole, muttered under her breath, and the man elbowed her hard in the gut. She seemed familiar, but I couldn't quite place her.

"Yeah… I'm here to enlist," I said, maybe a bit redundantly, considering the situation.

"Fantastic!" The man beamed, opening the door a bit wider. "Why don't you come on in, and we'll get you all situated."

The recruitment office was empty save for us—just a small building with few numbered desks. The man led me to the first desk and rounded it, Nicole at his side. When he turned slightly to begin tapping at his computer, I could read the name on his uniform. *Vasco.*

"Alright, are you a witch, dear?"

"Er, yes."

"Delightful. What type?"

Type? "I—"

"Describe your abilities for me."

I hadn't used magic in years. Everyone knew witches couldn't set things on fire with their minds or shoot electricity out of their fingers or anything actually interesting, so I'd never seen many practical benefits to it. Plus, it was dangerous. Too dangerous. My magic was very blunt, not at all subtle—if I was lucky, people tended to faint when I used it, and that didn't seem very useful in my line of work. And if I wasn't lucky… But that had only happened one time, and I'd resolved to forget about it.

Even in this "modern age" when everyone was supposed to be super accepting of witches, I'd probably get mobbed on the spot if someone suspected me of using magic. That incident yesterday had been a case in point.

"Sometimes," I said, then hesitated, unsure quite how to put it. "Sometimes, I can make people pass out, and then I feel strong."

"Right, a Drainer then. What's your name, dear?" He asked, fingers hovering over the keys, probably ready to look me up in that wonderful database of theirs. What if they accused me of avoiding conscription? That was worth a hefty fine, even jail time, by the queen's new decree. But they couldn't punish me for avoiding military service for only a couple of weeks when I was literally signing up right now to serve. Right?

I smiled widely at him. "Is that really necessary? Can't you just give me a uniform and ship me off?"

He frowned, bushy eyebrows bunching together. "We need your name to access your records."

I chewed my chapped lips, tasting blood. "So, if I did something, let's say, potentially illegal and it was in my records, would I not be able to enlist?"

His companion, Nicole, whose name tag read Salma, straightened and rested a hand on her gun. I saw her and Vasco share a nervous look. Salma... she was the woman from last night, I realized. The one who fought Minnie. I scowled.

"What did you do, dear?" Vasco asked, eyes slightly narrowed

I laughed, and Vasco smiled hesitantly. Salma only frowned. "Oh, nothing, I was just kidding." I smiled apologetically. "Sorry, my sense of humor is a bit screwed these days," I said, leaning forward conspiratorially. "My therapist thinks it's the stress." Like I could afford a therapist.

They didn't relax much, but Vasco attempted a chuckle. "Look, dear—"

"Hey, silly me, I completely forgot about that drug den I wanted to report!"

They stared at me blankly, and Salma leaned forward, powering up a tablet. "A drug den, you say?"

"What's your affiliation with said den?" Vasco asked, frowning.

"No affiliation, I just saw something *really* incriminating on my way here." I beamed, giving them the address to Big U's warehouse. I didn't think of myself as a snitch, but I wasn't about to support the illegal narcotic trade if it didn't benefit me. Especially if ratting them out could possibly benefit me.

"So, anyway, with that out of the way"—and the soldiers sufficiently buttered up, I hoped—"I'm Isla Byrne. Isla is spelled like the beginning of 'island,' not like your eyeball." I sighed. "You'd be surprised by the number of people who think my name is 'eye-la.' And Byrne is B-Y-R-N-E, not burn." I pantomimed burning my hand, but he wasn't looking.

"Yep, I have you right here," Vasco said, leaning closer to his computer. "Oh, you're actually on the potential conscription list. You had your sixteenth birthday recently and your blood isn't in the database."

I faked a laugh. "How ironic. Well, that just works out perfectly, doesn't it?"

"She's the girl you and Mila went to test last night," he said, turning to Salma, "when you ended up recruiting that other girl instead, remember?"

My heart leaped in my chest at the mention of Minnie.

"So, do I need a blood test, or..."

Salma turned to me, eyebrows raised, black eyes glinting. "Why weren't you at the orphanage? Bryce said you... left?"

Both of them were watching me now. "Yeah, just a little change of address recently. Independence, lost childhood, all that."

Vasco frowned contemplatively at his screen. "We don't have any record of an official withdrawal from the public care system here—"

"That's right, all the paperwork was filed recently and is probably still going through." I frowned too, as if concerned. "Is it really not showing up? I hope it didn't get lost in the process... Anyways, I suppose it won't really matter, now that I'm going to be a proud member of the New Coranti Armed Forces!" I grinned, a little forcefully, at the pair. Maybe I was laying it on a tad thick, but they seemed to buy it.

"Right, well, your health records all seem relatively up to date, and you don't have any disciplinary..." Vasco's face softened, and he met my gaze. "Aw, sweetie, I'm so sorry."

"We honor your sacrifice for the good of Coranti," droned Salma, even her harsh, cynical features drooping a bit.

"It's fine," I muttered around the rising lump in my throat, though it wasn't. I didn't want to hear their "your sacrifice" nonsense any more than I wanted to join the war that killed my father, but here I was. "It was a long time ago."

"Well then, you just need to sign a few forms, and you'll be off to Tori to train." The capital, home to both Coranti's new military stronghold and the original seeds of the Witch revolution over nine years ago, was right across the lake from Monta. It was also where I grew up until my father was conscripted seven years ago and they shipped me over here due to an overflow at the Tori Orphanages.

"Hey, Ben, what—" Captain Akins cut herself off, clearly not anticipating my presence when she entered the office from a side room in civilian clothes. Her eyes passed over me once dismissively before returning to squint at me again. "Hey, I know you."

I swallowed. "You hired me for your party, ma'am."

She nodded, relaxing. "Oh, that's right. You're enlisting, huh?"

"Yeah. Ma'am."

Salma's eyebrows rose. "Miss Byrne just needs to sign a few things and she'll be good to go, Captain."

"Okay." Akins yawned, lowering herself into one of the chairs meant for waiting would-be soldiers. "Byrne, huh? Sounds familiar." She hesitated. "But I suppose you told me your name when I hired you." I most certainly did not, but I wasn't about to tell her that.

"Actually, Miss Byrne was a resident at the Monta Orphanage until recently, when she turned sixteen," Salma hinted, and I scowled.

Akins' eyes widened noticeably, and she turned back to me. "Isla Byrne, that's right! I completely forgot about you in that chaos with the one-armed girl. Do you know her?"

I gritted my teeth. "We've met."

Akin nodded, eyes alight. "Now, that girl there is what I call a patriot. And now you too, I suppose. So brave, so young, so ready to fight for her country." Yep, that was me. Brave. Totally not trying to get the actually brave one to see reason and desert.

I signed a few papers, a contract for five years of service, paying close attention to the policy on deserters, and—oh right, I was getting paid. Goodie. Salma handed me a ferry ticket, already paid for.

"Oh, we'll be on the same ferry," said Akins.

"You're going to the capital too?"

"I'm stationed there. Captains don't usually do recruiter jobs, but I was in town, and when my friend Ben here told me about the job, I figured I'd help Sergeant Salma out."

Salma nodded sagely. "Oh, right, you and Vasco are the best of buds. You must be really good friends, huh? I don't sleep in the same bed as my friends, and I sure don't kiss them on the mouth, so you two must be really—"

"What are you insinuating, sergeant?" snapped Akins, her tone making it clear that captain was higher ranked than sergeant. I should probably learn these things if I was going to be part of the army—what rank was I, even?

Salma paled slightly. "Nothing, captain." She swallowed. "Especially considering fraternization between a sergeant and a captain would qualify as disrupting the chain of command and get said soldiers demoted or worse."

I faked disinterest, but inside I was jumping up and down with glee. I was hardly officially recruited yet, and I could already blackmail who I was nearly halfway certain was a fairly high-ranking officer.

Vasco and Akins were glaring daggers at Salma, who, looking very much so like she regretted speaking, averted her gaze onto me. "Welcome to the New Coranti Military, Private Byrne." Well, at least that answered the question of my rank. I shook her extended hand, and then, in turn, Vasco and Akins' hands.

"Here, let me gather my things and we can walk to the ferry together," Akins said in a strained attempt at cheeriness, trying and failing to get rid of the tension and the murderous look Vasco was giving Salma.

"You know, that's alright, I'll just meet you there." I plastered on a smile. If there was one thing I really didn't want, it was more one-on-one bonding time with my favorite Captain.

"You sure?"

Very. "I just need some fresh air."

The air at the wharf was anything but fresh. It smelled like dead fish, body odor, and some pungent chemicals by the lake-side warehouses, but I'd decided to pay my buddy Big U one final visit for old time's sake. And to wipe down that room just in case there was anything that could possibly incriminate me should they go through with a raid. Better safe than sorry.

Big U wasn't there, but I was glad for my foresight when my old, gross blanket was stuffed in my duffel bag and a few stray light brown hairs were floating away across the lake.

The ferry docks were only a couple blocks down from Big U's warehouse, and though I'd thought I'd get there at around the same time as Akins, considering my brief detour, I didn't see the tall Captain anywhere. With about thirty minutes until our ferry left, I decided to go ahead and board the boat, elbowing past the line of scowling passengers waiting to buy a ticket.

"Hey, I already have a ticket," I told the man at the ticket station, flashing the paper Salma had printed for me, signed Recruiter Sergeant Benjamin Vasco. He adjusted his glasses and squinted at the paper, eyes widening slightly at the New Coranti Military emblem in the corner. "Thank you for your service. You can go right ahead to the Premium section."

I met the glares of the growing queue I'd just bypassed with a grin and a wink as I flounced through the boarding gate. Maybe this whole military thing wasn't going to be so bad after all. I found the Premium section without much difficulty. It was a large balcony on the top of the ferry, looking like what I could only assume a cruise ship looked like, with some fancy tables and padded lounge chairs aplenty. I chose a chair in the sun and plopped down, sliding my duffel bag beneath the chair as I got comfortable.

"There you are, Private. I was starting to wonder when you'd get here. What took so long?"

My satisfied smile slid off my face. Of course, Captain Akins was already here. I straightened, turning to face Akins, who had moved across the deck to situate herself on the lounge chair right next to me. *Deep breaths, Isla. She's your boss now, not some stranger you can be rude to and never see again.*

"Hello, Captain. Sorry for the delay, I just had to stop for some goodbyes before I left."

"Of course, I understand. You know, when I was your age..." I yawned, and though I didn't have to fake it—I was exhausted—I may have exaggerated the noise. Blissfully, Akins took the hint and stopped talking.

I smiled at her innocently. "I'm sorry, ma'am, but it's been a long morning and I didn't sleep so well last night—"

"Ah, the pre-enlist jitters. Happens to the best of us."

My smile became just a little more fake. I'd had no idea I was going to enlist last night.

"Well, do you think I might be able to take a little cat nap on the way over to Tori? We're not setting off for another half hour and it's a two-hour ride."

"Of course, of course."

With a sigh, I leaned back into the comfort of the lounge chair, which was ages better than how I'd slept last night, and attempted to block out the noise of passengers boarding the ferry below.

"Want some earplugs? Always helps me."

I opened one eye to stare at Akins, but for once I didn't want to avoid her. "Yes, please."

She handed me a pair of little foam earplugs, the kind they gave out on airplanes, she said, and showed me how to fit them into my ears.

This time, when I closed my eyes, the hubbub faded to the background, and the gentle warmth of the late-summer sun enveloped me like a warm hug. As always, it was hard to quiet the voices in my head before I faded off to sleep, the whispers of magic and monstrosity twisting just out of my reach.

But within only half an hour, I was asleep.

•• ———————— ••◉•• ———————— ••

I was eight years old again, and terrified, hunched over in the hall outside our apartment.

"It was an accident, Dad! I didn't—I didn't—"

"Hey, it's alright, sweetheart." He wiped at my tears with the pad of his thumb, but they just kept falling in an inescapable torrent.

"It's not, it's not alright, she's not waking up," I sniffled, rubbing at my nose with the back of my hand, smearing snot all over my face. My father nudged the body out of the way with his foot and crouched beside me. Oh Omili, the *body*—

"Nobody's mad at you, sweetheart. I know you didn't mean it."

"But—but—"

"Hey, listen to me. There's no need to cry. Just tell Dad what happened."

My eyes were red, and my vision blurred with tears, rendering the still woman on the floor into a shapeless blob.

"I-I was just standing in the hall, practicing the—the—" I waved a shaking hand at the cards, scattered all over the hallway. "That trick you showed me, but—" I leaned my head into my father's shoulder, soaking his jacket through with tears.

"Shh, shh…" He ran his hands through my hair, making comforting noises under his breath as I sobbed. "What happened, sweetheart?"

"I messed up the trick, Dad, and—and the cards were everywhere—" I hiccupped. "Then, Ms. Borough, remember? The mean one with the cats and the son who stopped visiting last year, who cries and watches her soaps real—really loud on Sunday afternoons?" I gestured at the door across the hall. "Ms. B-borough from apartment 3B."

"I remember."

"She—she slipped on the cards, and she broke the heel of her fancy shoe, and then—" I swallowed, struggling to get the words out. "She started yelling at me, Dad, and I was so scared, she looked really scary."

"Shh, yes, she was a mean lady," he said reassuringly.

"And—and she grabbed me, and she started shaking me and yelling at me and she was so loud, and I was so scared and I tried to pull away—"

"And you pulled her energy instead. All of it."

I blinked at my father's blurred face, still sniffling quietly. "Y-yeah, I guess."

He gave me a big hug, squeezing me tight. "Don't worry, Isla, sweetheart, this is a good thing."

"W-what?"

"It means you're powerful, sweets. Powerful like me. You just have to learn how to use it—"

"No. No." I shook my head fervently. "I don't wanna learn, Dad. I don't ever wanna use magic ever again, not ever."

He tsked softly, still running a reassuring hand through my hair. "It's alright, sweetheart, you'll come around. You're in shock. You go to your room and lie down now, and I'll take care of the mess."

I nodded mutely, and he helped pull me to my feet.

"I'm so proud of you," he said with a reassuring smile. "We'll talk more about this tomorrow, alright?"

But the next morning he was called out of the military reserves for the war, and I was shipped off to the Monta Orphanage before he was even dead.

I got the letter and the useless medal only two months later, telling me they *honored my sacrifice.*

# 6

*"Who was Cecile Omili? A legend? A scientist? A rebel? A genius? The answer, in my professional opinion, is indubitably: All of the above."*

—*An In-depth Biography of the Witch Who Shaped Our Modern World, written by Lei Nosser with annotations from Queen Isabella Ladrine of the New Coranti Monarchy.*

I woke sweaty and chilled to the bone. The sun had gone behind a cloud, and the sudden chill off the lake was enough to make me wish I was really in a bed, with a blanket and a pillow and a father to tell me it was all going to be alright.

Or... maybe not.

I thought I'd stopped reliving that moment in my nightmares years ago, but talking about my stupid magic with that stupid recruiter had sent my thoughts spiraling in a direction I didn't like.

I rose from my seat and stretched with a yawn, not at all rested. I pulled the earplugs from my ears and inspected the scenery. Tori, in all its glory, stood before us. We'd be docking soon. To the east were the Sinea mountains, and the sun was now hovering high above. I squinted in the glare off the water, temporarily blinded. It must've been around ten in the morning now, which meant I'd gotten at least a couple of hours of sleep.

Could've fooled me.

"Good morning, Private," grumbled Akins from her lounge chair nearby, where she was squinting at a cell phone screen as she typed.

"Good morning, ma'am."

Akins turned dark eyes on me, and I noticed a wrinkle between her eyebrows that seemed out of place on her otherwise youthful face. When she spoke, it was slowly and succinctly, leaving no room for doubting what she meant.

"You didn't hear anything at the recruiting office today."

I wanted to be a smart-alec and make a snide joke about my apparent deafness, but I sensed this wasn't the time. See? Growth.

"Of course not, ma'am. My ears and my eyes—and I suppose my mouth—are shut." I closed my eyes, mimed locking my lips shut, and covered my ears.

Akins relaxed back into her seat with a chuckle. "As you were, Private." I took that as a cue to open my eyes and mime retrieving a key to unlock my lips. Because that's the sort of person I was. Of course, my lips weren't even metaphorically sealed—I would proudly blab about Akins and Vasco, especially considering Akins had good as confirmed the rumor herself just now. But I wouldn't tell a soul— at least not until I'd blackmailed the good Captain for everything it would get me, and Minnie and I were far, far, away.

"So," she said, pausing to read a message on her cell phone, "are you still good for my party?"

I straightened. "Your party? Isn't that taking place in Monta, ma'am?"

She raised a thin black eyebrow, not even bothering to look up from her phone. "Did you not look at that address I gave you?"

"I didn't recognize the street name, but I figured it was just a part of the city I wasn't familiar with. I haven't exactly had time to look up a map in the past few days. Ma'am." I was getting really good at this whole formal address thing. The key was to say it sarcastically in my head, and then I'd remember to say it normally out loud. "Does that mean the party is at the capital?"

"Of course." She scoffed. "I rented out the Chamberle banquet hall and everything. I told you this was a big deal." I didn't recognize the venue, but it sounded fancy.

"Right. Then, I suppose if I'm not shipped off to war in a week, it would be my honor to work the party."

Akins chortled. "Don't believe everything you hear about the New Coranti Military, kid. We don't just 'ship people off' to—"

"My father was sent to the front lines the day he was called to serve. He died shortly after." My tone was harsh and clipped. "Ma'am."

Her face sobered. "I'm sorry, kid. We don't ship rookies off to war, how about that? I assume your father was a trained soldier?"

"He joined the army reserves before the revolution and was called out by the queen when the war started." I swallowed. "He was training to be a cobbler."

"A cobbler? Like, the dessert?"

I glared at her. "Like the people who make shoes—" I cut myself off before I could call her a foul word. "...ma'am."

"Well, cobblers aside, you'll have at least two months of intensive schooling and physical training before you're promoted to active duty. Normally we'd train you more, obviously, but the war being how it is..." She trailed off, powering off her phone. "We're docking. Get your things ready, private, you're about to be in our glorious nation's capital."

I resisted the urge to tell her I'd lived most of my childhood here—it wasn't worth it.

I slipped the earbuds in one of my many pants pockets; I didn't think Akins wanted them back now that they'd been in my ears. They were probably meant to be disposable, but I figured they might come in handy. Duffel bag in hand, I followed Akins down to the main deck, where passengers were rising from their seats and filing towards the docking gate as an automated voice boomed from the speakers, telling us to form an orderly queue so we could all disembark once the ferry was securely in the harbor. The line formed was certainly less than orderly.

I followed the Captain like a duckling trailing her mother as she blazed a path to the nearest subway with her uniform. I frowned, just now noticing the change of outfit. She must've changed while I was sleeping. She paid for both our tickets with some kind of special pass, and we boarded the underground train with a chorus of stares following us. Akins ignored it, and only a few stops later, with the car deadly silent, she gestured for me to get off.

Soon, we were back in the warm late morning air, which was considerably cooler than it was yesterday, standing outside a tall, narrow building on a crowded street.

I cleared my throat. "This isn't the military complex."

"You've got some acute observational skills there, Private." Akins gave me a sideways look, and I got a great view up her nostrils. Ew.

"So, why are we here?"

"I just have to stop real quick for an errand. You can wait outside."

"Great," I muttered to her turned back as she disappeared through a sliding glass door. "I don't suppose anyone wants to see a magic trick?"

Crickets, and a few glares. Alright then.

Finally, Akins met me back on the street and we descended back into the subway tunnels. No one seemed surprised to see a military officer walking in their midst, but I guessed Tori had a stronger military presence than Monta.

"You're pretty busy, huh?"

Akins kept her eyes on her mobile phone, fingers tapping furiously. "Yeah. I'm the highest-ranking officer in the city right now. Well, besides the queen, of course. All the higher-ups are off fighting the Nillaesce. 'Only reason I'm still here is that I'm serving a term teaching recruits."

"So you might be my instructor?"

"I sincerely hope not."

Ouch.

She laughed. "No, no, I like you, kid, it's just... being more experienced than my fellow instructors, I've been given the... special cases."

"Oh." The subway rattled along, and the occasional light flashed past as we sat in silence. "I hope you don't perceive this as rude, ma'am, but you seem pretty young to be the highest-ranked officer in Tori."

Akins laughed again. She sure did that a lot.

"Just about everyone in the military is pretty young these days, Private. Did you know the queen herself is only thirty-seven?"

I frowned contemplatively. "So she must've had kids fairly young, right? Wasn't Princess Daphne nineteen when all that stuff with her went down a couple of years ago?"

"Sharp memory, Private, but I wouldn't mention that name around the royals."

"The royals?"

"Yeah, the 'palace,' as it is, is right on the grounds, and the queen runs the whole place—supervising the training and all that. She's not big on ruling from a distance."

Interesting.

"But why?"

"What, about the princess? I would think it's common sense, considering what happened—"

"No, why is everyone so young? Ma'am."

"Right. Guess that's common sense too, though. The pre-revolution military was filled with old dudes, and when the witches took over, prominent revolution members filled the vacant leadership positions. Most of them were pretty young, and all women."

"Were you in the revolution?" Against my better judgment, I was actually curious about the answer.

"Sure was. I was only twenty at the time. Omili, it feels like I've aged two hundred years in the last eight." Akins rubbed between her eyes with a sigh, closing her eyes for the briefest second before returning to her phone. The screen had dimmed, and as she tapped in her passcode to reopen it, I looked over her shoulder as subtly as I could. Five-eight-eight-six. Couldn't hurt to know the mobile phone passcode of the highest-ranked officer in Tori.

We rode in silence for several stops, as I tried—and failed—to ignore the curious, nervous glances of the other passengers in our car. The number of people in our car slowly decreased until finally, Akins stuck her phone in her pocket and stood just as the subway pulled into the final stop. I looked around the now-empty seats and wondered if anyone else on the subway was getting off here. Didn't look like it.

I followed Akins out of the militaristic terminal and up a steep set of stairs, where she swiped some special identification card and the doors before us *whooshed* open. Beyond them sat a round receptionist desk with a bored-looking man stamping papers.

"Name?" he asked before we had even gotten to the desk.

I glanced at Akins, who looked back at me expectantly. I cleared my throat. "Byrne. Isla Byrne."

He swiveled his chair over to a large monitor, where he clacked away. "Just enlisted this morning, huh? Vasco's done all the paperwork, but it doesn't look like we have your blood in the records. I suppose he didn't administer a test?" he muttered under his breath. "Typical."

"No, but I don't really think I need a blood test—"

"Standard procedure for all female soldiers. We just need to, firstly, check that you do in fact have supernatural traces in your bloodstream, and quantify how much in order to place you."

*It's just a needle, Isla, it's just a needle, it's just—*

"Miss?"

I breathed deeply, and stuck out my arm, inner elbow exposed. That was where they took blood from usually, right?

The man raised an eyebrow at me. "*I* don't take blood samples. We have an infirmary for that." He pointed vaguely away from the desk before nodding to the tall woman behind me. "Perhaps Captain Akins can take you?"

She sighed tiredly. "I don't have time to ferry recruits around the complex, I've already had this one following me around like a lost puppy since Monta. I'm very busy, you know."

I frowned. Just because we were going to the same place didn't mean I'd been trailing her like a lost puppy—had I?

"Of course, ma'am. Here, kid, I'll just give you some directions," he said, already grabbing a loose piece of paper and scribbling something down. "After you get your blood taken and tested, you can come back here to wait while the results come in. Then we'll get you all situated with your instructor and group." He handed me a hastily drawn map of this section of the complex.

"Thank you," I mumbled, already turning away, leaving my duffel bag on the floor. But I wasn't going to the infirmary. Sure, I'd get my blood tested, but first I wanted to find Minnie. Find out what group she was in, and how I could manipulate my blood test results to get in the same group as her. I didn't really have a plan for getting her out of here, but I knew I had to find her first.

It didn't take much sneaking about to find the dormitories, on the second floor, a series of rooms full of bunk beds reminiscent of the Monta Orphanage. I peeked into several of the rooms, all vacant, and realized what a moronic idea this had been. Of course, the recruits wouldn't be in their dormitories in the middle of the day. They'd probably be training, but where?

I walked into dormitory C7 and plopped down on one of the bunks with a defeated sigh. It wasn't very comfortable, just a thin mattress on a wooden rack, but hopefully, I wouldn't be sleeping on one of these for very long. As soon as I could find Minnie, convince her to leave with me, and figure out how to leave without getting arrested, we'd be out of here. It couldn't be that hard, right?

I stretched and stood, ready to go get the blood test over with, and saw a flash of movement out of the corner of my eye. I froze. I probably—scratch that, *definitely*—wasn't supposed to be here. I peered around the corner of the door into the adjacent room, where I'd seen the motion. It looked empty from here and I relaxed slightly. I was probably just jumping at shadows. It had been a nerve-racking morning.

Slowly, I moved out into the hall to get a better view of room C9. The first thing I saw was a messy pile of newspapers and what looked like toilet paper near the foot of one of the bunks, which was odd and a bit unhygienic, but not what had initially caught my eye. A single dot of light appeared on the pile. I frowned as the dot grew, realization clicking in. My eyes followed the path of the light in the dusty air, and I moved slightly to the right to get a better view of the source.

A girl, probably about my age, stood by the window, holding up a magnifying glass to the bright morning sun and grinning demonically at her rapidly widening dot. She wore black fishnet sleeves under a standard-issue white top with the New Coranti Military emblem over the heart and shiny black leggings that definitely weren't in the recruit dress code. Her black eyes were wide in glee, the borderline insane expression accented by sharp black eyeshadow. Her skin was almost as white as paper, but I was pretty sure it was mostly powder—if only from the fact that the glimpses of her skin visible through her sleeves was slightly less pale than her face, which was framed by a bob of light blonde hair.

I stepped forward, relieved that it was only a recruit and not someone more important. I pulled over a conveniently placed stool to help me reach the fire alarm and covered it with my hand, waving away the faint smoke rising from the girl's budding fire.

The girl at the window jumped in alarm, shifting the magnifying glass, before making the same relieving discovery I had and scowling at me. "What are you doing?"

I rolled my eyes. "That's such an amateur move. You have to cover the smoke alarm first, or at the first whiff of smoke you'll get drenched and the authorities will be right on you."

She scoffed, focusing back on her arson. "I'm no neophyte, punk. I *want* to be caught."

Well, that was new. "Excuse me?"

"I want to get kicked out of the military, dipstick."

"Oh." Would that work? Had I just found me and Minnie's way out? I wished, but, alas, no.

"Now uncover the fire alarm so I can get dishonorably discharged."

"Sure, get yourself arrested, I don't care," I said, removing my hand and stepping down.

The girl bent down, grabbing a thick book from her makeshift kindling and throwing it at me. I caught it with a grunt, brushing off a stray piece of toilet paper. At least it looked clean.

"'A recruit will be discharged dishonorably during training under any and all charges of unnecessary violence, destruction of military property, fraternization with a superior officer, arson, or other reasons as ruled by the General in Chief.'" She quoted, deadpan, nodding at the book she'd thrown at me. "Section thirty-seven, chapter four, clause thirteen."

I looked down. The book was titled: *So, You've Enlisted in the Coranti Military? Here's Your Helpful Guide To All the Relevant Handbook Rules, compiled by Andrew Wilkins.* The cover depicted a young man, probably in his early twenties, wearing a military uniform and an obnoxious grin. I flipped it over, searching the inside of the back cover and, sure enough, there was a publication date.

"This is extremely outdated. It was published two years before the Witch Revolution, and the military is run by different people now. I doubt the queen would let you off of military service just for arson." I smiled grimly. "Plus, I'm pretty sure this was meant for voluntary recruits, not conscripted soldiers. You'd probably have to break your leg or something like that."

The girl glowered, and I extended my hand with a grin. "I like you. What's your name?"

"That's none of your business, idiot. Leave me alone."

I shrugged, turning to face the hallway. "Suit yours—"

The blare of an alarm over the intercom froze me in my tracks, and I looked first at the uncovered fire alarm, then over my shoulder at the girl. I really didn't want to be here when she got arrested for arson. No way was I getting incriminated in this.

"It's not the fire alarm," muttered blondie the nameless arsonist sullenly, eyes on her decidedly *not* burnt papers.

"Then what is it?" I asked, just as a voice crackled over the speaker in the hallway.

"We need a supernaturally-specialized doctor at the training grounds ASAP, and all recruits to their dormitories. There has been an incident on the training grounds. I repeat, a supernaturally-specialized doctor to the training grounds ASAP, and all recruits to their dormitories. There has been an incident..."

I swallowed, exchanging a glance with the would-be arsonist. She had a decision to make, and I needed to get out of here.

# 7

*"The urban legend of the witch-killer 'Darkheart' is one made of shadows and fear, not logic and fact. There is no hard evidence I have found of one all-powerful witch-killer murdering hundreds of witches over the last twenty-four years. If anything, I would cite these mass killings to a group of genocidal maniacs, not one sole individual with more power than the whole Supernatural Ground Division of the New Coranti Army."*

—*Darkheart: Ghost Story or Threat to Public Safety? Debunking Coranti's Most Terrifying Rumors, written by John Eckelvi.*

•• ▬▬▬▬▬ ••●•• ▬▬▬▬▬ ••

I bolted for the stairwell, the girl right on my heels. She followed me down two flights of stairs and out onto a hallway on the first floor, seeming to think I had any idea where I was going. I didn't, and all the hallways were beginning to look the same. At the next intersection, I whirled to face her.

"Where should we go?"

"The cafeteria?"

"What, you hungry?"

"No," she said, scowling. "It should be pretty much empty this time of day, and all the important people who might be there will be off investigating whatever went down at the training fields."

"Good plan, you lead the way." We slowed to a brisk walk, and I followed her down several more stark hallways before they opened into a large room filled with tables. "So, why weren't you at the training grounds?"

The arsonist barely spared me a glance as she led me to a table in the corner. "Bathroom break, naturally."

"Naturally."

She squinted at me, apparently just now noticing my lack of uniform. "Who are you, anyway?"

"New recruit. I was supposed to go get my blood tested at the infirmary, but I suppose you could say I went for a... bathroom break."

She smiled at me, and it was startling how much the slight motion changed her features. With a sigh, she extended a hand.

"Vera Roberts, conscripted witch, Holder specification."

I shook her hand. "Isla Byrne, conscripted witch, and I'm going to be honest with you, I'm not quite sure what all that specification stuff is about."

Vera rolled her eyes. "You're really new, then. That's the basics of what they teach you."

"Mind enlightening me?"

"You'll find out soon enough anyway, but whatever. You know how magic works, right?"

An image of a woman collapsed in a hallway flickered across my vision, and I shuddered. "Sort of. I know only women can be witches, and magic involves taking the energy from other people, right?"

"Er, not necessarily. Guess you're a Drainer, then?"

"Sounds familiar."

"Alright, so there are three basic types of witches—and this is all hereditary, mind you, so you can only be a witch if you come from a witch family, and you can only be a Drainer if you come from a Drainer family, and so on. Anyways, magic is all about the exchange of what they like to call 'Life Energy,' though I don't think even the scientists quite understand it. It was pretty much taboo to study it before the Revolution, so the only pre-Revolution data we have are some really weird hypotheses."

"I couldn't care less about the history or science or whatever, just cut to the chase."

Vera scowled at me. "Fine, I'll let you get the boring lesson then," she said, crossing her arms over her chest.

"Don't be such a baby. I just want to know—"

"How about you go get your blood tested before they find out you're not where you're supposed to be?"

She had a point, I realized with a frown. "How about you shut up?" I muttered spitefully, just to have the last word, rising from the table and leaving the cafeteria.

The makeshift map was meant to help me get from the front desk to the infirmary and wasn't much use from the cafeteria. Vera probably knew, but no way was I going back to ask her. At least I was on the right floor now.

I wandered the halls until I found someone to give me directions. Honestly, you'd think there'd be more people here, but this area seemed nearly abandoned.

"Excuse me, I'm a bit lost."

The boy, who had been power walking like his life depended on it, slowed to a stop, brushing a shaggy mop of reddish-brown hair away from his face. He was probably about my age, though it was hard to tell between his tall frame and babyish face dotted with deep, pocked scars—either from acne or some sort of pox, I couldn't be sure.

"Sorry, I'm kinda busy right now—"

I frowned at his vaguely familiar face. "Do I know you?"

He smiled self-deprecatingly, looking like he'd rather be just about anywhere else in the world, and I realized where I recognized him from. "Probably."

I waved him off. "Doesn't matter. I just need directions to the infirmary."

He sighed tiredly, turning to point in the direction I'd come from. "Go that way until the hallway splits, turn left, pass the elevator bank, go through the doors to the medical wing, and then the infirmary is the second door on the right."

"Thanks," I said with my classic mischievous grin, "Your Highness."

He gave a small, tight-lipped smile back and flew off down the hallway as if I'd bitten him. I laughed softly, turning back the way I'd come. Akins had warned me there'd be royals wandering about the military complex, but I hadn't exactly expected to see the prince on my first day.

The general public, in my experience, had mixed opinions on the royal family. They didn't feel very "royal," in the traditional sense of the word—the queen may have been the most powerful witch in the country, maybe the whole world, but she really had just created the monarchy out of thin air eight years ago and plopped herself right on the throne, and she brought her kids with her. They were all over the news, all the time, to the point where I'd honestly rather they just told us depressing news from the war over another mindless news story about what Princess Alethia, first heir to the throne of Coranti at only thirteen years old, was doing yesterday.

I found the infirmary without much trouble. Past a pair of double doors marked "MEDICAL," the infirmary was a clean, well-lit room with several other doors leading off it. At the desk, a young man with a name tag that read only "intern" was typing at a desktop computer.

I peered around the room, hoping someone more qualified might be hiding in the corners, before remembering the announcement that had sent Vera and me scurrying from the scene of her almost-crime. Right. All the real nurses and medics and such must be at the training grounds.

I cleared my throat, loudly, and the intern raised his head from the keyboard, blinking rapidly at me. He bolted to his feet, stumbled, righted himself, and rounded the desk with a wide smile.

"Are you Isla Byrne? Bart at the front desk said you'd be coming by a while ago, so we've been expecting you."

I plastered an apologetic smile on my face and lied with the truth. "Sorry, I got a bit lost. These hallways all look the same."

He nodded sympathetically. "I completely understand. I've been working here for a couple of weeks now, and I'm still totally confused all the time." He rubbed his hands together. "Right! Let's draw some blood!"

I grimaced. "Are you really qualified to do that?"

"It's just a needle, don't worry, I do it all the time."

"Sorry, I just don't like the idea of someone sticking a needle in me and literally pulling my blood out of my body."

"Have you never had blood taken before?"

I shook my head. "No, my dad was pretty weird about it growing up. I think he had a thing against needles or something." I shuddered. If so, it was definitely something I'd gotten from him.

"It's very simple. I just stick this little syringe in your arm and take a smidgen of blood," he said, holding up an arguably not-so-little syringe. "Then I put the blood in this machine right here"—he tapped a simple aluminum cube, about as tall as my forearm, that was sitting on a side table—"and it analyzes your blood content! Pretty cool, huh?"

I only hmphed in response, jutting out my arm. "How long will the results take?"

The intern stepped forward with his torture weapon, still contorting his face into what I think he intended to be a comforting smile. "Oh, usually only about a half an hour. Now, you'll feel a slight pinch—"

I flinched, focusing on the open door instead of the needle in my arm.

"All done! That wasn't so bad, huh?"

I forced a thin smile as the intern slapped a bandage over the inside of my elbow and crossed, humming quietly, to the blood cube. Then, the humming cut off abruptly. He stood stock-still, staring at the blood he'd squeezed into the little well at the top of the cube. He turned slightly to gape at me, Adam's apple bobbing as he gulped.

"W—why don't you sit down there, m—miss," he said, backing away from me as he gestured at the row of waiting chairs, wide eyes flickering between the blood and my face.

I frowned, standing on the tips of my toes to get a better look at the blood. I didn't see a lot of blood, but there didn't seem to be anything wrong with it.

The intern scurried from the room, muttering something about the bathroom over his shoulder. What a weirdo.

Watching the puddle of blood slowly filter into the metal box with a whirring noise, I yawned and sat down in one of the uncomfortable plastic chairs. My foot tapped absent-mindedly against the chair leg as I waited for the results

A couple of minutes later that weird intern still wasn't back from his impromptu bathroom break, but the stomp of boots outside the infirmary door brought my attention from my tapping leg. I straightened in my seat, leaning forward to see the group just as they entered the room. I cleared my throat, ready to tell the four heavily armed soldiers that all the infirmary staff was gone at the moment, but they focused on me instead.

"Are you Isla Byrne?" one of the soldiers, a tall blonde woman, asked gruffly.

I narrowed my eyes. What did they want with me? "No, I'm not."

"She's lying. Take her."

I jumped from my seat just as the soldiers swarmed me, grabbing me roughly and yanking my arms behind my back. The cold metal of a pair of handcuffs clinked around my wrists, and the iron grip of two soldiers clamped down on either arm. I kicked my feet weakly, trying to free myself, but they had the audacity to put handcuffs around my ankles, too. What were they going to do, drag me?

That was exactly what they did, pulling me down countless identical hallways and ignoring my protests and questions. If I could have moved my arms even a hair, I was sure I'd be able to get out of these handcuffs, but, alas, it looked like I'd just have to wait. I tried to pay attention to where we were going, though all the hallways seemed to blend together. I knew for certain we went up at least seven floors. Maybe eight.

Finally, my entourage, complete with the blonde woman, who seemed to be the leader, the two goons holding me, and a shorter woman behind who I'd only seen in glimpses, stopped at a large pair of double doors. The leader reached for the buzzer by the doors, but before she even hit the button, a booming voice called for us to come in.

The room was about the size of my room back at the orphanage, with a table at the far edge and a single, lonely chair near the large doors. At the table sat Queen Isabella of Coranti, my favorite Captain, and two other women I didn't recognize. The soldiers shoved me roughly into the chair, attaching my handcuffs to the back, and the handcuffs around my ankles to the legs of the chair.

I smiled widely at the table as the leader and the woman who walked in the back approached it and the other two went to stand to either side of me. Goodie.

"What can I do for you fine ladies today? Why the special treatment?" I asked through gritted teeth, fighting to look as relaxed as possible despite the dread curdling my stomach. This wasn't good. This wasn't good at all

"Drop the act, Byrne. We've seen your blood," snarled the woman to the queen's left, nodding to the soldier who'd stayed behind, who I now noticed was carrying a little clear cup filled with blood. My blood?

"Excuse me?"

I tried to meet Akins' eyes, but she wouldn't look at me, and instead, my eyes found the queen. I'd recognized her instantly—the fiery red hair, pale blue eyes, and harsh, angular face that were all over the news almost constantly were a little hard to forget. She wasn't looking at me either, but she seemed to be more distracted than purposefully ignoring me. The only people at the table actually looking at me were the two strangers, one with spite and the other with caution.

"You're a murderer, Isla Byrne."

Omili above, they knew. I wet my lips, ready to rebuke the claim, but the same woman, the angry, dark-haired one on the queen's left, cut me off.

"No, never mind, that's too good a word for what you are. You're a mass murderer, for Omili's sake. You're practically Darkheart."

No, wait. I was no mass murderer. I'd just made one mistake, one time, when I was little.

"That's a bit of an exaggeration, Emilia. Based on the data—"

"I couldn't care less about the data. Look at that blood. Take a long, hard look. Do you see how black it is? I've studied blood for years, Tanya, and that right there is the magic of dozens of dead witches."

"The results from her blood test are just coming in now, actually..." muttered Tanya, the second stranger, as she tapped at a tablet screen. She inhaled sharply.

"I was right, wasn't I?" huffed Emilia.

"I... Yes. Going by average magic content in a witch, this young lady must have killed approximately thirty–one witches. Less if the witches were more powerful than average, more for less powerful witches, you get—"

I cleared my throat loudly, gathering the attention of the whole table. Akins still wouldn't meet my eyes, though. "Excuse me? Do I not get a say?"

"Murderers don't get a say, so no," said Emilia, red-faced, turning to the queen. "Your Majesty, I suggest we execute her immediately."

"Suggestion noted," yawned the queen, as she tapped a device in her ear and began muttering to it softly.

"Wait, wait, wait," I sputtered, calm facade shattering. I knew the military would kill me, but I didn't think this was how I'd die. I'd never even said goodbye to Minnie. "What grounds do you have to execute me? Just a bit of blood? What happened to justice, to—"

"*Justice* is when proven murderers get put down, and we have all the proof we need in that 'little bit of blood.'"

"So you're just going to ignore my testament? I'm no mass murderer. I don't even know how you deluded idiots got the idea that two seconds looking at my blood gives you the evidence to murder me in cold blood." I nodded respectively to the queen, who still very clearly wasn't paying attention. "Excluding you, Your Majesty. You're no deluded idiot." She was as much an idiot as the rest of them, but contrary to their apparent beliefs, I didn't have a death wish

Emilia the mean idiot leaned forward in her seat, a grim smile playing across her lips. "I'll humor you for a second, little murderer. Let's say you're as oblivious as you say, and you have absolutely no clue what we're accusing you of."

"I don't."

"I'm still talking. Don't interrupt me." She took a deep breath, rolling her neck. "My name is Emilia Morren, head of the Darkheart Oppositionary Department of the New Coranti Military. My sole purpose is organizing the hunt against Darkheart. Do you know who Darkheart is, little murderer?"

I nodded solemnly. Everyone had heard of Darkheart, though many, me included, believed him to be a nightmare tale told to little witches to keep them scared. The government had never acknowledged his existence before.

"To understand Darkheart, one must first understand the transference of magic."

"Isn't it hereditary?" I asked, feeling smart.

Morren gritted her teeth and kept talking as if I hadn't spoken. "As most people understand, all natural witches are women, and come from long and ancient lines of witches all of the same specification."

"Natural witches?"

"Tanya, will you please search up Byrne's family in that helpful tablet of yours?"

"Of course." I focused on Tanya as she typed, trying to ignore Morren's hateful glare.

"Well?"

"Father: Nicholas Byrne, deceased at forty-one years, served in the Coranti Military as a young man and was called out of reserves to fight in the war, where he was shot three times in the chest at the Battle of Split Peak. Mother: Anna Byrne, deceased at thirty-six years, also served in the Coranti Military, had a record of juvenile violence and crime, deceased in childbirth. Isla Byrne has been a ward of the Monta City Orphanage for the past eight years. No known siblings." Tanya furrowed her brow, typing at her screen. "We don't have Anna Byrne's analyzed blood in the records because she died before the revolution, so we can't know her status as a witch, but she has no ties to any known witch family lines."

"So that proves absolutely nothing, right? I still don't understand what makes you think I'm a murderer."

"I'm getting to it," snapped Morren. "The instant that intern saw the color of your blood, he had the sense to call security. Your blood is several shades darker than normal blood."

I scoffed. "So? What does that even mean?"

"It means… Right. Back to Darkheart. You know he's a mass murderer too, right?"

"Sure." I ignored the "too."

"When you kill a witch, you get a smidgen of their magic, about six percent. The rest is thought to be absorbed into the atmosphere. We're not about to go around killing witches for science, so we can't be sure what happens to the other ninety–four percent."

I frowned. "I didn't know that."

"Sure you didn't," laughed Morren. "You just killed those thirty–one witches for fun, right?"

"I told you, I—"

"So this magic is unnatural, some might even say cursed. There are two fundamental, unbreakable laws of magic that we know of, and murder breaks two of them. Killing different types of witches and getting their magic is the only way to have multiple types of magic. It's also the only way for a man to have magic, for example, Darkheart. Except for a sex change, of course."

"Darkheart is a witch?"

"Were you not listening, little murderer? Darkheart is a mass murderer who has killed hundreds of witches to get their magic. Now, here's the kicker. Have you ever wondered why he's called Darkheart?"

"Not particularly, no."

"He's called Darkheart because, when magic is taken forcefully by a murderer, it taints your blood. Every witch you kill turns your blood just a little blacker, until, after hundreds of murders, your blood is pure black."

"So he's called Darkheart because his heart pumps black blood?" I asked, deadpan.

"Oh look, the little murderer has a brain cell after all."

Tanya held up her screen, showing it to the assembled parties at the table before turning it so I could see. "The left image is what normal blood looks like when exposed to air, and the right image is Miss Byrne's blood sample from a half-hour ago."

I squinted at the two side-by-side images. The difference was definitely noticeable, but just looking at my blood without the parallel, I wouldn't be able to tell it was different at all. That poor intern must look at a lot of blood if he could see the anomaly. The very thought made me queasy. Not that I was squeamish or anything—alright, I was a little squeamish.

"So how do you know I wasn't just born with especially dark blood?" I leaned forward as much as my restraints would allow me. "You can analyze my blood, so can't you give me a lie detector test or something? That's a thing, right? I promise I'm no mass murderer."

Tanya frowned contemplatively. "I suppose a polygraph test couldn't hurt, could it?"

"I don't know if it would help," muttered Akins, looking only at Tanya. "She's a street magician. She lies for a living."

"Actually, I don't think of magic tricks as lies, per se. More like me showing you an alternative version of the truth and trying to get you to believe it."

"So, lying?"

"You're all out of your minds! Why would we give her a polygraph test when we have the proof of murder right here?" protested Morren.

"The girl has a point, Emilia. All of this supernatural blood analysis stuff is pretty new, considering this branch of science didn't even exist a decade ago. Maybe she just has some rare blood pigmentation disorder we haven't seen before?"

"Fine," Morren said grudgingly. "She can take a polygraph test. If it says she's telling the truth, we revisit the matter. If it deems her guilty, we sentence her to death, no questions asked."

Tanya and Akins nodded, apparently agreeing with this insane plan, and the three women turned to the queen expectantly.

"Your Majesty? What do you rule?" Tanya asked hesitantly.

"Sure, give her the test. Sounds good," the queen said through a yawn.

"Alright then. I'll get the questions and equipment prepared, and the test should be ready by the end of the day," chirped Tanya, rising to her feet and gathering her things. I gaped as the table members began to file out.

Tonight, I would take the test that could get me sentenced to death, and all I had to do was avoid talking about that one time I accidentally killed someone. No pressure.

# 8

*"Polygraph tests are highly circumstantial and faulty, easy to cheat and easy for an innocent to fail."*

—*What Is a Polygraph Test? an article by renowned behavioral scientist Elena Forcet.*

"Are you comfortable, Miss Byrne?" asked Tanya.

I struggled not to frown at the bright light being shown into my eyes. "Well, I'm—"

"Too bad, I couldn't care less how comfortable you are," muttered Morren. Goodie, she was here too.

"We'll start, then. I have a list of questions prepared, which an independent examiner will ask you. We're on a bit of a rushed schedule considering the severity of your alleged crimes, but I assure you, all necessary measures have been taken to validate your results. Good luck."

Footsteps, the slam of a door, and the bright light dimmed enough for me to see the person sitting across from me, holding a clipboard. I was still restrained, and my wrists were beginning to ache and chafe from having the handcuffs on nearly all day. I'd spent the majority of my day in a solitary holding cell. Apparently, the new monarchy slogan was "guilty until proven innocent," by the way they were treating me.

I focused on calming my breathing as assistants placed rubber tubes over my chest, stuck metal plates to my fingertips, and wrapped a thick band with a little clock-like monitor around my arm.

"Are you ready to begin, Miss Byrne?"

I swallowed the anxious lump in my throat, knowing the tubes and wires surrounding me were there to monitor my bodily reactions. I just had to stay calm and remember I wasn't guilty. Well, not completely guilty.

"Yes."

"Delightful. We will begin with a set of simple orientation questions, to test the equipment, then slowly shift into the more relevant questions." The examiner cleared their throat. "What is your full name?"

"Isla Anna Byrne."

"Where were you born?"

"Here. Well, not here exactly, obviously, but at the Tori General Hospital."

"Favorite color?"

"Blue. Navy blue."

"Have you ever held a weapon?" Slowly shift. *Right.*

"Define weapon?"

"An object designed to inflict bodily harm or physical damage."

"Er, no, I don't think so? Maybe a knife."

"Are you aware of the origins of your blood color?"

"What kind of question is that? I'm aware that my blood is perfectly normal and not tainted with creepy dead witch magic, so yes?"

"Have you ever stolen something?"

I swallowed. Might as well tell the truth. "Yes."

"Do you have a history of violence?"

"As I said, I don't really have a thing for weapons."

"Answer the question, Miss Byrne."

How was I supposed to avoid that one? Would you call that incident with my neighbor when I was eight a history of violence? The longer I paused, the more guilty I seemed, so I needed to say something fast.

"Well, us orphans tend to have a lot of pent-up anger and grief, you know how it is, so I've been in some fights before at the orphanage." I tried my hardest to sound like that was all I'd been trying to cover up.

"Have you ever killed a witch?"

"Not to my knowledge," I said sardonically, although it was the truth. I wasn't sure if Ms. Borough from apartment 3B had been a witch, though I didn't think so.

"Are you a mass murderer?"

"Wow, these questions are getting awfully blunt."

The examiner blinked baleful eyes at me.

"Not in my memory. The only two options I see are that I either committed said mass murder when I was super young, or I killed a bunch of people at some point during the last sixteen years of my life and the event was so traumatizing it blocked my memory. Both of these options seem ridiculous and unprovable, so no, I am not a mass murderer. Are we done now?"

"Please be patient, Miss Byrne, just a few more questions. Have you answered all questions asked truthfully?"

"As truthfully as I'm able."

"Have you intentionally concealed any relevant information over the course of this test?"

If that woman wasn't a witch, then technically that information was not relevant to the current investigation, right? I smiled and answered semi-truthfully, "No."

"That concludes the test, please wait calmly in your chair for the assistants to remove the test equipment. Thank you for your patience."

Who were they kidding? "Wait calmly in your chair." It wasn't like I was going anywhere with these restraints.

The same squad of four security-people escorted me back to my holding cell in silence. Based on how noticeably not executed I was right now, I assumed I'd passed the test.

They took off the handcuffs this time, and I curled up on the thin cot, ankles still bound, and tried to massage some life back into my bruised and raw wrists. This was really not how I wanted things to go, but what else had I expected from the New Coranti Military?

My sleep was restless at best, and I woke feeling even more sleep deprived than I had when I'd fallen asleep, if that was even possible. I'd woken up and fallen back asleep countless times during the night, but now I sat upright on the cot, knees tucked to my chest, waiting for the table of unqualified buffoons to decide my fate. Honestly, every day I was thankful that mind readers didn't exist. If someone could look into my head… Calling the queen a buffoon would be the least of my problems. Well, no, it would certainly be up there on my list of problems.

The *clunk* of several pairs of booted footsteps thumped down the hallway outside, a key turned, and finally, the door opened to reveal my favorite blonde security team leader. She jerked her head in my direction, and the goons stepped forward to secure the handcuffs back on my sore wrists and drag me out.

"So, execution or restitution, which is it?" I asked with my brightest grin, but they acted as if they didn't even hear me. Smile slipping, I repeated myself, words tripping over each other as the soldiers hauled me up several flights of stairs.

"Hello? Are you guys mute?"

Silence.

Then, a single gruff "No."

"Great, thanks. Lovely chat."

They brought me to the same room as yesterday and restrained me to the same chair, where I sat awkwardly as Akins, Morren, and Tanya all filed in and seated themselves at the large table. I tried to wipe my sweaty hands on the back of the chair to no avail. I didn't like handcuffs much, I decided.

"Where's the queen?"

"Her Majesty could not attend this morning, but she has already signed off on our decided course of action," said Tanya, tapping at her tablet.

"Which is? I suppose you haven't decided to execute me after all."

"Bold assumption," muttered Morren, but the sullen expression on her face told me what I needed to know.

"Delightful. Can we take these handcuffs off, then?"

"Not quite yet, Miss Byrne. We have, in fact, ruled that there is not enough strong evidence to sentence a bright young girl such as yourself to death."

I would bet that the vote hadn't been unanimous. Morren still seemed to think I was plenty guilty.

"So, what will you do?"

"You do have promisingly high magic content in your blood, and in such strained times, we need every witch we have. You will be trained to fight like any other recruit," Tanya announced.

"Forgive me if I don't jump up and down with joy, I'm a little… tied up at the moment," I replied, trying my very hardest to keep the bitterness from my tone. Training to fight in this war… that was what they thought I wanted, right?

"As there is no firm evidence against you, we wish we could presume you innocent. But frankly, we can't afford to take that risk, and thus you will be under strict guard at all times and will be supervised by the very best and most resilient instructors we have on hand. We want to trust you, we really do, but at the first hint of trouble, we will not hesitate to send you to a holding cell. Do you understand?"

"Yes."

"Wonderful. Now, yes, we can take the handcuffs off." Tanya nodded to the security leader, who stepped forward to unlock the restraints on my ankles and wrists. I stood as soon as I could, stretching.

Akins stood too, rounding the table and heading for the door without looking back. "Come along, Private, lessons start at seven."

Was she talking to me? I met Tanya's gaze, and she nodded for me to follow. What had Akins said? *I've been given the… special cases.*

"This is just fantastic," muttered Akins as she led me down two flights of stairs and several long, blank hallways. "The train wreck, the arsonist, the dimwit, and now, the alleged murderer. Sounds like the beginning of a bad joke, doesn't it, Private?"

"Yes, I suppose?"

"Yeah, it does." Akins chuckled mirthlessly. "The mental train wreck, the arsonist, the dimwit, and the murderer walk into a bar.

They kill Captain Akins, dance on her dead body, have a drink, and leave."

I forced a smile, unsure how to respond to that.

Akins pulled open the door to a small classroom with a huff and stood in the doorway for several seconds, blocking the entrance. Finally, she stomped inside and plopped into a spinning chair clearly meant for a teacher.

"Look at that clock, Private, and tell me what time it is."

My eyes followed Akins' extended arm to the clock over the whiteboard. "Uh, it's five minutes to seven, ma'am."

"Exactly," Akins growled. "So why in the world are we the only ones in this classroom?"

Someone woke up on the wrong side of the bed this morning. "Maybe because lessons start at seven, ma'am?"

"Don't get smart with me, Byrne. Punctuality is very important. I do not tolerate lateness."

I resisted the urge to tell her that, technically, no one was late yet. They still had five minutes.

"I'm here!" A frustratingly cheery voice called out, and a boy entered, slamming the door even farther open than it was already. I was pretty sure a vein popped up on Akins' forehead.

"Who are you?" Akins' voice dripped with disdain as she took in the nightmare that stood before us. Absurdly tall, probably taller than her, even, with bleached hair and electric blue tips that stood on end as if he'd been electrocuted. His face looked like that too—I'd never seen such a wide smile on anything but a skull.

"Edward Buck, ma'am. You're Captain Akins, right? Or am I in the wrong room?" Without waiting for an answer, the giant of a boy plopped down at one of the desks, the plastic chair creaking under his weight. I stifled a grin at the expression on Akins' face as I took a seat on the opposite side of the room as him.

"Yes," replied Akins through gritted teeth. "I'm Captain Akins. Welcome to Training Group 118."

"I'm so happy to be here! I think it will be just such a delightful change to train with witches." He turned to face me; teeth bared in a blinding smile. "Are you a witch?"

"What's it to you?"

His smile slipped slightly. "I'm used to training with normal enlisted soldiers, you know, just a bunch of boring eighteen-year-olds that are not magical in the slightest and very resentful, so I just thought that witches would be more... fun, you know, because you guys actually have a reason to fight?"

The gentle scratch of a chair shifting slightly against the linoleum floor brought all of our attention to the far-left corner of the room, where a girl had pulled out a chair. She flinched slightly when she saw us looking at her and lowered her head slightly.

"Don't mind me," she said to the floor, slipping into her chair. "I don't mean to interrupt."

She was willowy to the point of worry, with a thin face dominated by wide eyes behind large, round glasses with golden frames. Sharply contrasted against her dark skin was her yellow dress, pale and floral, and definitely not uniform. Looking down, I remembered I was still wearing my black shirt and cargo pants from after my shower in Monta. Was that really still not even two full days ago? So much had happened.

Edward wore a sharply fitted uniform, with the same white training shirt as I'd seen on the arsonist. Interesting. Only one of us was in uniform.

"Roberts or Bailey?" asked Akins, surveying a tablet she'd pulled from a desk drawer.

"Oh, uh, Bailey. Ella Bailey," squeaked the girl.

Edward turned to her with wide eyes. "*The* Ella Bailey? You're a legend! I've heard so many stories about you." His leg bounced wildly, shaking his desk like an earthquake. "Is it true you used magic to knock twenty recruits unconscious at the training grounds yesterday?"

"Just six, actually." Ella straightened her glasses, twisted her delicate gold ring, then started messing with her long, dark braid, like her hands couldn't sit still.

"And the instructor," added Akins bitterly, to Edward's amazement.

"It was an accident, I promise, I didn't mean to—"

"Luckily," interrupted Akins, "they are all showing signs of a full recovery, and Sergeant Fulke is going to resume teaching tomorrow."

"Oh, that's good news, right?"

I raised my head at the sounds of a scuffle outside. A loud string of very creative curses followed the two security goons into the room as they hauled my friend the arsonist in between them.

"I told you, I can walk, you scuttling scrap-bags! Put me down this instant!"

And they did, with a loud thump. The soldiers left, closing the door behind them, and with another curse, Vera stood. No one offered to help her as she adjusted her tight black pants and slouched into a seat between Edward and me.

"Vera Roberts, I assume?"

"The one and only."

"That's everyone, then."

Akins stood, replacing the tablet on the desk, and began to pace with her arms crossed behind her back.

"I am Captain Mila Akins, Supernatural Ground Division of the Coranti Army, and for the next two months, I will be your instructor. We will cover fighting techniques, basic war strategy, military hierarchy, use of firearms, theoretical supernatural instruction, and practical supernatural use on a battlefield. You will answer to me and obey my every order. You will have a curfew from twenty–one hundred hours to five hours every night. Every morning, you will report to this room at exactly six-fifty, and instruction will begin at exactly seven. You will wear the proper uniform given to you by the New Coranti Military. Is this understood?"

We answered in a strange mix of nods, attempted salutes, vocal affirmation, and grunts. Akins sighed, sinking back into her spinning chair.

"The past eight years have molded us into an... unconventional military training program, and yet we do have our constants. This group breaks most of them. A mix of non-supernatural and supernatural recruits, we are a small training group of only four choice individuals. Ella Bailey, diagnosed with severe clinical anxiety, a powerful witch, and yet a liability on the battlefield. Edward Buck, a horrible soldier, and apparently so annoying that absolutely every instructor in the department begged not to train him."

Edward's ever-present smile began to droop.

"Vera Roberts, attempted arsonist with a history of juvenile violence and destruction of property. And, of course, Isla Byrne, possibly a mass murderer, who is currently not being executed due to the fact that most of the evidence against her is flimsy at best."

Ella, Vera, and Edward all turned to me with wide eyes and I grinned back, daring to wink. They all flinched, even Vera.

"You may ask why such an odd and dysfunctional group is being trained at all, and at any other time in Coranti history, you probably wouldn't be. But this is wartime, and we need all hands on deck. We're outmanned enough against the Nillaesce army as it is without turning away capable witches. And Edward. Personally, I believe my efforts would be better off elsewhere and that the lot of you are hopeless, but far be it from me to question orders from above." Akins snorted. "So, let's learn."

# 9

*"To be a* nornei—*or witch, as the monsters are known across the mountains—is to be an abomination, struck down by the deities. All* nornei *must be purified in holy death for their souls to reach Auris and Lerein."*

—*What is a* Nornei? *written by Edricko Nort, Nillaesce High Priest beneath the Leitoi.*

••———————— ••●•• ————————— ••

"Are you paying attention, Byrne?"

I lazily raised my eyes to meet Akins' gaze. "Of course, ma'am. Always."

She huffed, muttering something under her breath about being reduced to a school teacher, and I grinned. Teachers hated me. "If you've been paying attention, then surely you can tell me who is thought to be a pioneer in defining modern witchcraft, nearly two hundred years ago?"

"Easy." I faked a yawn, stretching enough to catch a glimpse of Ella's notebook, scanning her neat handwriting quickly for the answer. "Cecile Omili, of course."

"That's… correct." Akins sounded surprised. She was a little too distracted to deduce that I hadn't moved across the room, into the seat directly behind Ella Bailey, because of a bad draft. No, I'd moved because I'd marked her as the type of person to take neat, detailed, easily cheatable notes. As always, I was right.

I relaxed back into my seat as Akins continued blabbering about magic theory this and boring history that. I wasn't here to learn. I was still determined not to use magic, ever, and I wouldn't need what they were trying to teach me about the battlefield because I wouldn't be *going* to the battlefield. I was here to get Minnie and get out.

A small wad of paper bounced onto my desk, disrupting my brainstorming, and I scowled in the direction it came from. Vera raised her eyebrows at me, and with a long-suffering sigh, I grabbed the note and unfurled it under my desk. On it were written two different messages, in two different handwritings, with two different pens.

First, written in plain black ink and a messy scrawl that looked more like chicken scratch than anything a human would write: *Hey Byrne. Alleged murderer, huh? Who'd you kill?*

The second was simple, clean, block letters in bright blue ink. *Hi, Isla. This is Edward. I just wanted to let you know that I intercepted this message because Vera here can't throw to save her life, and though I don't approve of the crude question, I'm very curious about the answer.*

I frowned, crumpling the note back up and tossing it at the trashcan. I didn't look to see if it went in or not.

"And now I'm tired of dealing with you morons, so I get a two-hour break before physical training. Eat lunch, use the little witch's room, whatever, meet me at the training grounds at thirteen hundred hours. Understood?"

Akins pinched the bridge of her nose and began gathering her things before pausing.

"We'll have a quiz tomorrow on everything we learned today, so you might as well study too. Dismissed."

I ambushed Akins on her way out the door. "Where's my duffel bag?"

"We already moved it to the group dormitory room," Akins said dismissively, pushing past me, medals jangling.

"Which room is that?"

She paused, raising an eyebrow. "The one on the opposite side of the complex as the normal dormitories, behind a secure, locked door, for the safety of the other recruits."

I gaped, unsure why I was even surprised. "What?"

"Morren's idea, not mine."

Muttering a curse under my breath, I followed her out the door, only to find myself face-to-face with two pairs of eager eyes. Well, face-to-empty air and face-to-chest, more accurately. With everyone standing up together, I could see that Ella was around my own height, maybe a bit taller, but Vera was nearly as short as Minnie and Edward… Well, he was one mountain of a person.

"You didn't answer my question, Byrne," said Vera with a scowl, not looking at all scared of me despite asking me, as she so delicately put it, who I'd killed. Edward looked a bit cowed, though, tucking himself slightly behind Vera as if she were a shield. Which was in itself a hilarious image.

"Do you really want to find out?"

I stepped forward, and almost without noticing, they moved out of my way. Ella actually jumped backward as I passed, fingers flying to her ring in a gesture that reminded me of Minnie fiddling with her necklace. When I was out of their lines of sight, I smirked. Sure, I didn't want the people who could actually do something about it thinking I was a murderer, but a reputation amongst my peers couldn't hurt, right?

•• ———————— ••●•• ———————— ••

"Excuse me, miss? I think I'm lost." I smiled at the woman before me, wearing a uniform similar to Akins', only with fewer medals.

"Well, where are you supposed to be?"

"I'm not quite sure, ma'am. I went for a bathroom break, and when I got back, my group was gone."

The woman muttered something under her breath which I decided to pretend I hadn't heard, especially the choice curse words and the bit about stupid, useless recruits. She pulled a small touch-screen tablet from her massive pockets and began tapping at the screen.

"Group number?"

I frowned, as if deep in thought, going with the idiotic recruit role she'd assigned me. "I'm sorry, ma'am, I don't remember. I'm new, and I'm no good with numbers at all."

"Fine, your name, then?" asked the woman with a long-suffering sigh, opening a new window on her tablet.

"Minerva Aberle."

I craned my neck to get a look at the woman's name tag as she typed. Fulke. That name sounded familiar.

"Here you are. You really are fresh off the boat, aren't you? Just joined yesterday?"

I wondered what other information was on that little profile—hopefully it didn't mention the long, curly, dark hair, the skin tone, the height... or the whole born-without-one-arm thing, because this sleeveless shirt wasn't really the best at hiding the fact that I had, in fact, two very functional arms.

"Group 107 should be in the mess hall right now, taking a midday break." Fulke looked at me sternly over her sloped nose. "Don't forget that, alright? Group 107."

"Uh, where's the mess hall?"

"First floor, it's the big room. Just ask someone down there less busy than me if you can't find it." She stormed off with heavy, pained steps, like someone struggling to get back strength lost.

"Glad you're recovering well from being Drained yesterday morning, Sergeant Fulke!' I chirped at her disappearing frame. She flinched.

The cafeteria wasn't hard to find once I made it to the first floor. All I had to do was follow the noise of conversation and clinking trays from what sounded like multiple training groups. Taking a deep breath, I summoned all my bravado and peeked my head around the corner.

It was nowhere near as abandoned as yesterday morning, when Vera and I had hidden out here. A sea of white uniform training shirts and brown pants sat crowded together in groups, talking and eating off trays. I scanned the room for a familiar mass of dark curls, to no avail. She was probably hidden by one of the taller recruits.

"Do you know where Minerva Aberle is sitting?" I interrupted a rather large girl with mousy brown hair who was in the middle of a conversation with her friend.

She scowled at me, muttering something to the sharp-faced girl next to her before replying. "Who?"

"Short? Long, curly, dark hair?"

"I don't know who you're talking about," huffed the girl, giving me a dismissive wave. "Sorry."

I sighed. I knew Minnie hated it when people used her arm—or lack of one—as her main identifying feature, but most of the time it ended up being the thing most people remembered. It was a last resort for me, always.

"The one-armed girl?" I said grudgingly

"Oh, her?" replied the first girl's friend, her eyes lighting up in recognition. "She's..." She scanned the room briefly, arm raised. "She's sitting right over there, by the silverware stand."

I followed her extended arm and saw the silverware stand in question. I still didn't see Minnie, but it was a start.

"Thank you," I muttered half-heartedly over my shoulder, already several feet away.

And there she was. Laughing with the girls sitting next to her, dark curls falling around her shoulders.

I was standing at the end of the table and she didn't even notice my presence. "Minnie?" I pushed closer, squeezing between two tables to reach her seat. "Minnie?"

"Isla?" Minnie exclaimed, whirling around in her seat. Her eyes were wide as saucers, irises like two little chocolate circles in a pool of milk.

My face split into a grin, and I opened my arms for a hug. "Miss me?"

"Who's this?" asked the girl to Minnie's right with a giggle, poking her shoulder.

Minnie barely turned her head to address the girl, still gaping at me like she'd seen a ghost. "Uh, Isla, this is Abby, Abby, this is my best friend from Monta."

I shook Abby's extended hand briefly, not really paying attention to her.

"What are you doing here, Isla? Did you break in or something?"

I rolled my eyes. "I enlisted, dummy."

"For me?"

"No, Minnie," I deadpanned, "I joined the New Coranti Military out of my patriotic spirit and my love for my country."

Minnie laughed and gave me a quick, one-armed hug. Apparently whatever hostility she'd held for me the night before she left had disappeared.

"This is so exciting! What changed your mind?"

Nothing. Nothing changed my mind.

"I guess something you said stuck," I replied with a sheepish smile. "Now, can we talk in private?"

"What for?" Minnie looked around at the packed tables around us, and the odd mix of people who couldn't care less what we were talking about and, the more substantial party, people obviously eavesdropping. With my black shirt, I probably stuck out like a sore thumb in a sea of white uniforms.

"I'd just like a little space, that's all." And, maybe, trying to convince a girl with a heart of gold to *not* die heroically was something best talked about away from blabbing mouths.

"Alright. I don't think the Sergeant will mind if I pop out for a little bit," she said, nodding her head to an older woman sitting with what appeared to be other officers at a table near the windows. Minnie turned to her new friend, whose name I'd already forgotten. "Hold my seat, will you?"

"Of course."

We wove between crowded tables and out a side door. Minnie stopped in the hallway outside, but I just scowled at the three other recruits camped out here for a break from the chaos of the mess hall. Instead, I walked until I found a stairwell and started going up the stairs.

"Where are we going?"

"Away."

"You know there are elevators, right? No one ever uses the stairs anymore."

I plopped down on a stair just above the landing and smiled at Minnie, patting the spot next to me. "Exactly."

"So," she said, lowering herself to sit beside me, "Isla Byrne, rebellious spirit, cynic, pickpocket, and magician extraordinaire, joined the New Coranti Military of her own free will." She squinted at me suspiciously. "Are you sure they didn't grab you after I left? I wouldn't doubt it."

"No, really, I joined of my own volition."

"Recently, huh? You haven't even gotten a uniform yet."

I sighed. "I went to the recruiting office right after I saw your note, but the whole process got a bit... delayed." I noticed myself subconsciously rubbing at my still red wrists and forced myself to stop before Minnie noticed. She was observant, and I didn't feel like explaining to her why I'd spent the night handcuffed in a cell when I still wasn't quite sure why myself. I knew I hadn't gone on a homicidal spree, I knew it, and yet, somehow, I still felt guilty. Like I'd escaped an execution I knew I deserved.

"So, what group are you in? I would think they'd put you in my group, 107, with all the recruits from the past few weeks, but I—"

"Run away with me," I blurted out.

"What?"

"I can figure out a plan, we can leave, we don't have to stay, we, we—"

"No."

"Minnie, you've had your taste of the military, I'm sure it was exciting, how patriotic you are, now please—"

"No."

"Just listen, just think rationally for once, just realize that this will get you killed—"

"No!" bellowed Minnie. "Bleep it, I said no. Seriously, Isla, this is why I didn't want to talk to you before I left." She sighed, holding her head in her hand, voice softer now. "I knew it. I knew you'd try to convince me to leave. I want to fight, Isla. You were out in the world, doing what you wanted to do with your life, however misguided that may be, stealing from tourists or whatever. I was tired of being cooped up there, in that bleeping orphanage, hearing about brave witches dying at war. I was tired of being helpless as the riots get worse and anti-witch hate crimes are happening left and right. I was tired of watching the news keep focusing on a battle months ago to hide the fact that we're losing this war, because we are. We're losing, and I'll be bleeped if I'm not going to do something about it."

I swallowed, fixating on a crack in the wall across from our stair.

"Don't you see, Minnie? You're right, Coranti is fighting a losing war here, figuratively and literally. They don't have the support at home, and the military, this whole government, in fact, was hastily thrown together by a couple of revolutionaries. They're fighting against a larger, stronger, more organized fighting force with dedicated soldiers and more highly developed weaponry. If Coranti is doomed to fail, doesn't it make sense to get out now? To leave while we have a chance?"

I thought everything I'd said had made perfect sense, but Minnie looked appalled.

"Are you kidding?" She shook her head, laughing incredulously under her breath as her dark halo of curls bobbed around her face. "No, no, of course you aren't kidding. I've known you half your life, I know you think like this. I just can't believe you have the apathy within you to consider the death of hundreds, no, thousands of innocent people and shrug it off like it's no big deal."

"I'm not shrugging it off, Minnie. It's tragic, of course it is. But at least I have the sense of when to blame the higher-ups, pray for the lost souls, and *not* throw my life away in a hopeless war."

"But we have the power to change things. If—"

"No. No." I grabbed Minnie by the shoulders and shook her, hard, as if shaking her would knock some sense into her thick skull. "You can't make a difference, Minnie. You're just one girl with big dreams and some limited experience in hand-to-hand combat. You can't change the tide in this war, you have to understand that."

"But I can fight."

"You'll die."

Her eyes were steely, her voice steady. "Then I'll die fighting."

Omili above, this was going horribly.

"Fine."

# 10

*"We need every witch in this Omili-forsaken country on that war front."*
—*Lieutenant Sophia Goulding's statement in an article for the Tori Daily.*

I sat alone on the stair for some time, ignoring the grumbling of my dissatisfied stomach. I hadn't eaten since the stale sandwich they gave me last night, after the polygraph. I reminded myself it wasn't over, not yet. I still had two months to convince Minnie. She'd come around eventually, I just had to keep trying.

Two months.

"You look horrible," Vera muttered snidely under her breath when I finally made my way back to our isolated room. There were two bunk beds—that was four beds for three girls, with an adjoining bathroom and another room down the little hallway for Edward. This section of the complex was dead quiet.

Ignoring Vera, who sat perched on top of the bunk bed in the corner, I went into the bathroom, bolting the door shut behind me. I tested the lock, and when it held, I let myself relax. I stared into the mirror, watching pale, watery grey eyes rimmed with dark, sleepless circles. My face was taut, my skin was oily, and my hair was a wreck, far more hanging out of the ponytail than the two neat strands I usually allowed. It had been a long day and a half since I'd showered. Recently, I'd gotten used to a lack of sleep and a lack of showers, but now I intended to take advantage of everything free I could get my hands on. Maybe this whole military thing wouldn't be too bad after all.

I just really wished I'd grabbed some food while I was in the cafeteria.

I took a long, relaxing shower, enjoying the warm water, though they'd provided only a plain white bar in the way of soap. Rude. Soon, Vera was banging on the bathroom door and yelling at me not to use all the hot water, and my moment of bliss was over.

It had been nice while it lasted.

A towel rack, outfitted with three spotless white towels, hung outside the shower. I frowned at the names, written in decisive black marker strokes, in the bottom corners of the towels. They gave each of us our own personalized towel, but they couldn't be bothered to splurge on shampoo, at the very least? I scoffed, grabbing the towel marked *Byrne*, and toweled off quickly before wrapping the towel tightly around my body and opening the door.

"Hey Edward," I yawned, crossing the room to where a familiar duffel bag sat on the bed nearest the door. He raised his blue-tipped head, realized I was wearing only a towel, and flew backward towards the door, hands over his eyes and stumbling over his own feet. Vera laughed at the spectacle, a high-pitched sound that sounded almost like a fairytale crone's cackle.

"What—why—I was just bringing lunch," sputtered Edward, briefly removing a hand off his tightly shut eyes to grope around for a paper bag, which he threw in my direction. He had fantastic aim, even without looking. Interesting.

"I don't know what you're making such a big fuss about," I said, looking down at the towel. "I'm not naked or anything."

Edward grimaced, shuffling backward out of the door blindly, to a chorus of Vera's weird cackling laugh.

Clearly, he had never lived in close proximity with so many strangers before.

"You're supposed to change into that, I think." Vera pointed at the white uniform shirt and brown pants laid out next to my duffel bag on the lower bunk bed. I shrugged, reaching inside my duffel bag for a pair of cargo pants and a sleeveless black shirt identical to the one I'd been wearing before. Tucking the towel more securely under my armpits, I walked back into the bathroom to change.

Now fully clothed, I plopped down unto Ella's bunk next to her, to her alarm. "Notes, please. And a hairbrush."

"Ex-excuse me?"

"Give me your notes."

"I can help you study if you want," she offered with a small smile, reaching into her worn, patched bag for her binder.

I scoffed. "I'm not interested in studying."

"Then why do you want the notes?"

"To cheat the test, of course."

"Why? It's not like the grade is going on our records or anything. I'm pretty sure it's just to help us review the material and let the Captain know how she—"

"Blah, blah, blah. I couldn't care less about the material, or what dear Mila thinks. I do care that she'll decide to make my life more miserable by subjecting me to something tedious if I fail. Thus, the only answer is to cheat."

"But there's hardly any material we went over today, and we still have over an hour left in the time she gave us for lunch. I enlisted four months ago, and I've already learned all this content, so I'm sure I could help you—"

"Why'd you take notes if you already learned it?"

"Taking notes helps me study, and Captain Akins teaches slightly differently from some of the other instructors I've had, so I thought it was best to be thorough." She shrugged. "Plus, it wasn't like I had anything better to do."

What an oddball.

"Good for you. Just give me the notes, alright? Trust me, I used to cheat all the time back at school, it's a breeze after you've learned a few card tricks. It's all about learning where the eyes go first."

"Leave her alone, would you?" Vera hopped down from her perch, chucking a comb at my head as she crossed to where Edward had left the paper bag. "Eddie brought us sandwiches from the mess hall."

"Eddie? You haven't even known him for a day and he already gets a nickname?"

Vera smirked as I snatched the bag from her and peered inside. "It's a psychologically proven trick to make others feel mentally inferior to you—give them a really stupid and basic nickname that implies neither great consideration into the name or much care at all for the recipient. I read about it in a study nearly—"

"Shut up, Verrie." I stuffed a sandwich into my mouth and tossed the bag back to Vera as I raked her comb through my damp hair, pulling harshly at the knots until it satisfied me, then using the bathroom mirror to pull it neatly into my preferred style.

As I finished chewing the sandwich and thoroughly wiping the mustard off my fingers and mouth, I clambered to the top bunk with my father's black cards and began shuffling, letting the motion occupy my fingers so my mind could focus.

Minnie was brave, determined, and so... annoying. She was annoying and self-righteous, but right now she was the only family I had, and I was determined to get her out of this mess. Without her, I wasn't sure who I was. I wasn't sure I wanted to know. I—

"Cool trick."

I stopped shuffling the cards and raised an eyebrow at Vera.

"Cool... trick?"

She scowled. "That's what I said, yeah."

"That wasn't a trick, Roberts," I said, rolling my eyes. "That was just a distraction."

"Show me a trick, then."

"No time to show off now, I'm afraid." I hopped down from the bed, tucking the cards back into the small black velvet bag in the small interior pocket of my duffel bag. "I'm going out."

"Out? But we're supposed to be back for lessons in less than an hour. Where are you going?" Ella sounded remarkably like Minnie at that moment.

"Give Akins my love."

"Isla—"

I hurried out the door and down the stairs, beginning to wish I'd taken Minnie up on her countless offers to exercise with her. I was marvelously out of breath after the first few floors, and by the time I made it to the ground floor, I was wheezing.

Thankfully, I didn't need directions to find a door out of that maze of a complex; the whole building was equipped with signs pointing you to the nearest exit in case of a fire.

Today was more overcast than it had been the whole week, and there was a brisk chill in the wind that made me wish I'd grabbed my coat on the way out. The complex was on the edge of the city and seemed to serve as half military base and half training facilities for new recruits—and, apparently, it also served some function as a royal residence. The front door of the massive building dropped straight off onto the street, but the side door I'd exited from led onto a parking lot full of dumpsters. Goodie.

I made my way across the odious lot to the street and descended the steps to the subway Akins and I had taken here just yesterday. Mostly only military personnel used this stop, as there wasn't really much else down here. On the minus side, that meant fewer people to nab a ticket from. On the plus side, however, there weren't many people to notice as I ducked under the gate and made my way into the station.

Up the stairs I went at the Nella Station, onto a busy road a couple of miles from the complex and haunted by memories. I made my way down familiar streets, wandering like a ghost through a memory. There was my primary school, where I'd first realized that lies and subterfuge were easier than struggling to pay attention to the mind-numbing sludge of boring and useless facts they forced into our brains. I'd gotten caught countless times, but I got better.

My old apartment building was only a three-minute walk from the school, though I remembered it taking nearly seven when I was younger. I looked up at the building, hands in my pockets, eyes finding the second window on the third floor, on the side facing the alley, not the main road. My bedroom window.

What I was about to do was stupid, reckless, illegal, and definitely not something Minnie would approve of. Well, Little Miss Perfect never had to know, did she?

I carefully surveyed the area for witnesses, noticing only a homeless man asleep a little way down the alley. I'd seen a much better place a couple of alleys over, but either this guy hadn't done proper reconnaissance, or the spot was claimed by someone scarier. Probably the latter.

With a grunt, I clambered onto the bottom of the low-hanging fire escape, arms burning with effort. I'd done this before, countless times, before my father died. I'd made a game out of it, seeing how fast I could get up to my window without dying. Maybe not the safest activity, but I'd gotten bored easily.

I made my ascent up the rickety metal stairs, watching through the slotted floor as the alley below got farther and farther away. At the third floor, I peered through the dirty window. All the lights were off inside, making the room dim enough that I had to squish my face up against the bug-smeared glass to see anything but my reflection, even on a cloudy day like today. The bedroom door was cracked open, but I saw no light past it. Either the new inhabitants were broke and had to conserve electricity, were taking a midday nap, or they were at work. I guessed it was the latter and got to work on opening the window.

Just as I'd hoped, whoever lived here now hadn't noticed the window was broken and thus hadn't fixed it, giving me the chance I needed. It wasn't obvious that the window didn't work perfectly—in fact, the only way to really tell at all was from outside the window, which was how I knew, from my days entering and exiting this way for fun. The window locked just fine from the inside, but if you hit the window in just the right spot and twisted it just the right way as you pulled, the latch popped right open.

And just like old times, I fell through the window with about as much grace as a dying walrus.

The floor was still covered in the same pale blue carpeting I remembered, but, of course, all my furniture was gone. I wasn't sure what they'd done with it, but I knew it was government property until I turned eighteen. *Welcome to Coranti, where sixteen years old is a perfectly good age to get shipped off to war without your consent, but they won't give you your childhood dresser back until you turned eighteen.* All the legislature here was ridiculous and full of holes, the product of an incompetent government and unsatisfied citizens.

The carpet was clean, free of the black hairs from Angel, our massive hound, that had always clogged it when I was growing up.

Instead of the furnishings I'd seen here eight years ago, now the walls were plastered with all sorts of posters and artwork, and a large desk and chair took up the corner. A home office, then.

I pulled my knees to my chest with a sigh, leaning my back against the wall underneath the window, a slight breeze ruffling the top of my hair. What was I doing here? I'd been angry at Minnie, angry at myself, the master negotiator, for not being able to convince her to abandon her moral code to save her life. Angry at this whole war. Part of me wished I'd never been born in Coranti, where, through cooperation with witches, scientists had perfected a blood analysis test that could detect the magic in your blood. Anywhere else, no one could know whether I was a witch, and as long as I never used magic again, as I intended not to do, there'd be no way to prove it. Of course, in nations as strongly anti-witch as Nillaesce, proof wasn't necessary. Just a suspicion was enough to get you killed.

Coranti, the only openly pro-witch country in the modern world, a country run by witches, was supposed to be a safe haven for witches under persecution. It was supposed to be a place anyone could be free.

And yet, we were being forced to fight to the death for that freedom. What was the saying? Only freedom in death?

The turn of a key in a lock and shuffling footsteps froze the breath in my lungs. The new residents of apartment 3A were home.

# II

*"The Coranti-Nillaesce war shows no sign of ending soon, despite the significant military advantage of the Nillaesce. The unified witch forces present in Coranti for the first time in military history and the additional protection of the physical border of the Sinea Mountains between the two nations are doubtless the only reasons why the war continues to trudge on. From economic booms in countries selling supplies to both sides below the radar to the devastated refugees fleeing over the southern border, in this report I intend to discuss at length the many effects of the Coranti-Nillaesce war on politically uninvolved nations."*

—*Excerpt from a historical paper published anonymously in Lilta.*

I scrambled to my feet as quietly as I could, fumbling to get the window open wide enough for me to climb out. I stuck my head out, feeling my ponytail brush the sweaty skin on the back of my neck with a disconcerting prickling sensation. Coming inside, I'd been able to go headfirst, knowing that a relatively soft floor awaited me and I wouldn't fall three stories if I slipped. Needless to say, I wasn't so eager to swan dive my way out.

Outside, the apartment door squeaked open, and my heart started a frantic dance in my chest. I wasn't in my element here. I wasn't a burglar, for Omili's sake. I was a pickpocket. I was used to crowded streets and magic tricks, not being cornered in someone else's house, facing charges of trespassing and attempted burglary that just might send Morren over the edge and get me executed.

Past my raging heartbeat, I urged myself to take deep breaths and calm down. They just got home, right after lunch, or maybe on a lunch break? The first place they went wouldn't be their office, right?

I heard a muffled voice saying words I couldn't make out, then, much clearer and definitely closer, a deep voice in reply.

"Yeah, I'll be right in there, I just need to drop a few things off in the office."

Goodie.

Newly panicked, I realized I couldn't safely make my way out the window in time. I recognized every creak of the floorboards in the main room, and whoever was coming was nearly to the office. My head whipped back and forth as I looked for a hiding place, and I dove behind the door right as it opened.

Really, not the best idea.

I pressed myself against the wall, trying to control my ragged breathing so it didn't give me away. The man who entered, obviously in a bit of a hurry, didn't notice when the door bumped against me instead of closing all the way. While his back was still turned, I reached forward and slowly pulled the door open until I was hidden, wincing as it creaked slightly.

I heard shuffling and the scrape of a filing cabinet, and then the man left, pulling the door shut behind him. I stood frozen in place as the distinct, familiar creaks told me he was entering the kitchen, then stumbled toward the window. I contorted to squeeze myself through, feet first, and made it safely back onto the platform. I let out a shaky laugh, trembling in the sudden wind that chilled my bare arms. I grabbed the slightly rusted railing in a white-knuckled grip and began my descent down the stairs, not bothering to close the window behind me.

•• ———————— ••●•• ———————— ••

"Hello, Captain Akins. How's your afternoon going?"

Akins whirled on me with a scowl that could curdle milk and probably scare someone who actually cared out of their mind.

"You're late."

I pretended to check my watch with a pout. "Wait, do you mean it isn't really eight in the morning?" I shrugged, pushing past her. "Guess my watch is broken."

"Where have you been, Private? It is *far* past thirteen hundred hours."

"Using the bathroom." I met her eyes with a cool stare, daring her to call me out on the lie.

Akins raised a questioning eyebrow, and I heard Vera cackle in the background. "For two hours?"

"Sure."

She turned away from me with a grunt, gesturing at the three recruits lined up in some sort of fighting stance.

"Stand with the others. You'll regret being behind in physical training when you're fighting for your life."

I highly doubted it. Right now, my goal was to not have to fight for my life, at all.

We spent the next three hours learning various techniques for hand-to-hand combat we'd doubtless never use until Akins handed Edward a list of exercises to do and pulled the rest of us aside.

"We will spend the next two hours working with your supernatural talents. Byrne and Bailey are both Drainers, but Roberts is a Holder." Akins frowned, looking at her notes. "On second thought, Roberts, I'll work with you later." She handed Vera another long list of exercises and pushed her towards Edward.

Ella and I stood side by side while Akins paced as if deliberating how to teach us.

"We studied a brief overview of supernatural history and magic theory this morning, and now is the time to put some of those theories to the test." She cleared her throat. "Bailey, I already know you have a great deal of raw power and struggle with control, but Byrne, the only indication I have of your power is from your blood test." Akins turned and grabbed a large potted plant from the table at her side and plopped it in front of me. "Why don't you give us an example?"

I blinked at the wide leaves, then raised my eyes to Akins. "You can use magic on plants?"

"Of course, magic affects anything with Life Energy. Weren't you paying attention this morning?"

"Right, right, I remember you saying that," I lied.

I breathed in deeply through my nose, eyeing the plant in question. It was just a plant, no harm done if I killed it, right? I'd sworn never to use magic again, but that was on people. I placed shaking hands on the thin leaf, suddenly realizing I had absolutely no idea how to actually do magic. I'd been so focused on not doing it that it had never occurred to me where to start if I actually wanted to.

"Steady your breathing, focus on the energy you're attempting to Drain, place your hand on the organism if you must, and... Pull."

"Pull?" I tugged experimentally on the leaf, but nothing happened.

"Not the plant, you dimwit. Pull with your mind. Pull the energy."

I closed my eyes, rubbing the leaf between my fingers as I tried to concentrate.

And...

There it was. The energy. I could feel it, flowing through the plant, and, more noticeably, through Ella and Akins.

It was there.

I could take it.

I could pull and pull and pull until there was no energy left, and they'd be crumpled, motionless, on the ground

I could pull...

Gasping, I fell to my knees, breaking the connection.

Nope.

Not happening.

"Why don't you go first, Ella? Give me something to work with?" I rasped, forcing cheeriness as I pushed myself to my feet. That was a close call. Killing two people, even in a training accident, would be dangerous as is. With my current standing as an alleged mass murderer, I'd be executed without a second thought.

"I don't know, Isla, that doesn't seem—"

I grabbed her arm and shoved her in front of me. She stumbled, almost knocking over the plant.

"Go ahead, Drain the plant."

"Don't pressure her, Byrne, she—"

"I really don't think—"

"Drain—"

"No—"

Ella squeezed her eyes shut, ripping herself free from my grip, and I felt the tug as she did the same thing I'd done so many years ago. The line between physical and magical pulling was thinner than Akins believed, it seemed.

I'd never been Drained before.

I felt suddenly heavy and weak, the opposite of the light, airy, *powerful* feeling that came from Draining someone else.

And then, like a magical cushion scooping up my Drained mind, I felt the power, the raw energy. The Life Energy. It flooded my veins, the comfortable yet unsettling feeling I remembered from all those years ago when I Drained Ms. Borough from apartment 3B. But I wasn't Draining someone else now. I was Draining... Myself?

I took a deep breath and realized, with a start, that I had my energy back. I raised my eyes from Akins' slumped form to the pained wince on Ella's face.

"I-I'm so s-sorry," she whispered to Akins before turning to face me, straightening her glasses with shaking fingers then going to the ring on her finger, twisting, twisting, twisting. When she saw that I was standing upright, she gasped. "What—"

I raised an eyebrow at her. "I'm supposed to be unconscious, right? Like Sergeant Fulke, and the six recruits in your old group? Like Captain Akins?"

"I—"

"Have you ever killed someone, Ella Bailey? Have you ever pulled too hard, pulled all the life from them?" I stepped closer, staring intently at the dark eyes beyond her glasses. "Have you ever felt so powerful, so out of control?" My voice cracked and I realized how much I wanted, no, needed an answer. I grabbed her by the shoulders and shook her. "Have you?"

"Back off, Byrne. She's obviously having a panic attack." Vera shoved me roughly away from Ella's trembling form, and I stumbled backward, balling my fists to hide how badly my hands were shaking.

"Hey, Ella. Breathe in, breathe out. Focus on my face. Do you have any medicine?"

I turned with a huff, trying to calm myself down. Ella was lucky. She was out of control, yes, but she'd never really lost it. She'd never gone too far.

"What happened to Captain Akins?" Edward asked, coming to stand next to me. He stretched, and when I turned to face him, I was at eye level with his sweaty armpits. Gross. I briefly followed his gaze as he watched Vera sit Ella down and help her with her medicine, but all I could focus on was the plant, brown and wilted.

"Ella went all crazy Drainer on her and knocked her out."

"Cool."

I shuddered, thinking of the way all the energy had left my body. Of the way it suddenly hadn't, like I'd Drained... myself.

* * *

"What did you do?" Ella's voice was barely more than a whisper in the quiet dormitory, and I paused my card trick to meet her suspicious gaze.

"What do you mean?"

She narrowed her eyes. "I definitely Drained you. I know I did. I felt your energy enter me, but you didn't look Drained at all. How'd you do it?"

"You're mistaken. Your brain is muddled. You were really anxious, and you don't remember properly—"

"What." There was an edge in her voice now. "Did. You. Do?"

I swung my legs over the side of the bed, planting my palms on either side of me as I leaned forward to look down at Ella. "Listen carefully. I don't know what happened out there on the training field, but you're not going to tell a single soul. You understand me? Not a soul. If anyone asks, if Akins asks, I plopped right down there on the floor with her and had a little nap."

She nodded.

"Now, would you give me your notes, please? I've got some cheating prep to do."

I stayed up past when everyone else was asleep, pouring over the notes I'd missed this morning, my stomach sinking farther and farther with each word I read. I hoped I was wrong. I really, really hoped I was wrong. There was only one explanation I could think of for what happened today, but that didn't make any sense at all.

I couldn't be a Drainer and a Holder. It just didn't happen.

There were three universal types of witches: Donors, Drainers, and Holders, and each had a way to manipulate Life Energy. Donors could pass their own Life Energy to another living thing, Draining themselves. They were commonly trained as nurses and doctors, because of their non-violent talents. Only one Donor, the queen herself, had ever used her talents to fight; she was so powerful that she was said to be able to distinguish between different facets of Life Energy and push certain negative energies from herself into other people. It was actually very interesting to read about, and Ella had even provided little diagrams in the margins. Really, top caliber notes right here.

Drainers were the opposite of Donors, pulling Life Energy from other organisms and into themselves, giving themselves power and leaving the person, animal, or plant in question Drained. I skimmed that section of the notes, considering myself a bit of an expert on the topic already.

And finally, Holders. Until the last decade, Holders were not officially recognized as a type of witch at all. Of course, none of this was official at all until eight years ago, but scientists had never even speculated that there could be a third type until open research began in Coranti. Drainers and Donors worked outside of themselves, pushing and pulling energy around externally. But Holding was an internal magic. Holders could Drain themselves, becoming weak at times and storing the Drained energy within themselves to use at another time, when they could pull the stored Life Energy from inside themselves.

Donors pushed, Drainers pulled, and Holders navigated the careful balance of pushing and pulling within themselves.

What did that make me?

# 12

*"Detective Fetz was an odd man, by Nillaesce standards, though he found himself quite at home in the bustling and diverse streets of Coranti. Years had passed since his monumental journey over the mountains from Nillaesce to Coranti, but he would still recall those shivering nights with fondness on a cold, windy day in his office, a pipe between his lips."*

—*Tomorrow's Last Mystery, written by Roberta Tinn (a Corantian author, it should be noted).*

"Hey, Vera, wait up a moment."

"What do you want, Byrne?" Vera's tone was sullen as always, but she slowed for me to catch up.

"Just to talk to you about something."

Vera appraised me out of the corner of her eye as I fell into step next to her. "You put on the uniform."

I looked down at the pressed brown pants and the New Coranti Military emblem on my white shirt, then over at Vera. "You did too." I almost didn't recognize her without the skin-tight shiny black pants. She'd gone without the fishnet sleeves today, too, but her makeup was the same.

She shrugged. "It's a new day."

"My thoughts exactly." I cleared my throat, wishing Vera wouldn't walk so fast. I wasn't exactly in a hurry to get to lessons with Akins. "Are you ready for the test?"

"Get to the point, Islie."

I paused, frowning at her. "What did you just call me?"

"Just trying something out. What did you want to talk to me about?"

"I'm curious about Holding. What's it like?"

"Weird question."

"Well?"

Vera leaned against the wall outside the classroom and rubbed her chin pensively. "It's like... I don't know, I'd expect it's a lot like Draining, but instead of Draining from someone else, you're Draining yourself. Oh, and, of course, it's not immediate. With Drainers and Donors, you have to use up all that energy immediately. I don't Drain myself and then immediately get an energy spike, that wouldn't make sense. For example, yesterday, when Ella accidentally Drained Akins, she took nearly all the Life Energy of a full-grown, muscular woman and had to use it immediately. Her little stick body couldn't handle it, and it triggered a mental breakdown."

I thought of when I'd Drained Ms. Borough, so many years ago. I hadn't felt overwhelmed. I'd felt the energy flow through me in a single moment before it had been filed away. The only thing I couldn't handle that day had been the guilt of... well, the guilt of what I'd done.

Vera checked her watch, a thin black band I hadn't even noticed under the fishnet sleeves but was now in stark contrast with her pale skin. "It's six minutes to seven, we better go inside before Akins blows a fume."

"I heard that," muttered Akins from her wheelchair as we entered and took our seats on opposite ends of the classroom. "Just because I'm stuck in this wheelchair until I recover from being Drained doesn't mean you get to be insolent."

Ella was already here, and I chose the desk behind and to the right of her, ready to cheat off her if the notes written on my arm didn't work.

"Wonderful way to start our second day, everybody! Everyone is here on time, no tantrums on the way in the door"—this comment was obviously directed at Vera, who scowled and slumped lower in her seat—"and *nearly* everyone is in uniform."

I looked around the room, eyes falling on four white uniform training shirts and four pairs of crisp brown pants, as Akins rolled her wheelchair up next to my desk. She grabbed my right arm in cold fingers and turned it over, displaying the little black rows of words on my inner forearm.

"Please use Private Byrne's blatant attempts at cheating as an example of what is not permitted in the dress code: no writing on yourself in permanent marker."

Vera snickered and I gaped. My arms had been crossed or my forearm otherwise obscured the whole time I'd been in the classroom. No teacher had ever called me out on that one before.

"There's no rule in the handbook about carrying small, folded up pieces of paper underneath a watch band, but I would say it's generally frowned upon when taking a test."

Akins flipped my arm over, pulling back the faded blue watch and removing the worn paper I kept beneath, close to my pulse. I snapped out of my surprise and grabbed for the paper, but she ripped it out of my grip with a grin.

"Didn't think I'd find that one, did you?"

"No, that—"

She unfolded the note without care, and I winced as the little creases began to tear at the corners.

"Goodbye, sweetheart. I'll see you on the other..." Akins' voice faded off and she cleared her throat, eyes scanning the brief message and the tear-spotted paper as if seeing it for the first time. "So, not to help you cheat, then."

"That wasn't yours to read," I snarled, holding out an open palm, which Akins dropped the note into numbly.

"No, no, you're right, I'm sorry." Akins rolled back up to the front of the classroom, and all eyes were on me as I gingerly folded the paper back along the well-worn creases and tucked it back between my watch face and my wrist.

•• ▬▬▬▬▬ ••●•• ▬▬▬▬▬ ••

Two days later, Akins pulled me aside after hours of exercising and physical training during which I participated but refused to do anything magical. I wasn't one to go diving headfirst into unknown waters, let alone waters that could get me executed.

"I don't understand what your problem is, Private. You weren't conscripted. You volunteered for this."

I scoffed, crossing my arms, and my eyes found the skinny girl lifting weights across the gym. "Ella Bailey enlisted, but she doesn't want to be here either."

Akins narrowed her eyes. "How could you possibly know that?"

"I saw what happened at Minerva Abele's recruitment, ma'am. This government is completely screwed, but it's uniform on its health policies, for one thing. Ella Bailey enlisted of her own free will, and she isn't trying to leave."

Akins groaned. "Then what in the world makes you think she doesn't want to be here? Maybe she's just like Private Aberle and is determined to fight for what she believes in despite her disabilities."

I leaned forward, squinting up at Akins' cold black eyes and crooked nose. I spoke clearly and slowly, enunciating every word. "Because she's miserable. She cries in her sleep, her anxiety is off the charts, she has a picture of a little boy, probably her brother and most certainly dead, taped to her bunk. She hates it here, but she has a good enough reason to stay."

I yawned, cracking my neck, and began to back away.

"What?"

"Riddle me this, Captain. Minnie joined for Coranti, Bailey joined for the money, so what did I join for?"

"That's what I asked *you*, Private."

I shrugged and turned away, offering her only a lazy salute over my shoulder. "See you at the party, Captain."

I left with a smirk, feeling immensely pleased with myself. Until only a couple of minutes later, I ran straight into Vera.

"You joined for love."

I blinked at her. "Excuse me?"

"You asked Akins why you joined. I'm telling you."

I glared at her. "What makes you think I joined for love?"

"I don't think, Byrne. I know." She tapped her skull and gave an attempt at a smirk that looked more like a grimace than anything else. "I may not look it, but I'm *very* smart."

I rolled my eyes. "Fine, tell me then. How do you *know* why I joined?"

"Private Minerva Aberle. You used a nickname for her, you know why she joined, by my knowledge you haven't seen her in the last couple of days, and yet she's on the forefront of your mind." She tilted her head, inspecting me. "I'd wager it's familial or platonic love, though, because you don't strike me as the sort of person to give up everything you believe in for romance. And, of course, though you look flustered and surprised, you're not blushing, fidgeting, or showing any other signs correlated with romantic embarrassment."

I scowled, shoving my hands in my pockets. "I'm not flustered or surprised, you just caught me off guard."

"You're extremely defensive and quick to retaliate."

"You're judgmental and think you're smart."

She grinned her creepy grin, extending her hand like I had when we'd first met. "I think we'll get along just fine, Isla Byrne."

•• ———————— ••●•• ———————— ••

I opted for one of my pairs of black leggings and, of course, a sleeveless, high-collared, tight black shirt to go underneath my new magician's jacket. With a roll of tape borrowed from Akins' desk (without her knowledge), I got the dirt and dust off my hat, restoring it to a pristine, smooth black. I'd spent the last hour using what my father taught me of sewing to tailor the costume to fit better.

One hour until Akins' party, I stood before the bathroom mirror in full costume, feeling fantastic.

"I'm pretty sure my metallic black leggings would look better with that."

I didn't take my eyes off my reflection, inspecting the silky blue lining and the golden speckles dotting the interior of the black cape. "Won't fit."

"Are you sure?"

I frowned, turning to face Vera, who stood in the doorway to the dormitory with folded black pants in hand. "You're nearly a whole head shorter than me."

Vera snorted. "More like a couple of inches."

"They won't fit."

"One: I'm not that short, two: I have really stocky legs for my height, and three: these leggings are a little long on me anyway." Vera offered the black mound to me, and when I didn't move, she began to move away. "Fine, sorry for trying to be friendly."

I sighed. "Alright, I'll try them on."

The leggings were a little loose around the calves and cut off a bit higher above my ankles than they were supposed to, but Vera was right. The reflective leggings looked way better with the velvety exterior and starry blue lining of my jacket and cape. I fastened the silver buttons and completed the ensemble with a swish of the cape.

Yeah, I looked fantastic.

My first instinct was to run and show Minnie, but that wasn't really an option, so instead, I packed my bag of tricks, straightened my hat, and got on the first subway to Chamberle banquet hall.

The hall was gorgeous, resplendent, a hundred other big, fancy words that Vera could probably define on the spot. The theme was simple and dark, and the giant room felt like a haunted mansion from centuries ago. The chandeliers were draped in translucent black cloth, the tables decked in black, and the wait staff all wore storybook witch hats.

I found Akins easily enough, in a clean black dress uniform with buttons shined to the point of blinding. I rolled my neck and met her in an extravagant bow, brandishing my hat.

"Where do you want me?"

Akins gestured towards the large, circular stage in the center of the hall that all the tables faced. "You'll do a show up there after they do all the awards and things, and before, while everyone is milling around and dancing and things, you can choose any spot you like to do tricks for tips."

"What awards?"

"Oh, you know, mostly goofy stuff to raise morale, 'best hair' and that sort of thing. The Most Promising Recruit Award is the only one anyone takes seriously." Akins sighed melodramatically. "It's supposed to be a big honor for the instructor of the recruit that gets the award." She scoffed. "Not like I have a chance, with you lot."

I pulled coins from behind ears and cards from the deck to the *oohs* and *ahs* and light applause of the gathered military officials, all in dress uniforms like Akins. I didn't steal a single thing, as tempting as it was. I couldn't just disappear after the deed was done, here, like I could on the streets, and it would be much, much worse a fate if I got caught. By the time Akins called for them to take their seats for the awards, I had an audience excited for my performance.

Which, of course, I wasn't prepared for. Akins knew I was a street magician, right? My specialty was up close and personal, not far removed on a stage. I knew some tricks I could do, but I didn't have much experience with stages.

"Ladies, gentlemen, and Lieutenant Oswald, thank you for joining me tonight at the third annual New Coranti Military Gala. It's such a delight to see so many familiar faces, but let's just take a moment now to remember the ones who couldn't be here tonight, whether they're no longer with us or fighting for our freedom out in the mountains." Akins raised her glass, and the others followed suit. "To justice. To equality. To freedom and sovereignty for witches everywhere."

"To freedom!" echoed the crowd. I didn't join them. Akins blabbered on, awards were given out, and I stood in the corner, picking at where my black nail polish had smudged. Minnie's feet were probably a red-smeared mess. She'd fought Salma with her nail polish still relatively wet.

Akins won the award for best host of a New Coranti Military Gala, an honor presented to her, through laughter, by the officer who had hosted the first two galas. After the applause died down, she raised her microphone, the little trophy still in her other hand.

"Thank you, thank you, but now it's time for the real star of the show: the Most Promising Recruit award. Anyone recruited since this time last year has been considered, and yet the recruit we will be celebrating tonight enlisted less than a week ago. She's brave, strong-willed, and wholly unwilling to give up. Everyone give a hand for our most promising recruit: Minerva Aberle!"

# 13

*"Leave our country, filthy witches."*

*—Anonymous hate message painted on the wall of a suspected witch-run establishment after the owner was killed in a violent raid.*

I stood in the shadows, agape, as a familiar girl with a wild mane of dark curls bounded up the stairs to the stage, a wide smile on her face. Minnie was wearing a black dress uniform similar to most others in the room, just bare of any medals. She waved to the audience, and as they settled down, Akins continued her speech. She went on about all of Minnie's great qualities, how beloved she was by peers and instructors alike, how her training scores were already ahead of everyone in the program, both in the classroom and on the field. She even talked about Minnie's mothers, two witches who played an instrumental part in the initial rebellion before they were sadly killed.

A young man in a pointy black hat handed Akins a trophy, which she presented in turn to Minnie with a flourish. Pictures were taken, Minnie beamed, and then Minnie descended from the stage, trophy in hand. As she made her way towards a little corner alcove, I intercepted her.

"Congratulations."

Minnie barely looked up at me, leaning against the wall to examine her trophy. "Thanks."

"I'm not surprised at all."

"Neither am I," she mumbled through a mouthful of the provided chocolate. I rolled my eyes.

"You're very modest, you know that?"

"Just stop, Isla. I don't want to hear it." Minnie finally met my eyes.

I leaned against the wall opposite her. "Minnie, please, I haven't seen you in days, can we just talk? I promise I'll try not to insult any of your life decisions if you promise not to insult any of—"

"You just want me to do what *you* think is best for me, huh?"

I frowned. "Exactly."

Minnie huffed, rolling her eyes. "But what about what I think? Does that matter at all?"

"Of course, as long as what you think isn't stupid and/or suicidal."

"Shut it."

"I really am happy for you. Promise."

"I said, shut the bleep up."

"Wait, Minnie, I…" I drew in a deep breath, slumping my shoulders in defeat. "You're right. I've thought about what you said the other day, and I was an idiot to try to convince you to do anything other than what you thought was best." I smiled sadly. "I'm just going to stay with you. I'm going to fight by your side. And if we die, we die together."

Minnie only stared at me for a few heartbeats, and I stood there, unsure how she would react.

To my surprise, she stepped forward, wrapping her arm around me in a hug. I leaned over slightly to reciprocate the embrace, tears brimming in my eyes.

"I love you," Minnie said, her voice watery

I blinked.

Minnie never cried.

Akins' voice crackled over the speakers nearest us, and I could see her still standing on the stage, speaking into her microphone. "Please, take a few minutes to enjoy refreshments and, if you like, a bit of dancing, music provided by the Bad Witches Band. Then we have a delightful show set up for your entertainment."

I pulled away from Minnie with a grin. "That's me."

She raised an eyebrow. "What, a magic show? On a stage? I didn't think that was your style."

"It's not."

Minnie contorted her features into a mockery of concern. "Oh no, how will you pickpocket all these lovely people from so far away? Do you have a grabber hook or something?"

"Shhhhh," I whispered, raising a finger to her lips. "We can't have all the important people in here knowing my extracurricular activities."

Minnie snorted. "Extracurricular, my bleep. You…" Minnie's voice faded to nothing as something caught her attention over my shoulder. "Speaking of important people."

I turned to the deafening noise of a room full of metal chairs being pushed back as everyone who had been seated stood at attention. Even I straightened slightly as the queen entered, looking as regal as ever in a white dress uniform that put her in stark contrast to every person and decoration in the room. Behind her, in a simple buttoned shirt not unlike the clothes I'd first seen him in, was Prince Kayden. He was the only other person in the room not in uniform.

"Please, resume your seats. I apologize for my tardiness. Did I miss anything?"

"Oh, you know, just the entire award ceremony," Akins muttered under her breath before making the horrifying realization that her mic was still on and her snide remark had been broadcast to the entire hall. Her face was absolutely priceless. "Excuse me, Your Majesty, I am so sorry."

I struggled not to laugh, but the disapproving glare Minnie sent me just made the urge stronger. I tried to cover it with a cough, more or less successfully.

Akins scampered off the stage as the queen took the throne-like seat at the only white-clothed table, and life flooded back into the room.

"It's nearly time for your act, are you ready?" Akins asked under her breath, double-checking her mic was really off this time.

No. Not at all.

"Uh, sure." I hefted my little sack of goodies, all the things I'd need for any of my practiced tricks.

"Stage name?"

"What?"

Akins huffed, clearly impatient.

"You're in the military records as a suspected mass murderer, Isla Byrne. Just about everyone here has been briefed on you, so for the sake of my party, what's your stage name?"

"Nesryn Courell," I blurted out without much thought. It was a cool, magician-y name, I figured. "No, Nessie. Nessie Courell."

"Mass-murderer?" spluttered Minnie. Akins grabbed my arm and started pulling me towards the stage.

"*Suspected* mass murderer," I corrected over my shoulder as Akins hauled me up the stairs. Dropping my arm like it belonged to a decaying, maggot-filled corpse, Akins fiddled with the microphone. She tapped it a few times to test it, successfully quieting the crowds.

"Now, please welcome Nessie Courell, a talented street performer bringing back the lost art of non-magical magic."

Akins left me alone on the circular stage with her clip-on microphone, and I did a little spin, taking in the tables of important people, all focused on me. Goodie. Trying not to look at Minnie, I reached into my bag for the props I'd need for my first trick—two plain, paper napkins. One was already balled up, and I quickly tucked it in between the base of my thumb and palm, so that when I held my hand right it didn't fall. When I practiced, it fell a lot. Minnie had seen me fail this trick so many times... The other napkin I brandished to the crowd, so they could see it in all its slightly crumpled glory.

"Behold, great officers of the New Coranti Military, a paper napkin." That got a few chuckles, and I turned in a circle so everyone could see the unfolded napkin, careful to keep the balled one hidden in the shadows of my right hand.

"I am now tearing said napkin," I narrated, still rotating slowly. As I ripped the napkin to shreds, I started crumpling the pieces up so they formed a little ball, which I rolled between my palms, careful to tuck it into the spot where the untorn napkin had been. The untorn napkin I now showed the audience with a flourish.

"The napkin has been torn, crumpled, and rolled. And yet," I said, beginning to unfurl the untorn napkin to an audience of both wide eyes and bored ones, "it seems to have stitched itself back together again."

I walked the circumference of the stage, waving the untorn napkin before the audience to a chorus of applause, and let myself breathe. Stage magic wasn't that hard, really.

"For my next trick, I will need a volunteer from the audience."

I scanned the tables, looking for a familiar short frame, but Minnie's head of dark curls was nowhere to be seen. Disappointed, I chewed my lip and surveyed the raised hands before me.

"Your Highness, would you be interested in joining me on the stage?"

Prince Kayden Ladrine looked surprised I'd called him out—he hadn't had his hand raised.

"I don't know..." The queen sent him an icy look, and I got the idea he was only here for the cameras. "Sure. Yeah."

He made his way onto the stage, head lowered against the occasional flash of cameras. My smile was thin-lipped as I offered him a dramatic bow. The press hadn't given me a second look until I'd brought him up here. Not that I cared, not at all, but a little recognition for my hard work would have been nice.

I rummaged in my bag, pulling out my deck of cards—the work ones, not my father's nice ones—and made a big display of shuffling them thoroughly as the prince inched closer to me.

"I've seen you before," he hissed under his breath. I only grinned at the audience, giving him a meaningful look before dropping my eyes to my clip-on mic. He followed my gaze with a puckering of his lips.

"Pick a card, my prince, any card." Prince Kayden deliberated over the fanned cards I held before him, lip tucked between his teeth, and as the moments slipped by, I had to stifle the urge to roll my eyes. It wasn't blood science, he just had to pick a card. Literally, any card.

He pulled a card from the left side of the splayed deck, took a quick look, and went to return it to the deck, but I stopped him. "Wait, wait, give the audience a good look first. Don't want anyone thinking you're my accomplice." I gave the room a big, comical wink like we were all in on a big secret. A few people chuckled softly, and others leaned forward in their chairs to squint at the card the prince showed them.

"All good? Great." I held out the deck, still fanned out. "Replace it anywhere you like. Now—"

The lights cut out suddenly, plunging the hall into darkness with a chorus of surprised gasps and a flurry of movement.

"Stay calm, everyone, stay calm," bellowed Akins, and I realized neither of our microphones were working. The power was out, including the sound system. The static of handheld radios filled the air, and I caught brief snippets of urgent-sounding chatter.

"—no power, everywhere, it's all black. The whole city is completely—"

"—here either—"

"Your Majesty!"

"—no visual, but we can hear—"

"—working on the backup generator now, and—"

"Your Majesty!" Someone was shouting, and I squinted through the dark room, seeing only blurred movements. The only light came from the thin windows near the ceiling, but the sun had set hours ago and the faint moonlight wasn't much help. Usually, there'd be light from the city throughout the night, but the blackout seemed to have affected the whole city. What in the world had happened?

A wavering beam of light cut through the particles in the air, and I followed the path to the person who'd had the forethought to bring a flashlight to a military party. They stood one table away from the queen, in a dress uniform buried in medals, with a military-issue radio in hand.

"Your Majesty," they huffed, as the officers between them and the queen stepped respectfully out of the way and the chaos in the room quieted, now that there was a sliver of light.

"Lieutenant Oswald," said the Queen, still sitting calmly on her throne, apparently unconcerned with the hurricane of panic spiraling around her.

"Your Majesty, I have Lieutenant Goulding on the radio here. She's the highest-ranking officer at the complex tonight, and…" The lieutenant glanced at their radio, shuddered, and held it out to the queen. "And, well, I'll let her tell you what's happening."

They pressed a button on the radio, and after a burst of static, warbling, muted voices filled the now hushed hall. I found myself leaning forward to hear better and scowled, rolling back on the balls of my feet as if I couldn't care less. This completely predictable government collapse wasn't my concern. It was about time, honestly.

A loud string of colorful curses crackled over the radio, and Oswald cleared their throat loudly. "Lieutenant Goulding, I have a group of some of the nation's highest-ranking officers and *the Queen of Coranti* listening over my shoulder, so if you'd like to filter out the language, now would be a great time," they hissed. "Sophia? You there?"

More curses, than who I could only assume to be Sophia Goulding finally managed to get a coherent sentence together. "I didn't quite get that last bit, Arin, things are pretty chaotic over here." Another loud curse, and the sound of glass shattering. "I can't see a thing, the recruits are fighting, rather pitifully, for their lives, and we can't even tell how many people we're fighting, since—"

"Fighting? Who?" the queen leaned forward in her seat, resting her elbows on her knees, brows furrowed. "Are we under attack?"

Goulding cursed again, and then the sound of hurried footsteps. "Wish I knew, Your Majesty, I have no clue what—"

A loud *clunk* and static filled the room.

"Lieutenant Goulding? Goulding, are you there?" Oswald called into the mic.

"Yeah, yeah, I'm here. Uh, you're going to want to see this, Your Majesty. You got a window or something at that fancy party hall?"

The Queen stood and made her way to the exit, boots clacking on the tiled floor. "What are you seeing, Lieutenant?"

"The lights are back on at the complex, and we've got visitors." I elbowed through the crowd that had gathered at the window, all trying to see the complex. I caught a glimpse of the building, practically glowing against the disturbingly darkened city line.

Goulding's voice dropped to a fearful whisper, and despite the high radio volume, I could barely hear her as the queen exited the building and walked towards the single black car waiting for her. "A group of soldiers wearing the Nillaesce emblem…"

"And?"

Against my better judgment, I left the building, straining to hear what Goulding replied as the queen got into the car, radio in hand.

"And Darkheart."

# 14

*"To be a witch, I believe, is to hold the power in your hand to control the very forces that govern not only the human body, but every living thing."*

*——A Study in Witchcraft, written and revised by Cecile Omili.*

Pure pandemonium ensued as the officers tried to get back to the complex all at once. Some, like the queen, had ridden here in private cars, but the rest made a break for the subway. I didn't see Minnie anywhere, but of course, she'd be in the throng of fancy-uniformed people heading for the subway, so there I went.

The things I did for friendship.

I carefully removed my new jacket and cape, folding them gingerly and tucking them into the bag I'd brought for my trick supplies before diving into the crowd. The number of high-ranking officers who got the business end of my elbows in the span of ten minutes might have gotten me arrested if we weren't under attack from the most wanted criminal in the whole country, and probably the whole world.

And, of course, Minnie was running right into the thick of things as usual.

I spotted her, near the head of the crowd, somehow not completely buried by the taller people pushing past her. She disappeared again from my sight when we descended the stairs to the subway, but I caught a glimpse of her as she swiped one of those fancy military passes Akins had and was given immediate access. Why hadn't I gotten one of those?

What a stupid question.

Minnie wasn't in the same car as me, in fact, I didn't see anyone I recognized in the group of passengers around me. The seats were all full, so I stood, holding onto the bar. I made faces at myself in the darkened window as the civilian passengers gave fearful glances to the distressed military officials in dress uniform speaking hurriedly into their handheld radios. I looked like some sort of assassin from one of those action movies Minnie loved, in all black, tight-fitting clothes. I still preferred the whole outfit, with the jacket and cape, but I could totally rock the stealth agent look.

A thought occurred to me, and I turned to the person standing next to me, who I now recognized as Lieutenant Oswald.

"Hey, why wasn't the subway affected by the blackout?"

It took Oswald a second to realize I was talking to them, and when they did they only shrugged. "Uh, I don't know, kid. I didn't really think about it."

I frowned, eyebrows bunching together. "Doesn't it run on the same power grid as the rest of the city? When I was younger, there was a city-wide blackout and—"

"I told you, I don't know. It's probably on a different generator now or something." Oswald waved a dismissive hand at me. "I'm no expert."

"Something about this feels... very intentional," I mused, shifting my weight.

Oswald gave a sigh of exasperation and moved to the other side of the car.

I got off the subway with the horde of officers at the last stop as they flooded up the stairs and through the door Akins had taken me through just a few days ago. The bright fluorescent lights here seemed blinding in comparison to the dark streets and the dim light of the subway. Everyone seemed to know where they were going, and in a matter of seconds, I was alone in the foyer, dazed and confused, unsure where to go.

I cursed softly, looking around at the empty desk and white, identical hallways branching off. How was I supposed to find Minnie now?

I heard a loud crash and smiled. By following the sound of fighting, of course.

The training grounds had transformed into a battlefield. I stood, tucked into the shadows as always, and took in the heavy scent of blood, the staccato bursts of some sort of gunfire, the constantly shifting formations of the more advanced recruits, struggling to get close enough to the enemy line to use their magic. But there was no enemy line. The Nillaesce bled through the shadows like an illusion, and I recalled Goulding, over the radio, telling us she wasn't sure how many people we were fighting. I could definitely understand now. I caught the glint of light off some sort of ceremonial sword as it slashed through the air, leading its wielder in a precarious dance.

I squinted, sure I was seeing things. A sword? Really?

Then I saw Minnie, long hair billowing out around her as she counter attacked with deadly grace. She was one of the few Coranti trainees who had managed to adapt to the strange attack, swinging her gun like a club to block the advances of the sword wielding Nillaesce soldiers she fought.

I groaned, grabbing my head in my hands. Of course she got a gun and a fancy all-access pass. She was the "most promising recruit."

That's when I felt it. Subtle, at first, just the slightest tug at my muscles, like soreness from a long day of strenuous work. But as the feeling grew, I recognized it for what it was. And on the field, I saw Coranti soldiers begin to droop.

I cursed, watching Minnie stumble forward clumsily as the Nillaesce she was fighting pressed ever closer. I wasn't sure how, but we were being Drained.

I pressed my eyes shut, trying to replicate what I'd done the other day when Ella had Drained me. Somehow, I'd replenished my energy with stored energy somewhere inside me. I just had to figure out how to tap into it.

With a sigh, I fell to my knees, ready to fall asleep right there on the packed clay training floors, until finally, I felt the energy bubble up inside me. Without hesitation, I pulled, feeling the energy flood my veins as I pushed myself to a standing position on shaky legs. I looked around, breaths rattling in my chest, and saw that over half the Coranti soldiers were collapsed on the floor, and the rest, Minnie included, were still sluggishly fighting.

I struggled over to where she stood, wobbling, swinging her gun barrel weakly at the retreating back of a Nillaesce soldier. I frowned, confused and grateful, and without wasting a second I grabbed Minnie and started dragging her with me away from the chaotic training grounds. She was short but remarkably heavy for her size—the weight of muscles accumulated from long hours of exercise. Bleh.

As I skirted the edge, careful to keep Minnie and I in the shadows, I noticed the Nillaesce all across the makeshift battlefield pull away from the Coranti soldiers as their opponents slumped, energy drained. They all aligned in formation, forming a row on either side of the large hole in the brick wall surrounding the open-air training grounds. Had that been there this whole time, or had I happened to miss an explosion?

Out of the hole stepped a stocky figure wearing all black, complete with a majestic cape to rival my own and a full-face mask covering their features. With every step they took, Minnie's weight got just a little heavier in my arms, and I felt the pull against my buoyed strength grow just a little stronger. I paused, amazed, awestruck, and maybe even a little flabbergasted by the sheer power they held. It was so beautiful, so enchanting...

I gasped, hauling Minnie indoors and as far away from the masked figure as I could, feeling the heavy pull of their presence weaken a little bit with each dragging step I took through the nearly abandoned compound, until, with a gasp, Minnie's eyes opened. We stood alone in a white hallway, struggling to catch our breath and understand what in the world was going on.

"I thought magic only worked with close contact," I rasped, leaning against the wall.

Minnie laughed softly, pacing back and forth in front of me. "No, no, honestly, what has your instructor been teaching you?" She paused dramatically and I groaned under my breath. Just like Minnie to lecture and gloat about something she'd learned.

"It's completely dependent on the strength of the witch. Some very weak witches, like me," she added with a wry smile, "need to be physically touching whoever they're Draining or giving energy to. More powerful witches, like the queen, can use magic on multiple people from a short distance."

"And Darkheart?" I asked, sure now he was the masked figure.

Minnie shuddered. "That monster has killed hundreds of witches. He's… well, we just felt firsthand how powerful he is, didn't—" She cut herself off with a wince, bending over slightly and clutching her abdomen.

"Minnie?" I pushed off the wall and rushed to her side, grabbing her lightly by the shoulders and steering her into a sitting position. She coughed softly, removing her hand from her stomach to shoo me off.

"I'm fine, I'm fine."

I gaped at the red smeared palm she waved at me, panic and bile rising in my throat. "No, Minnie, you are definitely *not* fine." I could barely see the blood on the dark cloth of her fancy dress uniform, but under further inspection, there was a deep cut in the fabric over her side, revealing a sliver of red beneath.

The sight of the blood was making me feel light-headed, but I fought not to completely freak out, for Minnie's sake.

"You—you're bleeding," I stammered out, unsure what to do. What were you supposed to do when that much blood was oozing out of someone's side?

"Oh, that?" Minnie glanced down and started giggling hysterically. "Yeah, I might have gotten a little cut. From a sword, of all things. Can you believe that? This was not what I thought I was signing up for when I joined the New Coranti Military, but hey, it's kinda cool."

"Yeah," I muttered, staring down, paralyzed, at her quickly darkening uniform. "Really cool." I closed my eyes, struggling to regain my composure. I knew absolutely nothing about first aid short of slapping bandages on boo-boos. This was way out of my area of expertise. Oh, how I wished I could use a magic trick to heal Minnie.

"I mean, it's definitely a bad-bleep way to go, am I right?" Minnie giggled again, then started talking in a horrible Nillaesce accent. "Hey, welcome to the underworld of eternal torture, where all the witches go. How'd you die?" She reverted back to her normal speaking voice. "Oh, I was stabbed by a ceremonial sword." The Nillaesce accent again. "Woah, that's so bad-bleep of you."

"You're not going to die today, Minerva Lilianne Aberle," I muttered. With a resolved sigh and a quick prayer to whoever was listening, if not the Nillaesce deities, I decided I needed to get off Minnie's ceremonial jacket and see what I was dealing with.

My hands were shaking so hard that undoing the buttons was impossible, so I had to tear it. I felt a little bad about it because the uniform looked very fancy and was definitely on loan to Minnie since she was just a recruit. At least it was already torn and bloody before I started with it.

"Well, I guess a Nillaesce underworld-soul-guardian-person wouldn't say bleep instead of cuss words, huh?"

"Right, because that was the problem with your delusional conversation with yourself," I replied under my breath, starting with the cut in the jacket and ripping it open until I could see Minnie's formerly white undershirt, now red with fresh blood.

I tore off a long strip of the now shredded dress uniform jacket and pressed it to the gash in Minnie's abdomen. That was what you were supposed to do, right? Put pressure on it?

As I held back tears, my mind sluggishly moving, unsure what I should do, Minnie's musings became even more slurred with pain and blood loss. "I wonder, do Nillaesce people curse like we do? Are they too holy for that?"

My vision blurred as the tears fell, sliding in an unstoppable torrent down my cheeks. My trembling hands were still pressed to Minnie's wound as she slipped in and out of consciousness, so I couldn't wipe them away. I could only sob silently, tasting the salt on my lips and tongue through the haze in my mind.

"Y—you're not..." I choked out through the tears, fighting to breathe in enough air to talk. "You're, you're not dying t—today, Minnie."

I collapsed onto the ground next to her, fingers hovering over her neck, feeling for a pulse, willing her to keep breathing.

And there, feeling the steadily weakening pulse of her heartbeat beneath shaking fingers, I felt something else. I felt her energy and knew I could Drain it all in a heartbeat. I felt my energy and remembered Draining it, pulling it through my body.

In the last seconds of Minnie's life, I gave her mine.

I pushed.

And the world disappeared.

# PART TWO:

# THE WITCH

# 15

*"Oh please don't you leave me, darling, baby I can't bear to say goodbye, maybe you could hold me tight, and I would never leave your side."*

*—Lyrics from the hit song "Not Goodbye" by pop artist Jean Lycro.*

"We must proceed with caution, Your Majesty. This was a direct attempt on your life, and I fear you are no longer safe here—"

"No."

"Excuse me, Your Majesty?"

"All ten soldiers we managed to capture immediately took some sort of poison, ending their own lives the instant they fell into our custody. They came here without the pretense that they would make it out alive, only as an accompaniment to Darkheart. This wasn't a failed assassination; this was a message."

"What message?"

"The Nillaesce want us to know Darkheart is with them now."

Morren opened and closed her mouth, looking like she wanted to say something in reply to the queen's ominous declaration, but the blonde security leader cleared her throat. I supposed I should probably know her name by now, but I had very little interest in learning it, as each time we met I hoped it would be the last.

The members of the long table, including the queen, Akins, Morren, and that other lady, whose name slipped my mind, all turned to face me. I gave them a grin, and, when the guards relinquished their grips on my arms, a dramatic, flourishing bow.

The queen raised an eyebrow, gesturing towards the lonely chair facing the table. I crossed to it lazily, ignoring the hammering of my heart. I hadn't been dragged and I wasn't all chained up, so I supposed my situation had improved since the last time.

"To what do I owe the delightful gift of your presence, Your Majesty?" Maybe I was laying it on a bit too thick. I didn't care.

"You know full well why you're here, Byrne," snarled Morren, leaning across the table to sneer at me. I just looked back at her blankly, unimpressed.

"Well, you apparently do, but do you mind filling the rest of us in?"

Morren ignored me, turning to the queen instead. "Your Majesty, this is all the proof we need. She is not only a Drainer but also a Donor. I was right about her from the start—she must be a murderer. It's the only way."

"Wait a minute, Morren, slow your roll." I stretched in the chair, glad not to be wearing handcuffs this time. "This is just the same brand of ridiculous, far-fetched assumptions as last time. What's this about me being a Donor?"

"You gave Life Energy to Private Aberle."

I leaned forward to scratch my leg beneath the standard-issue brown uniform pants, trying my very hardest to appear nonchalant. "I fainted from the stress of a battle and my aversion to blood, and Private Aberle survived a non-fatal cut to the abdomen. What about that screams 'mass murderer'?"

"You didn't faint, Byrne. You were unconscious for too long, and the recovery path you followed was either that of someone who has been Drained by a powerful Drainer or that of a very weak Donor, Draining themselves too much. And Aberle should not have been able to drag herself all the way to the infirmary after that much blood loss."

I shrugged. "Medical miracles happen all the time, and you'd be amazed by the tenacity of the Most Promising Recruit," I yawned, rising from the chair and slouching towards the exit. I really shouldn't try to dismiss myself in front of the queen, especially considering my precarious situation, but I needed to see Minnie. "Let me know when you have any *actual* evidence against me," I called over my shoulder.

"Wait!" screeched Morren, and with a long-suffering sigh, I paused in the doorway. "Your Majesty, please, all the evidence together must convince you... the suspicious activity, the dark blood, the mother from a historically non-magical family—"

"Who were reported as non-magical during a time where being a witch could get you killed in this country," I interjected. "They were probably hiding their magic."

Morren huffed, clearly out of "evidence." "Just look at her eyes, Your Majesty!"

I laughed. "You want me executed because of my eyes?"

"They aren't natural."

"Grey is a perfectly natural eye color," I bit back.

"Yeah," agreed a voice from the doorway, drawing all the attention off me. "Just because less than one percent of the world population has them doesn't mean they aren't natural—barely two percent of the world population is witches, and yet I don't see you trying to claim *we're* unnatural."

I beamed at Vera, who stood with Ella and Edward at the entrance to the room.

Morren didn't look at all pleased about the rebuttal but prattled on as if Vera had never spoken. "They look so empty, so cruel, like there's no soul behind them at all."

"Seriously?" I asked. "If you care so much about souls, maybe you should cross the mountains right now and cuddle up with some Nillaesce, where you can drink the blood of witches and talk all night long about soulless eyes."

"You—"

"Emilia." The queen hadn't moved from her seat, but Morren recoiled like she'd been slapped at the mere sound of her name from the queen's lips. "Your behavior is bordering on unprofessional." Queen Isabella's cold blue eyes bored into me from across the room. She was definitely paying attention now.

The security team directed the rest of Group 118 to stand next to my chair, where we waited in silence as the queen inspected us, head tilted and pale fingers propped beneath her sharp chin.

"In light of recent events, I have been forced to make some very difficult decisions," she began, every word rolling off her tongue with careful precision. It was hard to see the similarities between her and her son—where she was confident and poised, Prince Kayden had seemed nervous and apologetic. "We are faced with a very unique situation, and I will not attempt to hide from you that our state as a nation is very perilous. We are walking the knife's edge between success and catastrophe."

I barked out a laugh, then tried to cover it with a cough when the queen stopped her speech to glare at me. Walking the knife's edge? More like narrowly dodging the swinging knife, losing energy and resources in a fruitless dance against an inevitable loss.

"We are the closest we have ever been to winning this war, and yet, every good witch we lose to the Nillaesce makes our efforts more and more strained. Last night's attack was just one more blow I can no longer tolerate."

"So? What are you going to do about it?" I asked, lounging in my chair as if I didn't have a care in the world.

"Did the queen give you permission to speak?"

I met Morren's glare. "Did the queen give *you* permission to speak?"

"Well, I—"

"Enough," interrupted the queen, her icy tone bordering on frostbite. "What I'm going to do about it, Byrne, is why I've gathered your group of misfits together this morning."

I narrowed my eyes. "Why?"

"This is your last warning, Byrne." The queen's glare could've cut glass, and I twisted almost subconsciously, pulling my legs from where I'd draped them across the arm of the chair and planting my feet flat on the ground. "I will not tolerate this insolence."

"Yes, Your Majesty."

"That sounded sarcastic."

"Nope, sorry, my voice is just like that all the time."

"I'd suggest you change it." I shrunk under the queen's gaze; fully aware this woman could have me executed in a heartbeat. She sighed, relaxing slightly as her eyes surveyed the four misfit recruits before her. "The juvenile delinquent, the mentally ill witch, the possible mass-murderer, and…" the queen's brows knitted together as she struggled for a word to describe Edward's role in the group. "And Mr. Buck. I have come to the decision that Group 118 is no longer worth occupying the time of one of our finest soldiers. Yet, we can no more afford to have you roaming the halls or locked up somewhere than we can afford to release you from service, and thus I am faced with quite the dilemma.

"I believe I may have a solution, however." The queen turned to Morren. "I know Miss Byrne has already made her acquaintance, but for those who haven't, this is the esteemed Emilia Morren, head of the Darkheart Oppositionary Department. She is the expert on all matters pertaining to witch genocide, stolen magic, and, of course, the hunt for Darkheart. In the past twenty-four hours, the DOD has become more essential than ever. Emilia, please explain to Group 118 the plan you proposed."

Oh, this was all Morren's idea? Goodie.

"Thank you, Your Majesty. Tanya, if you please." Morren rose to her feet, gesturing for the other woman, Tanya, to turn on a projector in the ceiling that displayed a map onto the wall behind the table. "You should all be able to recognize this map—here is Coranti, and here is Nillaesce." My geography had never been great, but I'd take her word on it. "This long mountain chain, the Sinea Mountains, is obviously the physical border between us and Nillaesce, and serves as the front lines in this war." Morren waved a hand below where the map cut off. "Down here is mainly just desert on both sides of the mountains for miles until you reach the Urki river and the Liltan border." Morren sighed. "Why am I giving you fools a geography lesson? This is your domain, Mila." Akins shrugged, not looking up from where she was typing at a laptop computer on the table before her.

"Anyways, here we are." I followed Morren's finger to the little star on the north bank of the Tori lake, then couldn't help but look southward, to the dot marked Monta. "Darkheart is rumored to have a base in the mountains, near Split Peak. You're going to find him, and you're going to kill him."

I burst into laughter. Loud, outraged, borderline delirious laughter. "Wow. You've got a real sense of humor, Morren. Who would've thought?"

"This is serious, Byrne," muttered Akins.

I wiped a nonexistent tear of mirth from my eye. "No, really, what's the plan?"

"You're sending four young, hopeless failures with less than a week of training on a dangerous assignment in the middle of a war front?" asked Vera.

"As I said, we've had to make some difficult decisions."

"Excuse me, Your Majesty," Ella piped up, voice shaking as she twisted her ring. "Our pay will still be sent to our families, right? My mother?"

"Yes."

"And the handbook says that if we're killed in service, the military will send compensation money to our families?"

"Also correct."

I frowned. I'd gotten no such compensation, but I supposed it was just like that stupid thing with my furniture. They'd hold onto it until I turned eighteen and was kicked out of the public care system. And what about if, no, *when* I died before my eighteenth birthday? Who would get the money then?

"Any other questions?"

I scoffed. "This is a suicide mission."

The queen narrowed her eye but didn't correct me. My mouth was suddenly dry.

"This is a suicide mission," I repeated, softer, more to myself than to anyone else.

"Pack your bags and say your goodbyes. You leave tomorrow morning, before dawn."

$$\bullet\bullet \quad \text{———} \quad \bullet\bullet\bullet\bullet \quad \text{———} \quad \bullet\bullet$$

The medical wing was nowhere near as abandoned now as it had been when I came here to get my blood tested. Nurses, doctors, and Donors pushed past me in a frenzy, calling things out to each other and moving patients around. It looked like a miniature hospital, almost, though I'd thought the wing was mostly for research and, of course, blood testing. You'd think that with the compound so close to the city they would just use a civilian hospital, but I supposed it made sense that they wouldn't want to clog it up. This place was packed with injured soldiers, mostly recruits, from last night's incident.

"Minerva Aberle?" I asked a woman who rushed by me in a white coat, half shouting to be heard. She just shook her head, pointing to an intern sitting at a desk in the corner, scribbling on a clipboard. I sighed, dodging important people off to do important things, making my way to the intern. I'd barely slept at all last night after I woke up from my... fainting spell. The instant they saw I was conscious and unharmed, they kicked me out of the infirmary and sent me back to my dormitory so someone else could have the hospital bed.

They hadn't let me see Minnie last night, and every time I closed my eyes I saw her blood on my hands, pain tracing creases in her face, her eyes drifting shut... Nightmares had plagued the brief, troubled sleep I did manage to get, and I'd ended up spending most of the night staring at the ceiling above my bunk, trying not to cry and hoping Minnie was alright.

But Morren had confirmed that Minnie was alright—or at least alive.

Now I wouldn't take no for an answer.

"Where is Minerva Aberle?"

The intern darted his head up, like a startled bird, giving me a quick glance before pushing the clipboard out of the way and opening a computer.

"Relation with the patient?"

Would they let me see her if I told him we weren't actually related? "Uh, sister." Close enough, right?

He frowned, squinting beady eyes at the screen. "Name?"

"Nessie Aberle."

"I don't have a Nessie Aberle in the system. How is it spelled?"

I sighed as if this happened all the time. "It's Nesryn, N-E-S-R-Y-N."

"No, still not coming up."

"Weird, but Minnie wasn't in the system either until she got hurt," I fibbed, making it up as I went. "Our parents were pretty private, you know—although, actually, you've probably heard of them." Some sane part inside of me cringed. Was I really about to try to use Minnie's moms to butter up an unsuspecting intern? Yes. Yes, I was. "Lily and Camila Aberle? Founding members of New Coranti and leaders alongside the queen in the revolution?" I batted my eyes at him as he confirmed my story in the databases, eyes widening like saucers.

"The Aberles were your moms?" He bolted upright, giving me a sloppy, but earnest, salute. "Your sister is in patient room 103, just down that hallway. Thank you for your service, I'm so sorry for your loss." For a panicked second, I thought he meant that Minnie was dead until I realized he was talking about her parents. I smiled at him, thin-lipped.

I found room 103 without much trouble and waited outside for a nurse to write something down on the chart in Minnie's room and leave before I slipped inside. She was lying on her back, eyes closed, arm sprawled across the thin blanket. I sighed, moving to the chair beside her bed. I shouldn't be disappointed—she'd almost died, it made sense she would be asleep.

Minnie opened one eye, peering around the room cautiously before landing on me. When she saw me, she smiled, opened both eyes, and hopped out of bed, looking terrifyingly weak and small in her hospital gown. I paled, reaching for her arm.

"Minnie! You shouldn't be standing up."

She shooed me off, walking unsteadily to the window, where she slammed the blinds down, then to the door, which she locked. "I'm fine."

Minnie returned to her bed, perching on the edge for a few seconds before wincing and grudgingly laying down.

"How do you feel?"

"Just fantastic. They've got me on all sorts of painkillers, and they say as long as I stay on bedrest—"

"Yeah, you're doing a great job of that."

Minnie stuck out her tongue at me. "Apparently, it's only a superficial wound, and the blood loss was really the main concern.

They just poked around in there to check that nothing important got sliced and then stitched me right up. I should be able to resume physical training in a couple of weeks but in the meantime…" Minnie patted the bed with a sigh. "They won't let me out of bed for another day, and after that I'm supposed to stay in a wheelchair for a few days, and even after that I—"

"Okay, okay, I don't need the whole treatment plan," I said, smiling. "I'm just so glad you're alright."

"Thanks to you."

I laughed. "What are you talking about? You saved yourself, as always. I just passed out like a wimp at the sight of blood."

Minnie's face was mirthless. "I don't know what happened last night, Isla, but I'm pretty sure you saved my life."

"You're delusional. Maybe you should go back to sleep," I advised. Minnie scowled at me, and I winked, pulling the paper bag out of my pocket with a flourish. "A recovery gift."

Her eyes widened. "What is it?"

"See for yourself," I said, handing her the bag.

Minnie grabbed the bag eagerly, peering inside. "Chocolate!"

"Fresh from that shop you like—the original one, in the Tori square, not that knockoff we used to go to in Monta."

Minnie beamed. "I love you."

I rolled my eyes. "You love chocolate."

"True," she conceded, taking a giant bite out of one of the chocolate truffles I'd gotten her. Well, *stolen* for her, but I wasn't about to tell her that.

"Minnie?"

"Hm?" she mumbled around a mouth full of truffle.

I smiled, trying not to cry. As long as she stayed on bedrest, Minnie would be alright. And if I wasn't back by the time she was back in training… I wouldn't be coming back at all.

This was the only goodbye I could bear.

"I love you too."

# 16

*"Conscription is now mandatory for all witches ages sixteen and above. Blood tests are mandatory for every biological woman aged sixteen or above. Failure to comply is equal to a fine of at least five-hundred Coran and imprisonment of up to ten years."*

—*Supernatural Conscription Act 1023 AL, s. 53.2*

The train rumbled beneath us, and I gazed out the smudge-covered window at the forested hills flying by as my fingers moved the cards around. I tried desperately not to think about Minnie. She would be fine. It would be weeks until she'd even be back in training, let along fighting the Nillaesce. I had promised her that I would respect her decision, and I fully intended to.

If I ever saw her again.

"Seriously, Vera, black isn't a color. Try again."

"Fine. Red. Specifically, a shade of red so dark that it looks exactly like black but is still technically red."

"Sure, sure, be obstinate. Red it is. What about you, Ella?"

"Yellow."

"What type of yellow?"

"Soft, dandelion yellow."

"Sounds pretty. Hey—"

"No," I said, cutting Edward off before he could ask me what my favorite color is.

"Oh. Okay."

I shuffled the cards one more time, then started practicing a sleight of hand card trick my father used to do, still looking out the window. The dark blight of a bombed-out town flew by, though it took me a second to see it for what it was. I'd forgotten aerial warfare had been more prevalent in the early days of the war, forgotten being recently orphaned and scared as I huddled in a bomb shelter with other scared children as the planes flew by above. It hadn't taken long to realize that bombing was getting neither country anywhere in this war, only an eye for an eye. There was still the occasional bomb siren, but I hadn't seen a Nillaesce fighter in the skies for years.

It was like my life was divided into two acts: before the revolution, with my father in Tori, when we were happy, and after, with Minnie in Monta, while the two of us struggled to piece our broken hearts back together.

"Well, my favorite color is—"

"Bright blue, yeah, we get it," muttered Vera.

"Why do you guys have to keep interrupting me? I could've said orange, for all you know."

"But you weren't going to say orange, were you?"

"Well, no, I was *going* to say electric blue, but that's not the point." Edward sighed. "Who wants to play a game?"

"Sure," I replied, voice sarcastically chipper. "How about the quiet game?"

"You're no fun."

"We're being sent on a dangerous, impossible death-trip into enemy territory. So no, I'm not feeling very fun."

"If we're all going to die, might as well make the best of a bad situation, huh?"

I sighed, collapsing my father's deck and smacking it on the table before me, making Ella jump.

"Do you know how to play Wild Knight?"

I won every hand easily and was starting to feel discouraged by the sheer ineptitude of my companions. If they were this bad at cards, how in the world were they supposed to kill the most powerful man in the world?

I snatched a steadily crumpling card out of Ella's grip with an enraged scowl. "I'm letting you use my most valuable possession, and you have the audacity to *twist* a card?"

"I'm so sorry!" She looked at me with wide, apologetic eyes, fingers flying to her ring. "I didn't even notice I was doing it. Nervous twitch."

"I don't care." I gathered all the cards, stopping the game mid-round, and did a quick count to ensure I still had a full deck. Feeling stupid for letting these ungrateful idiots play with my father's cards, I slipped them back into the black velvet bag, remembering the woman from the cafe I'd played with the day Minnie had left. That woman was good at the game, maybe even better than my father, and *she'd* never damaged a card.

It had been a long day of travel, and none of it first class. We'd taken a train east from Tori to Lorten, the second-largest city in Coranti, then switched at a station there to the train we were on now: a one-way ticket to a small mountain town, the Coranti settlement the farthest to the East and the closest to the border. There, we would be equipped with whatever they thought we needed to find Darkheart's hidey-hole in the mountains and let us loose. Then, maybe I could run away? Live in the mountains with no one the wiser and wait for the Nillaesce to win the war?

But I couldn't. I'd sacrificed so much for Minnie. I'd let her consume my whole life because I was scared that if I didn't, I wouldn't know who I'd become. I needed Minnie, and right now, she needed me. I just had to figure something out...

The cogs in the train's wheels kicked into action as the elevation increased, pulling us up the mountainside. I pressed my face to the window, trying to see the lake in the distance without success. I shivered in the warm train car, goosebumps rising on my bare arms. We were in the mountains. The *Sinea* mountains. Sure, we were still in the western foothills, nowhere near the war zone and pretty far north of any actual fighting, but that's where we were going. I'd spent half my life in Tori and half my life in Monta, but I'd never left central Coranti.

Until now.

The train pulled into the small station, and Akins popped into our car, which was empty except for us. Apparently, there wasn't a lot of traffic to a small mountain town abandoned by anyone sane enough to realize they would be the first to die when the Nillaesce won the war and stormed Coranti. The only visitors were tourists with a death wish.

And us.

"Chop-chop, soldiers. Darkheart awaits."

I scowled at Akins, slowly gathering my bag and moping off the train as if it would leave and take me with it. Wishful thinking.

Akins led us up steep roads past quaint shops and picturesque cabins, all boarded up. This used to be quite the winter retreat, as the signs for a ski lift boasted, but since the war started, I'd imagine it became less popular of a destination. Winter sports were all fun and games until there were Nillaesce soldiers breathing down your neck.

I paused in the middle of an abandoned road to dig in my duffel bag from my jacket. No one had objected when I'd worn my normal clothes today, not the recruit uniform, but my sleeveless shirt wasn't exactly suited for the mountain gusts. I shrugged on the familiar, worn fabric of my jacket and kept walking, not bothering to speed up to join the others. I wasn't in a hurry.

The inn was, of course, empty, but the door was open and the lights were on when Akins ushered us inside.

"Are you glad to be rid of us?"

Akins glanced over at me, eyebrows raised. "Are you glad to be rid of us, *ma'am*."

"You're walking us to the gallows and still insist on proper address?"

The hard lines of her face softened almost microscopically. "I like you, kid, I really do. I'm sorry things worked out the way they did."

"Are you kidding me?" I spluttered, indignant. "You're sorry things turned out the way they did? What in the world is that supposed to mean? You're quite literally sending me to my death, and my only crimes are having slightly dark blood, being a little squeamish, and, oh, how could I forget, *having grey eyes?*"

"I don't have any crimes," added Edward, very helpfully. "Ella can't help her anxiety, and... well, alright, Vera might actually have done some illegal things and be a very unpleasant person, but she doesn't deserve to die."

"Thanks, Eddie."

Akins sighed, rubbing her temples. "Look, I can't do anything about that, alright? You may think this is just some elaborate excuse to get rid of the lot of you, but I promise it's actually a very important mission."

I snorted. "Then why send a few untrained teenagers of dubious ability?"

"Are you really going to make me say it out loud?"

"We're disposable," muttered Vera, spite dripping from her voice.

Akins didn't exactly confirm the sentiment, but she didn't deny it either as she turned and rang the bell at the desk. I narrowed my eyes.

"I'll tell everyone about you and Vasco if you don't get us out of this," I blurted out before I could stop myself.

Akins froze. "You said you'd keep your mouth shut about that."

"And I will, as long as you get me off this mountain and help me and Private Aberle desert."

"But Aberle worked so hard to enlist. Why would she want to desert?"

"I…" I'd forgotten that I'd told Minnie I was done trying to get her to desert. "Just get me off this mountain."

I waited, on edge, for Akins to process my blackmail.

"Who's Vasco?" asked Edward.

"More importantly, who are you going to tell?" replied Akins, a dangerous sneer forming on her face.

"Uh, the queen. Your superior officers would be a good bet too."

"But how? The train is gone, and only I can authorize a return trip. What are you going to do, *walk* all the way back to Tori without supplies just to snitch on me?"

I lifted my chin defiantly. "I just might."

"Uh, sorry, you're with the military, right?" Akins and I both turned to face the girl standing behind the desk, opening a computer.

"What clued you in, the uniform?" Akins huffed, gesturing at her ensemble. The rest of us were in civilian clothes—Vera had donned her fishnet sleeves and reflective black leggings, Ella wore a yellow floral dress with a black leather jacket, and Edward's blue shirt was so bright it made my eyes hurt.

"Yeah, and that we don't exactly have any other patrons…" the girl's voice faded away under Akins' heavy gaze, and she cleared her throat. "Captain Akins? Three rooms, right?"

"Make it two. I'm out of here." Akins rustled in her bag and pulled out two small black radios, complete with New Coranti Military Emblem, which she shoved in my direction. "Send a brief update of your progress every night at exactly nineteen hundred hours. If you miss two updates in a row, we will assume that you have either failed or abandoned the mission and that you, Byrne, have been lying this whole time and are actually a mass murderer. Understood? And I will be the only one at the other end of the radio, Byrne, in case you were daydreaming about blackmail. Have two different people carry the two radios so they cannot get lost or destroyed at once, and if something happens to one radio, use the other radio to notify us about it. If you are successful, you will be promoted and celebrated as war heroes—which, conveniently enough, comes with a pay raise. Any questions?"

"What if we die?" I asked, partly just to be annoying.

"Let us know on the radio."

"What if we die *quickly*? Still going to assume I'm a murderer?"

"Yes. What else… All your backpacking supplies, including camping gear, two weeks of dehydrated food, and several water filters, are stocked up here for you. We have an associate who will teach you how to use everything and send you on your way. Your rooms are paid for for tonight, but after that, you're on your own. Good luck."

"Wait," I called after her, dread sinking in. This was really happening.

Akins only paused a moment in the doorway, a frigid breeze blowing through the open door as she held it open. "Goodbye, Byrne. I really do want to believe you're not a genocidal murderer. Prove them wrong, will you?"

I couldn't sleep.

Edward got his own room, while the three of us had to share a two-bedroom room on the ground floor. Technically, it slept three, but that was if someone took the couch. It seemed pretty ridiculous to me that we had to share a room when we were the only patrons and we could each have our own room, but no one was asking me.

I called one of the beds as soon as humanly possible, so since Vera seemed like the type to insist on a bed, I'd assumed Ella would be sleeping on the couch. And yet, Vera got all polite and insisted that Ella got the bed. Weird.

Vera snored like a bear, and Ella kept shifting and turning over in her sleep, rustling the covers almost constantly. I wasn't sure why I minded now. Back in the dormitory we shared, these things hadn't really bothered me; I was used to sleeping in a room with a bunch of other people. I was used to being the last one awake, staring wide-eyed at the ceiling, daring myself to cry. Daring myself to break down, to give in.

My father always used to tell me that if I couldn't sleep, I should paint pictures on the ceiling with my mind. After he died, I'd painted his face on the orphanage ceiling until sunlight filled the room and the paint washed away. As it turned out, I was a horrible painter, but the nice thing about imaginary painting was that you could pretend it looked however you wanted it to look.

Now, I painted Minnie on the ceiling, graceful as a bird and strong as... some sort of strong animal. I couldn't think of anything off the top of my head. A goat, maybe? She was definitely stubborn enough.

*Tap. Tap.*

I blinked, tearing my eyes away from the cracked white ceiling. Vera was still snoring, Ella was still fidgeting, and I still couldn't sleep.

*Tap. Tap.*

Groggily, I pushed myself into a seated position. What was that noise?

*Tap, tap, tap-tap. Tap, tap, tap.*

A definite rhythm was forming, a melody I'd heard far too many times. Unbidden, the words rose to my mind to join the tapping. *Oh please don't you leave me, darling, I can't bear to say goodbye, maybe you could hold me tight, and I would never leave your side.*

I must've dozed off at some point during my imaginary artistic ventures because there was no way this was really happening. Maybe the stress was getting to me. Maybe I was delusional.

Slowly and cautiously, as if moving too fast would scare the sound away, I planted sock-covered feet on the carpeted floor and stood. I crept towards the window, heart in my throat, bracing myself to see a bird or a squirrel or a figment of my imagination.

Instead, when I opened the blinds, softly lit by the crescent moon, were two shining black eyes and a head of dark curls.

G. N. Solomon

# 17

*"The New Coranti Monarchy is the most disorganized, corrupt, and useless*
*government to be set in place since the Seventh Liltan Confederation of 970*
*AL. With a faulty hierarchy, poor leadership, and disjointed mandates, it's*
*only a matter of time before this new regime falls."*

—*An Anonymous Commentary on the State of Affairs in New Coranti,*
*author unknown.*

I spent several seconds gaping as Minnie realized I had seen her and stopped the tapping, opting to bang her fist against the frame instead and mouth for me to let her in. I fumbled with the latch, turning it the wrong way at first and nearly hitting Minnie in the face when I finally pushed the window open with a gust of cold air. I shivered, reaching out to help Minnie clamber inside. I went to close the window, but Minnie stopped me with a cold hand on my arm.

"Don't close it," she whispered.

"Why not?" I asked, at full volume, not caring if it woke Ella and Vera.

Minnie didn't answer me, instead turning back to the window and gesturing for someone else to come inside.

If Minnie's presence hadn't tipped me off to the absolute and undeniable fact that this had to be a dream, the Prince of Coranti clumsily falling through the ground floor window of an inn in the Sinea mountains was proof enough.

I laughed. An uncomfortable, sleep-deprived, self-deprecating laugh, sure, but I'd take any laugh I could get these days.

"What's her problem?" whispered Prince Kayden, to which Minnie elbowed him in the side. I winced in sympathy—I'd been on the receiving end of that elbow many times during the eight years I'd known Minnie, and unfortunately, she didn't know her own strength. No, that wasn't right. Sure, she was very strong, but she *knew* she was very strong, so I supposed it was more that she didn't know how to use her strength amicably.

"She's going through a lot," Minnie hissed back behind her hand.

"I can hear you, you know," I said, reining in my hysterical laughter enough to speak, with effort.

She sighed, gently closing the window against the cold night air before stumbling over to my bed and plopping down without her usual grace. My eyes went to her midsection, obscured by her second-favorite green sweatshirt instead of a uniform or a hospital gown. Minnie's eyes were wide, forehead creased with pain, the expression eerily similar to that time when she was ten and got in a fight with an older boy who made a rude comment about her recently deceased mothers. Being young and scrawny, she wouldn't have stood a chance in a fair fight with the behemoth, so I'd darted in and tripped him. But not before he knocked Minnie down and kicked her, hard, in the ribs. Seeing her, trying so hard to be strong, to be solid, to be more than she could be... it was painful, both then and now. I'd rather pretend she was invincible, to always picture her at the moment she'd defeated Salma, like nothing could ever bring her down. Because what would I do if the strongest person in my life fell?

"You should rest," I said, helping Minnie pull off her boots and recline in the bed. "What in the world are you doing here?"

Minnie smiled feebly. "I came to see you, you dumb bleep."

I raised an eyebrow. "So, naturally, you brought Prince Kayden Ladrine of New Coranti with you?"

Her gaze darted past me like she'd forgotten the prince was there. I had too, honestly. He was surprisingly good at disappearing into the shadows for someone so constantly bombarded by cameras.

I turned, extending a hand to shake. "Isla Byrne, Your Highness." He accepted my hand, and I tilted my head at him questioningly. "But we've met before, haven't we?"

He nodded, chewing on his lip thoughtfully, eyes slightly narrowed, I thought. It was hard to really distinguish facial expressions in the dim lighting. "Twice. Nessie Courell, was it?"

I grinned. "Right."

"Call me Kayden," he said tiredly, running a hand through his messy reddish hair.

"Alright, Kayden, I assume you didn't come here as an escort to Minerva?"

"Are you asking me if I'm staying the night?"

"You're not very bright, are you?"

He blinked sadly in response as if he heard that a lot in his life and wasn't about to refute it. "I was just checking."

I clicked my tongue. "Right. So, is that a yes?"

"Yes." Kayden raised his chin defiantly, which was a useless gesture as he wasn't exactly short. I noticed, for the first time, that he stood slightly hunched and folded over himself as if by sheer willpower alone he could make himself small and insignificant. It was in sharp contrast to Minnie, who was shorter than most people and yet carried herself like a ten-foot-tall goliath. "I will prove myself, if it's the last thing I do. I'm coming with you."

I snorted. "You're coming with us? On our suicide mission?"

"Yes."

A horrible thought occurred to me, and I felt ridiculously dense for not seeing it earlier. "That's—that's not why Minnie's here, is it?"

"Of course it is." He tilted his head, a mirror image of me just a few moments before. "You have met her, right?"

"You've got to be kidding me," I muttered, sending a look at Minnie, who was already asleep. Or, equally likely, pretending to be asleep so she could listen to us talk when we thought she wasn't listening. She did that a lot.

Fake or not, Minnie needed her sleep, so I snatched the key for Edward's room off the bedside table and passed it to Kayden. "This whole inn is empty, pretty much, but unless you know how to pick locks, the only other room you can sleep in is room 107. It's right across the hall. There's one extra bed in there, just be careful: Edward's a light sleeper and he wakes up freakishly early, so maybe write a note or something for him so he doesn't panic when he wakes up to the prince crashing in his hotel room?"

"I know how to pick locks," he replied, monotone.

I blinked, surprised. I'd always thought lock-picking would be a cool talent to learn, but I'd never gotten around to it. "Oh. Did you want to—"

"But I'll just sleep in the room that's been paid for," Kayden added hastily, grabbing the key in my outstretched hand.

"Any chance you want to open a room for me?" I asked with a mischievous smile, though I knew before the words had even left my lips how he'd reply, and besides, there was no way I was leaving Minnie in here alone.

"Uh, no, sorry." Kayden trudged sheepishly from the room; shoulders hunched as if he regretted speaking in the first place. Why did the prince know how to pick locks? Bored royalty, I suppose, with loads of free time to learn quirky talents off the internet he'd never use.

I spun in a slow circle, surveying my sleeping options. Ella was curled up in the bed next to Minnie's, clutching the black leather jacket she'd been wearing when we got off the train to her chest like some sort of comfort blanket. I frowned. I hadn't really pictured her as the type to wear something like that, but people always surprised you. She looked even more small and fragile than normal, twisted in the sheets like she was trying to escape.

I huffed, realizing I couldn't just kick someone so pathetic looking out of bed for my own selfish reasons.

And by the far wall, still snoring softly, Vera lay slumped with one arm hanging off the side of the couch and her neck propped up on the arm. I winced at the awkward position. How she could sleep like that, I had no clue, but she would definitely have a terrible crick in her neck when she woke up. Vera had removed the dark, bold makeup she always wore, and a light flush covered her pale skin. Without her ever-constant scowl, her features looked soft and youthful, almost peaceful. It was disorienting, and I looked away, feeling like I'd seen her naked.

So that was how I ended up huddled on the floor, wrapped in an extra blanket I'd found in the closet. It reminded me of those two weeks I'd spent sleeping on the floor, wrapped in a threadbare blanket before Minnie had left. I lay facing the clock, which I hadn't noticed before, and I watched, frozen, as the minute hand ticked along. Two fifty-three. Two fifty-four. Two fifty-five.

I shuddered under the too-thin blanket, unable to shake the mountain chill that had followed Minnie in through the window. Groaning, I rolled over on the floor, trying to get comfortable. The blanket rolled with me, exposing a sliver of my back where my shirt had ridden up to the chill in the air. I cursed softly, not wanting to wake Minnie, and straightened the blanket. My head felt fuzzy, and I was so tired, but I couldn't seem to sleep. I counted sheep, painted pictures on the ceiling, counted my breaths, blinked rapidly, clenched and unclenched my muscles, every trick I could think of to fall asleep, if only for a couple of hours.

My eyes remained fixed on the clock as the minutes slipped by, eyelids heavy and yet refusing to close. At some point, they fluttered shut for just a few heartbeats, and yet when I opened them, the clock read six in the morning.

I couldn't just lay here anymore, so, knowing I wouldn't be able to go back to sleep, I pushed myself up from the floor with a grunt. My mouth dry and sticky, I stumbled to the bathroom to get some water from the sink, stretching as I went. The sun hadn't yet risen, but the room was lit softly by the barest hint of pre-dawn light through the window.

I slipped on my shoes, washed my face, and straightened my ponytail, still wearing my clothes from yesterday and not particularly caring. I was achy and tired, and I knew that would follow me through the day, a fact made worse by the knowledge that we were expected to leave today for our insane trek into the mountains. I was really not looking forward to sleeping outside on the cold hard ground tonight.

The door to room 107 was unlocked, though if that was from incompetence or because the prince had left it open for me, I couldn't be sure. Inside, as I'd expected, though the prince himself was splayed face-down on the second bed, Edward sat awake on the couch, flipping through a book.

"Why in the world are you reading at such an insane hour?"

"Hey, Isla!" Edward's head darted up, a wide smile on his face, and he slammed the book shut. "It's not even that early. Tons of people wake up at six."

I frowned. "Yeah, for work and school and stuff. Not when they don't have to."

"You're awake too," Edward countered gleefully. hopping off the couch with a loud creak to start making his bed,

"Couldn't sleep."

He frowned, hands stilling on the sheets. "Couldn't sleep? But it's the morning... What, you didn't sleep all night?"

"I got a couple of hours," I said truthfully, and, looking to deflect the conversation about my ever-worsening insomnia, I nodded to the book he'd abandoned.

"Aren't you worried about losing your spot?"

Edward returned to his tidying with a slight downward twitch of his lips, but he didn't fight my change of topic. "Nope! I remember the page number."

"You remember... the page number? Really?" I shook my head, not exactly surprised, and settled myself on the now-empty couch with a sigh.

The bed was so neat it looked better than when we arrived, and after analyzing the length of the overlapping cover on either side of the bed, Edward realized there was nothing more for him to do. He plopped down, shifting the immaculate sheets slightly as he bounced loudly on the ancient springs.

"So, what's up?"

I raised an eyebrow, forcing a smile as I gestured to the second bed, where Prince Kayden was still sprawled, breathing slow and even in sleep. "You may have noticed the royal elephant in the room."

"Yeah, the note he left me was a little vague." Edward grinned, grabbing a paper airplane from the bedside table and tossing it to me in a perfect arc that hit me square in the chest, where it bounced off and landed in my lap. I pried open the note, written in sloppy black pen: *Sleeping here. We are joining you tomorrow.*

"A little vague indeed," I said, tossing the note on the couch beside me, no doubt in my mind it had been Edward who'd made the airplane, not Kayden. I leaned forward, resting my elbows on my knees and my head in my hands. "He came here with my friend, who is currently very injured and even more stubborn."

Vera burst into the room, her bob of blonde hair spiked and unruly around her head and a livid scowl on her face that would scare Darkheart himself.

"It's six seventeen on my last morning in civilization and I'm awake," spat Vera, face splotchy with a dangerous combination of poor sleep and rage. "Why am I awake, you ask? Because some moron in this moronic little town decided to turn on a streetlight *right* outside my window."

Automatically, I turned to the window to see what she meant, but room 107 faced a small creek, not the street, and only darkness and vague shapes were visible.

"Which," Vera continued, "shouldn't be a problem, should it, because I *clearly* remember closing the blinds before I went to sleep last night on that horrible couch." She massaged her neck with one hand, wincing. "Why were the blinds open, Isla? Why are you awake? While we're on that subject, why is there a girl in your bed, looking half-dead and bleeding all over the place?"

I blanched. "What?" I demanded, scrambling to my feet. "She's bleeding?"

"So not the point," muttered Vera, not budging from the doorway as I pushed past her.

Minnie's eyes were still closed, lids fluttering slightly and face pinched, her hand lying on the bedspread in a white-knuckled fist. I stumbled over my feet in my haste to reach her. Her sweatshirt, a dark forest green, was even darker in a rough circle over the right side of her abdomen. My hands shook as I leaned forward to pull back the stained fabric to reveal the bandages around her middle, soaked through with red. Bile rose in my throat as I took in the mess. Of course she'd traveled halfway across the country and reopened her very, very recent injury in the process.

I turned to face Vera and Edward, hovering hesitantly on the threshold. Well, Edward was hovering. Vera looked ready to fall asleep against the doorframe.

"Vera, check if anyone is here, and Edward, go find a… I don't know, a first aid kit or something." My voice wavered slightly, but I tamped it down, fighting to seem in control. I couldn't freak out about a little bit of blood.

They didn't argue, just exchanged a glance and left silently in opposite directions. I turned back to Minnie, unsure what to do. Unwrap the bloody bandages, or leave them on until I had something to replace them with?

"Minnie," I whispered, struggling to keep the anxious bite from my tone. "Minnie, I need you to wake up."

She only lay there, still as a statue, and a horrible thought occurred to me. Heart in my throat, I lunged forward to grab her cold wrist in my fingers, and for a few tense seconds, I couldn't feel anything over the rush of terror in my veins.

But there it was. A steady, even pulse.

I breathed out a sigh of relief, lowering myself to sit on the bed next to Minnie. Then I slapped her, lightly, on the face.

"Come on, Minnie, wake up."

I slapped her again, a little harder this time, and her fist unclenched and clenched as she squeezed her eyes tighter shut.

"Bleep, that hurts."

I grinned, so glad that she was awake that I forgot she was injured. "I didn't slap you *that* hard, did I? If the terrifying Minnie Aberle admits to being in pain, it must be really bad…" My voice trailed off, following her gaze to her bandaged abdomen, and I realized that, of course, it hadn't been my slap she'd been complaining about.

Minnie waved off my concern with a weak wave of her arm, forcing a pained smile that didn't reach her eyes. "I'm fine, really. It just hurts a little when I—" She inhaled sharply, eyes fluttering closed for a second before she blinked them open again, dark eyes watery with pain. "When I, you know, breathe. Other than that, fine. Just fine. Absolutely, one hundred percent, completely, utterly, fine. So, stop worrying."

"You're bleeding. Bad."

Minnie raised her head off the pillow to take in her midsection and the red stain soaking through, one eyebrow raised in mild annoyance. "You've got to be bleeping kidding me. This is my second-favorite sweater."

"I feel like I shouldn't have to say this, but you need to take care of yourself, Minnie. You can't just go romping around the country when you're *supposed* to be on bed rest."

Minnie smiled, gesturing at the simple black duffel bag sitting near the window. "Be a dear and hand me my bag, would you?"

With a huff, I stood and grabbed the bag, which was startlingly heavy. "What do you have in here, a bunch of rocks?"

"Unfortunately not, but I do have chocolate."

I rolled my eyes jokingly, but I couldn't stop thinking about the blood. That much bleeding couldn't be normal, right? Was that even a lot of blood, or did it just look that way because of the way it spread through the fabric? She didn't seem to be showing signs of blood loss, but she was also very tough and exceedingly stubborn, so that didn't mean much. I doubted she would show any symptoms of just about anything until she was ready to keel over and die. Honestly, it was probably her biggest flaw.

"Want a piece?" Minnie asked around a mouthful of chocolate, offering a small brown truffle to me.

I gaped at her in feigned horror.

She groaned, at least having the decency to look mildly embarrassed as she popped the truffle into her mouth, the last piece barely swallowed. "Bleeping soy allergy, right." She squinted at the paper bag I'd given her before I'd left Tori. "You sure these have soy lecithin in them?"

I shrugged. "Maybe they don't, but I'm not really desperate to try." I shuddered, remembering the hives and diarrhea I'd gotten last time I'd accidentally eaten soy. Instead, I snatched the bag from Minnie and stuck it back in her duffel bag.

"Hey," she protested, if a little half-heartedly.

"What are you doing here, Minnie?"

"You followed me, now I follow you."

I sighed. "How did you even know where I'd gone?"

"You remember my new friend Abby Morren? I introduced you to her when you came to the cafeteria, and her mom is the head of the DOD, so she—"

"Emilia Morren?"

"Oh, you've heard of her?"

"Yeah, we've met a few times."

"Abby heard her mom talking about some top-secret mission with some… interesting personnel choices, and, well, I won't bore you with the story, but I put two and seventy-two together and got seventy-four. Once I figured out you were leaving—by the way, why didn't you tell me about your homicidal tendencies?"

"You know, I don't think you'd believe me if I told you why they think that. My *blood*, of all—"

"Oh please, I know you're not a murderer. Anyways, I just had to come with you, and on my way out of the infirmary you'll never guess who I ran into."

"I—"

"It was Kayden!"

"Not *Prince* Kayden?" I asked, eyebrows raised.

Minnie waved a dismissive hand. "Oh, he hates those bleeping titles."

"Did you just censor yourself by saying *bleep* instead of cursing?" Vera stood in the doorway, looking mildly offended on behalf of vulgarity everywhere.

"Yeah, it's kind of her thing. She's got the mouth of a sailor but doesn't want to be the one to accidentally teach the kids at the orphanage foul language."

Minnie jumped to her own defense. "I mean, honestly, it's really genius if you think about it. It's like one blanket curse word that works in every situation but won't ever get you in trouble."

"It sounds weird," grumbled Vera, stepping aside a split second before Edward barreled past her, brandishing a large bag reading "First Aid" in large block letters.

"I," he panted, dropping the bag on the floor with a rattle that made me flinch and leaning over to catch his breath. "I got the bag. She isn't dead yet, right? Did I make it in time?"

I stood and hauled the bag over to Minnie's bed, pulling out a roll of white bandages and surveying the red mess of her abdomen. "Time to change your bandages. Don't die on me, alright?"

# 18

*"To be lost is a beautiful thing, for the truest freedom comes in the loss of control."*

—*Excerpt from an ancient Nillaesce book of poems.*

Eyes closed, I let myself be aware of the energy around me as we stomped upward through the forest. It was almost overwhelming, here, surrounded by a growth of living things instead of the solid buildings I'd grown up with. Experimentally, I pulled on the branches whipping past my ankles, and felt the exhilarating rush of energy flow through my veins. I shuddered, cracking open one eye to watch the withered plant disappear beneath my feet.

A grin overtook my face, and I started Draining every plant I passed, tucking the Life Energy carefully away within myself as I went. Before, Draining had been negative in my mind, forever intertwined with memories of a dead woman and a shaky vow. But I could feel the power now, and I could only wonder at the power I could hold if I practiced.

It was addictive.

Terrifyingly, beautifully, chillingly, wondrously addictive.

Though I had to carefully tuck the power away to not get overwhelmed, I got the feeling that I could pull and pull and pull until the whole forest around me was wilted and black, and still never be satisfied. It was such—

My thoughts were interrupted by the crack of boots stumbling over roots and a grunt from Minnie. I whirled to steady her, unease twisting in my stomach. She was always so graceful, so steady, that to see her stumbling on the forest floor was unnerving, to say the least.

"You shouldn't have come," I grumbled, struggling to stay upright with both of our packs on my back and Minnie leaning heavily on my arm.

Minnie's smile was faint, but at least it was present at all. "I'd like to see you *try* to stop me."

"Oh, you and your silver tongue."

In truth, though I'd been opposed to the idea of Minnie hiking around with a sliced-up midsection at first, I'd realized the benefits outweighed the negative. We were away from the complex, with no authority figures breathing down our necks. Maybe a few nights on the cold hard ground would wear away at Minnie's unflinching sense of duty and honor and get her to run away with me and desert this mission. I knew I was supposed to be accepting of her decisions, but she'd already technically abandoned her training to join us, which was the first step to completely deserting.

Minnie's breathing was growing ragged, though she tried to hide it, and when I spotted a small clearing just off the path, I pulled us toward it.

"Come on, everybody, we're taking a break."

Vera scowled. "We've barely been hiking for two hours, and about as fast as a crippled snail. You seriously want to take a break?"

I glared right back at her, settling Minnie on a relatively dry log to rest. "I'm sorry, we're literally walking to our death and you're complaining about the *pace*?"

Ella started spinning around like a headless chicken, patting every pocket on her person and even bending over to rummage on the ground.

"What are you looking for?" I asked, unscrewing my water bottle lid and taking a long swig before passing it to Minnie.

Ella's eyes were wide with panic and her voice was little more than a distressed croak. "I can't find my ring."

"The gold one?" Vera joined her in her search.

"It was—it *is*—my mother's. It helps me focus."

"If it helps, you can borrow this ring while we look." Vera handed her a simple black band from her own finger without hesitation.

"I can't keep taking your things." She hesitated "You must be freezing, are you sure you don't want your jacket back?"

I was surprised by the surge of disappointment I felt that the black leather jacket wasn't Ella's after all—for a second, it had endeared her to me. A soft-spoken girl who wore yellow floral dresses and a rough leather jacket seemed like someone I could genuinely be friends with, but now I saw she really was just the weak, pathetic girl I'd thought she was from the start.

"No, really, it's fine. And take the ring. Your fingers need something to distract them."

I cocked an eyebrow. "You know, you didn't strike me as the chivalrous type, Roberts."

Was she... blushing? "Yeah, well, you know, I like to, uh, help... people. Yeah." Vera pivoted, hiding her face from view, and started rummaging aimlessly through her pack.

"Really, Isla? This is a new low, even for you." I glanced over at Minnie, who shoved my water bottle back at me, splashing water on the front of my shirt.

"What?" I asked, screwing the lid back on and returning it to my bag.

"Tell me you didn't steal that girl's ring."

I frowned. "No, I—"

"Why would Isla steal her ring?" Edward was hunched over, tying his shoelaces in increasingly intricate knots.

Minnie snorted. "Oh, didn't she tell you? She's a *professional* thief. It's her *occupation*. It's what she does."

"I thought she was a magician," Kayden said, coming to sit next to Minnie on the log. I scowled. I'd been about to sit there.

"Magician by day, pickpocket by night," Minnie mocked in a sing-song voice, derision heavy in the curve of her lips.

"More at the same time, really, but that's not—"

Vera jabbed an accusatory finger in my direction. "A thief, huh? Does that explain why I somehow lost my lighter the other day?"

I rolled my eyes. "No, your disorganization explains that."

"What do you need a lighter for?" Ella asked. "Do you smoke?"

Vera looked disgusted by the prospect. "Of course not."

"Then what? That's the only reason I thought people carried around lighters."

"I use it to, uh, to..." Vera looked around as if waiting for an idea to come to her, before finishing lamely: "To light birthday candles."

I snorted. "We need to work on your lying skills, Vera. That was horrible."

"Yeah, well, the stupid magician pick-pocket girl would know about lies, huh?"

"And, apparently, your comebacks, too."

"Isla, stop deflecting," Minnie broke in with a long-suffering sigh. "Did you steal the ring or not?"

"Minnie, honestly, I don't understand what your problem is. It's not like I go around stealing for fun—I did what I had to do, and now that we're in the middle of the woods, what possible motivation could I have for stealing some ring that's probably not worth much anyway?" I splayed my fingers wide in a display of innocence and gestured to my pack. "I swear I didn't steal it. You can search me and my bag if you like, but you'll only waste your time looking there."

Minnie huffed. "Fine, I believe you. Let's just keep walking, alright?"

"Are you sure you don't want to rest for a little longer?"

Minnie pulled herself to her feet, trying to hide how hard it was for her and failing magnificently. "Let's just go. The last campsite before the formal trail ends and we're in the thick of the mountains is about ten miles away. We'll camp there for the night."

I was just the slightest bit jealous of Minnie and her easy leadership. She was so forceful and yet somehow so persuasive that it made it nearly impossible not to listen to her.

We walked in near silence for over an hour, all focused on the ground in front of us and our own whirling minds. Apparently, I was more focused on my mind than the path.

Ella Bailey. She'd corrected herself and used the present tense for her mother, which suggested she was still alive, but first, she'd used past tense, which might imply that she thought of her as out of the picture. She couldn't have left, because then Ella wouldn't still be so fond of her, so she must have been injured in some way, making her daughter the provider? Was that why she needed the money so bad? What—

The packed earth flew up to meet my face as my foot caught on a root, and I threw out my hands to stop my fall before the rocks could smash into my face. The rough path dug into my palms, and when I pushed myself up they were red and speckled with pebbles. I grimaced, brushing them off, and that was when I felt the pain shoot through my right index finger.

I cursed, scrambling to my feet, right hand cradled in my left. The stinging of my palms was already beginning to fade, making my finger hurt all the more in contrast. At least it wasn't my dominant hand.

"You alright?" Minnie asked, stepping forward to examine my hand.

"I'll be fine," I grumbled. "It's not my leg or anything, I can still walk."

And walk we did, only pausing once for a quick lunch before loping off again.

I Drained several more plants as we went, and practiced Holding the energy within myself, even going so far as to try giving Minnie some energy, though it was far more difficult than Draining. When it worked, I shuddered, failing to push away the ominous chill that swept through me. I could push, pull, and hold Life Energy.

What was wrong with me?

I couldn't be a murderer—I *wasn't* a murderer.

I hadn't killed dozens of witches for this power.

I wasn't a killer.

I wasn't a killer.

I wasn't a killer.

But what if I was?

Would that be so bad?

I frowned. Of course, I wasn't a killer. What was I thinking?

"We're here," chirped Minnie, plonking her bag, which she'd insisted she was well enough to carry after lunch, down on the picnic table. "Say goodbye to civilization, because this is the last table you'll see—"

"Ever," Vera interjected with a dejected scowl.

"...for the rest of this mission. Are you alright?"

"Oh, I'm just fine. The fact that we're marching to our deaths, however, is not alright."

I frowned. "Hey, you stole my line."

"I really don't appreciate your negative mindset, you bleeping pessimist, whatever your name is."

"My name is Vera."

Odd. Minnie was usually great with names. Was she pretending not to remember just to annoy Vera? If so, it was working.

"I don't care. If everyone keeps acting like this mission is destined to fail, then of course it will."

I snorted. "You know they don't actually expect us to succeed, right?"

"Guess we better prove them wrong," Edward said with a demonic grin.

Minnie turned to face him, pleasantly surprised. "That's the spirit."

My eyes flitted over to Vera; whose scowl had only deepened at the interaction. I got the feeling she didn't care much for Edward.

"You're just a stupid pile of two-week-old dirty laundry. Who even invited you, anyway?"

Minnie jutted out her chin, hand flying to her hip in a defiant stance. "I invited myself."

"You can't just tag along on top-secret government missions."

"Oh, so it's a secret mission now? I thought it was a death march."

"You've done nothing but slow us down all day," snarled Vera, stepping up so she was face-to-face with Minnie. I'd been right—they were about the same height, if Vera was just slightly taller and a bit wider.

"Like your attitude has been a real motivator."

"You're a drain on resources."

"You're an egotistical bleep."

"You're a disappointment to your stupid idolized moms."

It was just like that day on the playground, but now Minnie was bigger, stronger, and her opponent wasn't ten times her size. One would think seven years might also change her explosive tendencies, but alas, Vera never stood a chance.

Minnie had never been one to pull her punches, and I winced as Vera went stumbling from a blow to the face. But Vera growled—I kid you not, actually *growled*—and launched herself back at Minnie with terrifying ferocity. Taken aback by the brute force of all of Vera's weight hurtling towards her, Minnie fell to the ground, crying out as Vera's knee hit her injured side.

She didn't stop fighting, though, gritting her teeth and headbutting Vera, which shocked her into loosening her grip on Minnie's arm. Minnie yanked free and whirled on the slightly larger girl, a manic gleam in her eye.

"Now would be a great time to help me break up this fight," I stage-whispered to Edward, the largest person here. "Preferably before Vera gets her face smashed in, but feel free to take your time."

Edward's eyes were wide in horror at the bloody brawl unfolding before us. I really hoped all that blood was from Vera's nose, though I suspected Minnie's wound had opened up again. I was going to kill Vera.

If Minnie didn't beat me to it.

Minnie rained down blows on Vera, who mounted some fledging resistance but was, all things considered, the far weaker fighter. I gave Edward a pointed look, and he scrambled forward, grabbing Minnie by the shoulders and hauling her back.

"Careful with the injury," I called at him from the sidelines.

Minnie thrashed in Edward's grip, yelling several creative combinations of bleeped-out obscenities at Vera, who leered back at her, blood oozing from her nose.

Shrugging off Edward's hand, Minnie plopped onto the picnic bench with a grim, set face. Edward scuttled off to help Vera stand, and I slid down next to Minnie.

"Want to explain what in Omili's name *that* was about?" I asked, crossing my arms.

Minnie stuck out her lip and started prying off her new hiking boots, identical to the pair I'd gotten, which was not an easy task one-handed. "You heard what she said about my moms."

"You've heard worse. What was different this time? What set you off?"

"It's just something about that Vera girl." Minnie shuddered. "She's just... I don't know. So aggravating." She sent me a sidelong gaze. "If I'm being honest, she reminds me of all the things I don't like about you."

We both looked over at Vera, who was bellowing at Edward and adamantly refusing the jacket Ella thrust at her.

"Thanks," I deadpanned.

Minnie groaned, massaging her feet. "Ugh, I hate backpacking."

"You've never been backpacking before."

She glared at me. "I went backpacking today, and it was enough for me to know I hate it."

"Fair enough."

"Will you bring me my chocolate?"

I scoffed. "Get your own chocolate. Why should I?"

"Because I'm not wearing shoes." Minnie gestured to her boots, scattered on the dirt beneath her feet, as if the answer was obvious.

"And whose fault is that?"

Minnie made a face at me, and I made one right back. She looked hopeful when I stood, but I wasn't about to indulge her sweet tooth, and instead went to check on the object of Minnie's wrath.

Vera sat on a log across the campsite from Minnie, scowling and pressing a bottle of cold water, fresh from the icy stream gurgling near the campsite, to one of the many bruises blossoming on her face. She looked a little rough around the edges, but I doubted she'd have any lasting damage. Without really thinking about it, I ran the fingers of my left hand over the finger I'd hurt while we were walking. I didn't think it was broken, probably sprained, or something akin to that. Sure hurt though.

"What's the time?"

Vera glanced over at the thin black watch circling her wrist but didn't raise her eyes to meet mine. "Just past eighteen hundred hours."

I hmphed. "We'll need to make the radio report thing soon, then."

Vera just grumbled in reply, shifting her impromptu ice pack to another bruise.

Leaning forward, I lowered my voice so only Vera could hear me. "You got off easy, Vera Roberts. Count yourself lucky you didn't say something worse."

# 19

*"It was, in fact, a tragedy to behold, the downfall of Detective Fetz's good associate, Mr. Robert Tonwin. He was a beloved man for both his delightful anecdotes and insightful political commentary, and one of his most humorous traits was his fondness for predicting ridiculous and impossible events. On one stormy afternoon, the good detective recalled, his associate had proposed a future in which witches ran the world. The mere thought brought a chuckle to Fetz's despondent lips even now."*

—*Tomorrow's Last Mystery, written by Roberta Tinn and published, clearly, before the Witch Revolution.*

"This is Captain Mila Akins," crackled the voice over the handheld radio. "I am confirming your transmission has been received. Over."

The radio dissolved into static, then cut off completely, delving us in silence.

"What, no *thank you, brave soldiers, for braving the mountains on this dangerous and noble quest, we are forever indebted to you*?" I quipped, tossing the radio to Edward, who caught it easily. "Honestly, at this point, I'd be fine with a *good job* or even a *hope you don't die*."

I got a few half-hearted chuckles, which made Vera's lips twist ever downward. "Just shut up, Byrne. You aren't funny."

"Oh, how you wound me, my sweet Vera."

Edward leaned forward to pat me awkwardly on the back. At least, it was awkward for me; I doubted he had any concept of the word. "I thought that was very funny, if it makes you feel better."

"It doesn't," I replied drily.

We'd set up camp as best as we were able, with the brief instruction we'd gotten this morning as they saddled us up with all this hiking gear. The sun had already sunk out of sight below the trees, and I wrapped my arms around myself in the deepening chill as the light faded from the sky. After a quick dinner of jerky, crackers, and water so cold it was painful to drink, our morbidly solemn party turned out for our tents.

Well, *tents* was a bit of a stretch. We'd each been given a tarp to go beneath our sleeping bags and another tarp to go above, along with a few stakes to prop the upper cover up. The man who'd given us the gear we'd been supplied had insisted they would be easier to carry and set up than a real tent, but I suspected the New Coranti Military just hadn't been willing to splurge on a mission bound to fail. It was a miracle they gave us any gear at all, which I supposed was a testament to the last strings of hope they held that we might, maybe, actually pull this off.

They should have known better than to have hope in us.

After checking that Minnie's bleeding had stopped, washing the wound, wrapping her in fresh, sterile bandages, and struggling not to pass out from the sight, I started preparing myself for sleep. At times, it was terrifyingly easy to forget she was injured at all, with the way she acted. But at others, it was all too clear she was more hurt than she let on. I left Minnie with a single push of energy, the flow of Life Energy in and out of my body becoming more and more familiar the more I practiced. It made me wonder if maybe I could begin to pinpoint the specific frequencies of Life Energy the most advanced witches, like the queen, were said to be able to manipulate. I'd heard that she was able to apply her energy to things like speed or eyesight.

"I propose a challenge," announced Edward as I slid off my boots and climbed inside my sleeping bag. In a loose circle, the rest of our party was doing the same.

"What challenge?" asked Ella. She'd grown even quieter since she'd lost her ring if that was possible, and though her fingers still flitted along where it'd been, it was as if she'd lost a shield. My hands flew to my little velvet bag of cards, stored in the safest, waterproof packet of my backpack, and I felt just the slightest bit of remorse for what I'd done.

"Since we're so close to Nillaesce territory, it only makes sense to lighten the mood by seeing who does the best Nillaesce accent."

I rolled my eyes. Though being separated by the Sinea Mountains, Coranti and Nillaesce were descended from the same ancient people and thus shared a similar language, if in different dialects. Before the Witch Revolution eight years ago, the two nations had been allied and traded freely between themselves. Though Coranti had always been slightly more liberal with witchcraft than the vehemently religious, anti-witch theocracy of Nillaesce, it had never been wise to give open displays of your witchcraft. And before the revolution, when Witch-led science was yet to flourish, there had been no scientific way to test for magic. Thankfully, the New Coranti government had kept the supernatural blood analysis technology under lock and key, saving witches around the world from varying levels of persecution.

"The best accent?" Vera scoffed. "That's stupid."

The second Vera spoke in opposition, Minnie seemed to decide it was a great idea. "That sounds so fun! We should do that."

"I'll go first," said Edward, clearing his throat in preparation, before belching out a string of words almost indecipherable by the way he stretched and pulled them. I thought I recognized "fairy"— or was it "very"?

I laughed. "That was horrible, Edward."

Minnie snorted. "I want to try. I've seen enough old Nillaesce shows, I'm sure it won't be too hard, right? It's pretty much just Corantian with stress on different syllables."

I raised an eyebrow. "I think?"

"Here goes: Ahr'm gon'ta goey to da stir."

"Seriously, Minnie? Have you ever heard a Nillaesce accent in your life?"

"I'd like to see you do better."

I jutted out my chin. "Fine. Watch me." I opened my mouth, ready to amaze them with my linguistic expertise, then suddenly couldn't remember the way the Nillaesce vowels worked. Vera snickered at my hesitation, and I glared daggers back. All I could think of was how they pronounced the word bird—like it had a "T" stuck on the end. "Birdt flah. Birdt flop da wangs and flah."

A roar of uproarious laughter peeled from Kayden's tent, and I stuck my head out to scowl at him.

"I-I'm sorry," he rasped out as his fit of laughter waned, wiping tears of mirth from his eyes. "It's just—none of you have a clue, do you?"

"Rude," huffed Minnie.

"I've actually met some Nillaesce, you know. There was a brief time after my mother rose to power—"

"Oh, right, you're a prince." Vera yawned across the circle, interrupting him. She made a fair point—it was so easy to forget he was related to the most powerful witch in Coranti when he stayed so quiet and hunched all the time.

"Uh, yeah, right." Kayden coughed uncomfortably into his sleeve. "But I, I was saying, after the revolution and before the war officially started, there was a brief period of negotiations when the..." His voice faded off as he realized no one was really listening anymore.

With a yawn, I slid my cards out, ready to do a little shuffling, a little practice, a little anything to busy my fingers and calm my mind before I slept.

But I couldn't. I tried to turn the cards around my fingers, to let them slide across my knuckles like I'd practiced a thousand times, but the pain in my finger was still too strong, sending a jolt through my body whenever I bent it. I squeezed my eyes shut as the others laughed around me, oblivious to my rising panic. I couldn't shuffle. I couldn't do anything.

"That was definitely worse than Edward's, Vera," Minnie snorted.

"Shut it, Mi—" Vera hesitated, frowning. "Mi—"

I laughed, a real, hearty laugh that warmed my insides and made me temporarily forget about sleights of hands and sprained fingers and the inevitable doom hovering over us all.

"What?" Minnie looked between the two of us, confusion knitting her brow.

"She—" I struggled to wheeze out the words through the laughter knotting my stomach, devolving further into hysterics whenever I tried to speak. "She's mad because—because—" I clutched my midsection, tears of laughter pricking my eyes.

Vera scowled in her tent; arms crossed over her chest.

"Because your nickname ruined her—her little mind trick," I finally managed to say as the laughter subsided, straightening my sleeping bag.

"Her... mind trick?"

"Oh right, Minnie is a nickname! What's her full name again?" Vera sat up, setting her tarp wobbling on the weak supports.

I started laughing uncontrollably again.

"Isla Anna Byrne, don't you dare tell her what Minnie is short for."

"It's not even that embarrassing," I choked out.

"Tell me."

"Don't tell her."

"Min—" I began.

"Don't you dare!

I grinned demonically. "Minerva!"

Vera cackled. "Minervie!"

And on they went, bickering and joking like a group of old friends. Even Ella and the prince spoke from time, their words fading into the background as I stared mournfully at the deck of cards in my lap.

Without thinking, my fingers slid to one of my many pockets, feeling the weight of a thin gold ring in my hand. I raised it slightly to catch the last glimmers of sunlight through the trees, watching the glint off the beautiful twisting bands all interlocked together in a graceful logic.

It was a gorgeous trinket, sure, but, more importantly, I was fairly certain it was real gold.

I felt just the slightest bit bad about taking it, but if Minnie decided she wanted to run away, we'd need money for passage to one of the island nations west of Lilta. I'd done some research on the library computers during my time at the complex, and there were several carefully neutral islands who weren't openly against witchcraft where we could... disappear.

I'd knocked steps one and two of my ever-adapting plan out of the park—if a bit accidentally. Minnie was away from the complex and any authority figures, and I had the means to get us away from Coranti for good.

Step three sounded the simplest but was near impossible in execution—the actual act of convincing Minnie to leave with me, without forcing it on her. She needed to make the decision for herself.

That would come in time, I was sure.

It had to.

The sunrise was beautiful, the light filtering down to our campsite over the ridge of the mountain peak above and bathing the tents in beautiful golden light. Vera still snored, but at least there was chirping birdsong to accompany her out in the mountains. I sighed, glad for the best night of sleep I'd gotten in days, weeks, months? There was something to be said about falling asleep exhausted. A soft smile flickered on my lips and I closed my eyes, relaxing back into my sleeping bag with another contented sigh, hoping to maybe fall back asleep in the time it took for Minnie to spring out of bed and wake us all, a favorite pastime of hers. For the first time since I'd watched her almost die before me as I was helpless to do anything, I was just the slightest bit glad for her injury. She never slept in until sunrise, ever... except yesterday and today, apparently.

But the rustle of fabric and the clatter of a make-shift tent falling made me open my eyes again.

I rolled over quietly in my tent to face our quiet circle, disturbed by Kayden, who was struggling to right his tent without making even more noise and failing miserably. Leaving his tarp and supports in a pile on the ground with a loud sigh, he stomped off away from the camp, leaving the rest of us in the soft quiet filled with breathing and the ever-present burble of the creek.

I didn't know much about Prince Kayden Ladrine, but he was acting so weird, and I got the sense he was hiding something. Or was that just my paranoia speaking? It had been rather vocal lately. Still, it couldn't hurt to follow him, right? Even if he was probably only marching off to use the little prince's room.

Our illustrious prince stood facing a tree stump decorated with a mop of brown, dead moss, pacing with his hands behind his back. I was just glad I hadn't stumbled in on him taking a pee.

"No, no, that's stupid." He paused his pacing, facing the stump with determination. "Hello, Minnie—" he cut himself off, muttering under his breath as he paced. "Is it too intimate to use a nickname? I hardly know her. But is it too formal to use her full name when she goes almost exclusively by Minnie?"

Kayden sighed, facing the stump once more, and I had to stifle a giggle so he wouldn't hear me. Was—was the stump supposed to be Minnie? Oh, Omili, it was. And the moss was supposed to be her hair… it was too much, and I missed some of Kayden's conversation with stump-Minnie bent over trying to quiet my laughter in the shadow of the trees.

"Hello, Minnie. I know I've barely known you for a few days, and I didn't know you at all before that party, but I saw you, and I could never forget you. Of course, you didn't notice me. Why would you notice me? I'm just a worthless prince without a crown. My mother hates me, and she'd rather make my thirteen-year-old little sister her heir than—Omili, I'm rambling again."

He rested his head in his hands, shaking slightly in the mountain breeze. I almost felt bad for the guy. Kayden shook his head with a sigh, starting again.

"Hello, Minnie. I think you're the strongest, most—no, I *know* you're the strongest… girls like confidence, right?" He scoffed. "Minnie, you've got a billion times the confidence I could ever muster—that must be enough for the both of us, right? Wow, the both of us. That sounds like I assume we'll get together or something. Is that confident or just arrogant? Like I'd know, I've never felt either—don't be self-deprecating, Kayden."

If this dude's exterior ramblings were this jumbled, I definitely did not want to know what the inside of his head was like. Must be a mess up there.

"Hello, Minnie… Who am I kidding? Like I'd ever have the courage to pull this off. Like you'd ever notice me. You're amazing and fantastic, and I'm not the type to actually muster the courage to stand face to face with someone and tell them how I feel." He swiped the moss from the stump and sat down with a sigh. "What am I doing? This is ridiculous. It would be easier just to leave a note or something…" His eyes widened visibly, and he darted to his feet. I scrambled out of the way as quietly as possible as he walked right past me back towards the camp, eyes alight with his genius idea.

I still wanted to go back to sleep, but I stood frozen in the middle of the woods, processing what I'd just witnessed. This boy, this *prince*… he liked Minnie. As in, holding hands and flowers and fancy dinners liked her. Which wasn't a problem in itself, I supposed, but if…

A cold finger of dread curled in my stomach. What if Minnie felt the same way? What if she'd gotten attached to him? What if his note proclaiming his feelings for her was the thing that kept her from me when I'd worked so hard to keep her by my side?

This could be very, very bad, but I would fix it. I always did.

# 20

Minnie was still asleep when I made my way back to camp after an invigorating stop by the stream to splash the sleep off my face. I stayed in the shadows of the trees and watched Kayden draft a note while the rest of our group snored around him.

I snuck around the back of the tarp circle to fish around in Minnie's backpack for that infernal stationery and pens she carried everywhere. The stationary and pens she'd used for the note she'd left on my duffel bag, the day she'd formally enlisted. Sighing, I returned her backpack to order with a single pen and a single card in my clutches and sat down on a log to wait for Kayden to finish with his letter.

He took his sweet time with it, pausing several times to steel himself and collect his thoughts, even balling up his note and starting over completely at points, and I dared to hope he wouldn't go through with it.

But he took a few deep breaths, closed his eyes, and tip-toed less than stealthily over to the pack I'd just abandoned to stash the letter. The second he was gone, I darted over, grabbed the letter, and hid myself away back on my log. I didn't have long before Minnie woke up.

*Hello, Minnie,*

*How are you? Sorry, that's stupid, but I'm great, thanks for asking. I just—the weather's been great lately, huh? I know, I know, I can't make small talk in a letter, so I'll stop beating around the bush. I think you're great. I'm sure you know that, but I figured I'd tell you that I think you're great, and I feel great when I talk to you, and I'd like to get to know you better if you'd like. That's it. Bye, Kayden.*

*P.S. I'm sorry you had to read this; I completely understand if you don't feel the same way. In fact, I anticipate it. It's fine. My feelings won't be hurt. Well, maybe they will, but I'll pretend they won't. Bye again.*

I chewed at my lip, staring at the hastily written and yet very deliberate pen strokes. What to write, what to write? I supposed I could just toss it in the stream and be done with it, and Kayden would probably assume she'd ignored the note—but what if he asked her about it? I couldn't risk that. Plus, Minnie would never ignore a letter like that.

I uncapped Minnie's pen and set to work forging a note in Minnie's curly script and occasionally blunt tone, toeing the careful line of rejecting him politely enough to be believable but harsh enough that he stayed away.

I slipped the note in Kayden's pack without incident when he left to use the bathroom, only to realize that Minnie wasn't even awake yet. Sending a glance at Minnie's ever-slumbering form, I made my way back to Kayden's toppled tent only to run straight into Edward.

"Wow, it sure feels good to sleep in, huh? That's what hiking all day will do to you. Where's Kayden?"

I blinked at Edward, wondering how his mouth could keep up with how fast he was talking.

"Uh, I'm not sure. Guess he went to the bathroom or something."

Edward's head bobbed up and down like some creepy marionette. "Right, right, are you excited for a delicious breakfast of dried camping food?"

I sighed, feeling more tired just being in his presence. "You know, it's crazy. We're in the midst of beautiful, lush nature, and yet we're eating factory food? There must be some sort of delicious wild berries around here somewhere…" I hinted, and Edward's face lit up.

"Great idea! I'll look in this direction, you look in that direction, alright?"

I nodded, lips pressed into a tight smile, and he darted off away from the stream, massive feet nearly knocking over Vera's tent as he went. He reminded me a bit of an overeager puppy, and for a few heartwarming seconds, I smiled at the memories of my father and our dog, Angel.

"Morning, Isla," yawned Minnie, and I whirled to face her.

"You're awake!"

"Yeah, why are you acting so weird?"

"No reason—oh, hello, Kayden."

"Good morning?" Kayden twisted his hands together nervously and sent a furtive look in Minnie's direction before turning to put up his tent.

With a groan, Minnie pushed herself into a seated position, leaning heavily on her arm. "Let's do this! The earlier we start, the farther we can walk before we run out of sunlight."

"Goodie." I yawned, stretching my sore legs. "I say we take our time. What's the hurry, anyway?"

"The hurry is that there's a genocidal murderer and a witch-killing army roaming these mountains," snapped Minnie.

I shrugged. "Fair enough. Where are we even going, anyway?"

"Come on, Isla, I wasn't even formally briefed, and yet I get the sense I know more about this mission than you do."

"I wouldn't really call what we got a 'briefing' per se," I hedged. "It was more of a 'we hate you, so we're sending you into the mountains to chase the most dangerous man in the world. Have fun!'"

The clatter and *thunk* of tarp supports falling and hitting an unsuspecting skull drew my attention. "I hate the world," grumbled Vera, voice muffled beneath her tarp.

"Sorry!" chirped Edward, stepping gingerly past the supports he'd knocked over. "Oh, Isla, you're back already," he wheezed, out of breath. "I found some berries!"

Minnie frowned at the muted purple berries he held in an extended palm. "I don't recognize them," she said. "Do you think they're poisonous?"

"Sure hope not." Edward grinned, revealing purple-stained teeth. "I already ate a whole handful."

Minnie let out an exasperated sigh, turning to bellow at Vera, "Wake up, you lazy bleep!"

"I'm awake," growled Vera, poking her head out of her collapsed tarp, her bangs sticking up around her face.

Ella was already folding up her tarp and rolling it to fit in her backpack, sliding the stakes and ground cover in beside it. Slowly, we all began to follow suit, some more neatly than others.

"Let me help you lace up your boots," I said, gesturing to Minnie's bare feet on the rough ground.

"I can put on my own shoes, Isla," she sighed, reaching for her hiking boots. Minnie always preferred slip-on shoes she didn't have to tie for convenience's sake, as it was difficult for her to tie tight knots one-handed.

"I know you can, but if the boots aren't tight enough you could hurt your ankle or worse." I gave her bandaged abdomen a look. "You're already broken enough as it is." I winced. "That sounded bad, I'm sorry—"

Minnie laughed softly, sitting down at the picnic table and shoving her untied boots on her feet. "Just tie the bleeping shoes, peasant."

Nobody but Edward decided to partake in the mystery berries, which was probably for the best because he had to stop several times after we started hiking again to retch. He wasn't dying, though, I didn't think.

The path grew steadily steeper as we went, and devolved into a jagged, twisting, and narrow trail from the smooth, flatter one we'd followed yesterday. For many segments, we had to walk one-by-one, but when the path widened out again Vera ambushed me and pulled me to the back of the pack.

"I need to talk to you."

I gave her a sidelong glance, taking in the bruises and cuts mottling her face, before focusing back on the path before my feet. Minnie was leading us at a brisk pace, and I didn't seem to be the only one feeling the burn. My legs were aching already, and I could've sworn a poltergeist was steadily adding rocks to my backpack.

"What, what do you want, Roberts?" I huffed, breaths of cold air rasping my lungs when I tried to breathe.

"I think I'm having an allergic reaction to Ella."

She sounded serious, but I had to stop walking for a second to gape at her.

"An... allergic reaction? To Ella Bailey?"

"I mean, not to *her*, but to her soap or something?"

I panted out a laugh and started walking again, ignoring the muscles that screamed for me to keep standing still. "You've got to be kidding me."

Vera scrambled to catch up. "No, seriously, listen to me. I think it might be a real problem."

"Fine," I said, deciding to humor her. "What are your symptoms?"

"My breathing is erratic, I get all sweaty, my heart starts getting tachycardic on me, talking is weird and uncomfortable, and it's like my brain goes on vacation."

"And all this while you're around her?" I asked, deadpan.

"Yeah."

"My diagnosis: you like her."

Omili above, was she *blushing*? I'd never seen Vera's skin any other color than deathly pale or bruised sickly yellow, and the red flush splotching her cheeks was in vivid contrast to my mental image of her.

"W-what?"

"You like her," I repeated in a sing-song voice.

"What do you mean?" Vera asked, high-pitched.

"Seriously, Roberts, have you never had a crush?"

"A... crush? Like, a romantic interest in someone?"

"Sure, if you're a dictionary."

"No, I haven't. Why, have you?"

I snorted. "Tons. None of them ever went anywhere, though."

"I wonder why," Vera said snidely

I glared. "Really, trying to help you here."

"Sorry," she grumbled.

"What are you guys talking about?" asked Edward, stepping easily into stride beside Vera, his long legs eating up the terrain below without apparent effort.

"Oh, you know, our past romantic pursuits," I said.

Edward seemed to decide he would just add himself right into the conversation, gaining a far-off look in his eyes. "I used to have a girlfriend. Her name was Chloe. We were pretty serious."

I pretended to act interested. "That's so cool."

"She broke up with me a couple of months ago, before I was conscripted." He shrugged it off, like he didn't really care, though his face said otherwise. "What about you, Ella? You're drop-dead gorgeous, so I'm sure you've had tons of romance in your life."

Ella laughed, a tinkling sound like a fairy from a children's movie. "Stop it, you big teddy bear. *You're* the gorgeous one in this friendship."

I rubbed the spot between my eyes. I was no good at navigating social webs. I must have missed when these two became the best of friends. They kept talking beside me, but I noticed Minnie and Kayden walking ahead of us and strained my ears to hear what they were saying.

"...alright, Kayden? You've been even quieter than normal this morning."

Kayden just looked at her sadly, and I gathered he must have received my note. "I'm fine, Minnie. It's just"—he waved a hand in the air—"you know."

I shuddered in anticipation, wishing I had some popcorn. Minnie hated poor communication.

"No," she replied, voice icy. "I *don't* know. Tell me what's the matter."

Vera elbowed me hard in the side, bringing me back to the conversation around me. I glared at her, trying to convey *I'm not going to be your wingman* with the look.

"Come on, Ella, tell us about your romantic life," said Edward, before quickly amending: "unless you're uncomfortable talking about it."

I noticed her fingers go to where she usually wore her mother's ring and felt a twist of guilt.

"Yeah, I've had a few girlfriends, but it never lasts long. They always leave when they realize my anxiety isn't cute or quirky but a real mental disorder with problems of its own." She swallowed, twisting the black ring Vera had let her borrow. "And since the accident, well, it's been hard."

Boring. I tried to focus back on Minnie and Kayden, which they helpfully made easier for me by raising their voices.

"I can't believe you! You have the *nerve*—"

"Why are you yelling at me?" Kayden shouted back.

"I just wanted to ask how you were, and you started acting like it's *my* fault that you—"

"That I'm just a 'bleeping spoiled princeling without a clue,' huh?"

I beamed proudly at the use of a line I'd written in my forged note, before realizing it might have been a tad too aggressive.

"Stop putting words in my mouth!" bellowed Minnie, and the muted conversation about tragic pasts, blah de blah, walking beside me hushed to watch.

"Maybe if you stopped being such an arrogant bully, I could."

"Arrogant bully, huh?" Minnie was walking on his left side, so she twisted around and started walking backward so she could shake her fist in his face. Well, as close to his face as she could get. "I'll show you an arrogant bully, you abnormally tall, coddled, baby-faced idiot!"

"Face it, Minnie," Kayden yelled back, "I'm not that tall, you're just short."

"You did *not* just call me short," screeched Minnie, dropping her pack on the ground. I stifled a grin as I increased my pace to catch up to them. I don't know how Kayden had ever dreamed they would work out together; Minnie was so volatile and dangerous, like a housecat with razor-sharp claws, and Kayden was... Well, I didn't know him well enough to make as accurate an analogy to his personality, but it would suffice to say that though he seemed shy and docile, I suspected there was more to him, beneath the surface.

Not that I was in the business of psychoanalysis.

"I'm not going to fight you, Minnie."

"Why? Because you know you'll lose?"

"Yes!"

I gulped in the fast-thinning mountain air, legs straining to push me up the rocky trail towards Minnie. Grabbing her arm and shoving Kayden out of the way to diffuse the conflict, I buckled over to catch my breath as my dear prince went stumbling into Edward.

"H-how are you guys not," I wheezed, struggling to speak through the exertion, "not out of breath?"

Minnie snorted, yanking her arm free of my grasp. "I've spent too many years telling you that you need more cardio in your life for you to ask me why you're out of breath from a brisk hike."

"I'm sorry I'm not interested in waking up at ungodly hours in the morning to go on runs before school."

"It's good for your heart," chided Minnie, thumping her fist on her chest. "I'm going to live until I'm one hundred and twenty, and you'll be long dead in a pile of junk food."

"Yeah, if all the chocolate doesn't kill you first. I probably eat healthier than you."

"A healthy lifestyle is twofold: diet and exercise."

"So, I eat well enough and you exercise, and together we make a healthy human being?"

Minnie smiled weakly, throwing her pack back on her shoulder and fiddling with the buckle securing the other strap to her stump. "Sounds good to me."

"You would think your fight with Vera would satiate your blood lust for at least a few days, but you looked just about ready to launch yourself at the princeling. Care to explain?"

Minnie stared down at her hand, which she clenched and unclenched into a fist. "I don't know. It's stupid, but I-I don't know, I guess I sort of like talking to him?" A frown tugged at the corners of my lips, but I fought it back, for Minnie's sake. "He's so nice, and calming to be around, and a great conversationalist—"

"I'm sorry, what does this have to do with you picking a fight with him?" My voice was icier than I'd meant it to be.

"It's annoying, that's all. I like talking to him, I like how I feel when I'm with him, and I start to get hopeful. Then I panic and start self-sabotaging." She sent me a sheepish look. "You remember what happened with Tom."

I paused contemplatively. Maybe it would have been better to let Minnie fight Kayden after all—a bloody nose between them could be the killing blow in any possible relationship. "You mean when you gave him a black eye because he said you were pretty?"

Minnie's warm umber skin darkened a shade at the memory. "No need to rehash ancient history, Isla."

I huffed a disbelieving laugh. "That was only a year ago!"

Minnie shushed me, and, watching her eyes alight with mirth and embarrassment, I didn't feel bad at all for the stunt I pulled with the letter. It had hurt to see the pain on her face as she'd argued with Kayden, but I knew it would be justified when we were far from here eating grapes on an island somewhere. And I'd been right in my precautionary measures after all—it looked like, just maybe, Minnie might reciprocate some of Kayden's same feelings. I shuddered to think what might have happened if I hadn't followed Kayden away from the tents and intervened. Love could do dangerous things to your heart.

Wasn't my walking beside Minnie here proof of that?

As long as nothing could stand between us, as long as I could keep Minnie safe and away from this horrible war, we would be alright. Because we had love, determination, and most importantly, each other.

# 21

*"Sometimes, of course, I do find myself entrenched in the most paralyzing fear—that quintessential terror that someday, perhaps not far in the future, they will find me. What then? Will it all be for nothing, all my research, all my hard work, simply because the blood in my veins is infused with some indescribable quality? Will they not see that magic is but the science we are yet to understand? Perhaps, if I might continue to study this beautiful and tragic phenomenon, one day magic will be just another understandable constant. It is this, my dream, no, my driving need, as strong as the forces that bind us to the earth, that one day witches will be freed from the burdens and stigmatization placed upon them."*

*——Excerpt from the personal journals of Cecile Omili. Currently displayed in the hub of the New Coranti Military Headquarters in Tori, with the caption: "We Did It, Omili."*

I hated hiking.

My back and shoulders ached from the weight of my backpack, and my legs, sore from yesterday's walking, screamed in protest as they hauled me up the ever steepening and narrowing path. Before the war, people hiked these trails for recreation. We passed several beautiful waterfalls, I was pretty sure, but I was too busy trying to readjust my backpack into a more comfortable position to really appreciate them.

And all the while, Minnie pushed us to keep a steady speed.

"When are we stopping for lunch?" whined Edward, dragging his feet. Honestly, it was frankly quite difficult sometimes to remember he was actually the oldest person here, at eighteen years old.

"Soon," Minnie called back over her shoulder, not breaking stride.

"How soon?"

"Shut up, Edward," I snapped. "You and Minnie are the only actually athletic ones, but you don't see the rest of us complaining, do you?"

"Just because I was a starter on my school team every season in three different sports doesn't mean I'm prepared for a steep, off-road, multi-day hike through—"

"Literally no one cares, Edward." I looked over to Vera, walking next to Ella and staring at the taller girl with poorly masked admiration that Ella was either oblivious to or did a good job ignoring. "Back me up, Vera."

"Uh, I don't know. What do *you* think, Ella?"

I wanted to simultaneously claw my eyes out with my fingernails and travel back in time. It was like me expressing Vera's feelings to her in words gave her the will to act on them—in her own weird, creepy way. If only I'd nodded and confirmed her theory about the allergic reaction.

Though she tried not to show it, Minnie was beginning to breathe heavily, her steps becoming sluggish, her motions jerky.

"Lunchtime!" I called, yanking her to a stop.

Minnie glared daggers at me. "We're on a thin trail barely wide enough for two people walking side by side, carved into the side of a mountain." She gestured at the steep and heavily wooded slope above and below us. "Where in the world do you want to eat?"

"Right here on the path," I said, crouching down to sit on the rock-strewn earth and pulling Minnie with me.

We ate a quick lunch of jerky and dried fruit, then Minnie shooed the others along, telling them she'd catch up, as we stayed back for me to look at her cut.

Had I mentioned how much I hated the sight of blood? Specifically, Minnie's blood?

After cleaning the wound of any sweat and dirt that had managed to get beneath her bandages since this morning, I patted Minnie's skin dry and wrapped clean bandages around her middle.

"Honestly, the things I do for you," I sighed, using some of my water to wash the stray streaks of blood from my hands. Minnie was quiet a few seconds too long, and I glanced over, ready for a joking retort. Instead, her eyes were filled with a sorrowful heaviness, and she rose to her feet on unsteady legs to come stand beside me on the rough cliff where the path dissolved into the forested mountainside.

"You know I appreciate you, right? I feel like I don't say it enough."

I twisted my lips into a wry grin to hide the emotion seeping into my face. "Getting soft on me, Aberle?"

"Seriously, Isla, you followed me into your worst nightmare, and for what?"

I lightly elbowed her in her non-injured side, looking into the leaves just beginning to gain the rusty brown and vibrant hues of autumn.

"I followed you, you followed me, what does it matter? What matters is us, Minnie." My hand imitating her flowery script flashed in my mind, but I didn't feel guilty. No. This was all for her, for us. "We're together, and we always will be. That's what matters."

Minnie sniffled, rubbing at her nose with the back of her hand. I sent her a disbelieving look. "Did I manage to get Minerva Aberle, the toughest witch in the New Coranti Military, to tear up?"

"No," mumbled Minnie, wiping at red eyes. I watched her quietly, taking in the way her dark eyes flickered across the trees, absorbing in the world around us, and knew this was the best opportunity I'd get to broach the subject of running away again.

"Minnie?" I asked after the tentative silence had stretched out too long.

"Hm?"

"I've made plans. I've done the research. I have the means. I have you, you have me, holding hands on the cliff. All you have to do is jump."

Minnie raised one thick eyebrow. "Are you asking me to jump off this cliff with you? Because the answer is no. I have a lot more to live for, and I think you need a therapist."

I snorted. "No, dimwit, I was trying to be poetic." I reached for her hand, lacing my fingers with her icy ones. "I know I said I'd accepted your decision, and I have. But the circumstances have changed, and I'm just asking you one last time. I think we should desert. Before you shoot the idea down, please, hear me out." I raised my left hand in a placating gesture, and Minnie's face remained blank, staring ever forward at the sloping woods below. I took that as a sign to proceed.

"They don't expect us to succeed. They don't expect us to come back alive at all. Do you know what that means? That means freedom." I didn't mention the minute detail about me becoming a wanted fugitive if we missed a radio in—I'd like to see them *try* to catch me. "We can go anywhere, be anyone, do *anything* we want. And, more importantly, we won't be dead in a couple of days."

Silence fell again over the path as the noises of the rest of our group faded away. Finally, after an excruciating period of quiet, Minnie turned her head to lock her eyes with mine.

"I think I'd like that, Isla," she said, voice the barest whisper, almost faint enough to be carried off in the breeze. She cleared her throat. "I think I'd like that a lot." Minnie gave the trees another glance, as though saying goodbye, before shouldering her backpack and walking off. "Can we talk about this later?" she called over her shoulder, her usual confidence seeping back into her voice.

I gaped in disbelief, adjusting my bag and trotting after her. "Yeah, yeah, we most certainly can."

I struggled to catch up, pushing my unwilling legs farther and farther up the steep, winding path until it felt as though I'd climbed all the way to heaven. Ironic, considering I'd never see inside those golden gates. Not according to the Nillaesce.

I finally managed to catch up when the small group stopped for Minnie to examine her map, brow furrowed.

"Wh-what's going on?" I wheezed, legs wobbling beneath me as I fought to get my breath back.

"Right now, we're just off the Old Mickenso Trail, facing east," mused Minnie, tilting the map, oblivious to Vera peeking over her shoulder at the creased paper. "And Split Peak is right..." She lowered the map, pivoting to face the jagged mountain top towering above the forested valleys in the distance. "There. Our best intel suggests that the—"

"What do you know about 'our best intel'?" interrupted Vera, snatching the map from her. "You weren't even there when we were briefed." She hesitated, then amended. "Not that we were told anything *actually* useful."

"I have my sources," Minnie snapped, yanking the map back. "Anyways, everything we know about Darkheart's 'lair' seems to suggest he's hiding out somewhere in the mountains north of Split Peak." Minnie sighed, folding the map and returning to her bag, which was a painstaking process one-handed, but no one offered to help. "Keep an eye out for evil genocidal creeps, I guess."

I shuddered.

"So, we keep hiking towards Split Peak, then?" I asked, eyeing the imposing peak. I'd never been this close to it before.

"Unless we see something that inclines us otherwise, yeah."

Split Peak. Site of the infamous first major battle of the war, and the farthest north of any skirmishes since. The battle that killed my father.

Several millennia later, the sun was no longer visible beyond the thick curtain of clouds obscuring the sky, and the air was heavy with the scent of imminent rain. I took several sips of water from my bottle between rasping breaths, my lungs, feet, legs, back... *everything* ached.

"We'll stop here," announced Minnie, dropping her bag to the ground with a resounding *thunk* in a small clearing not quite as nice and neat as the campsite we'd stopped at last night.

"But it's only a quarter to seventeen hundred hours," Vera said, eyeing her watch.

"So? The light is only going to get worse from here, and in under an hour, we'll probably be walking through a storm. Best to set up camp now, while we're at a decent spot and have enough light to set everything up."

Vera grumbled her agreement, and as we unloaded our bags and set up our water-resistant tarps, my blood was humming with anticipation. It was later. I was almost scared to approach Minnie, for fear she'd changed her mind. But she'd practically agreed to leave, in Minnie-speak. I was so close.

"Are you sure these tarps will keep our sleeping bags dry?" asked Kayden, running a hesitant finger over his already assembled substitute tent.

Minnie walked over to stand by him, limping just slightly. "Probably not, with the wind. Might be best to knock it down over you when you're ready to sleep."

"You've got to be kidding me," groaned Vera across the clearing, kicking over her stakes with a vehemence born of pent-up frustration.

"What if I'm claustrophobic?"

Minnie and Kayden stared at each other in complete silence for a few seconds too long, and I felt the urge to run over and push them apart. This moment felt... personal, tender, and everything it took to form a bond between two people I would rather keep separate. Seriously, even with my intervention and their spat this morning, it was like these two kept orbiting back to each other.

Minnie opened her mouth to speak, and her voice came out low and soft, like she and Kayden were the only two people in the world, though I was standing only a few feet away. "Maybe—" She cut herself off, clearing her throat and backing away quickly. When she spoke again, the words were clipped and formal. Much better. "It's the tarp or the rain, Your Highness. You choose." She hesitated before walking away, voice softening slightly again. "Just close your eyes and pretend it's a blanket or something. You'll hardly notice it."

After an early dinner and too much bickering to bear, I returned to the clearing from my foraging for sticks small and dry enough for kindling. Minnie was counting off her one-hundred-and-thirtieth push-up, and the rough bark scratched against my palm as I clutched the kindling tight in my clenched fist, smaller sticks cracking under the force. With a sigh, I stepped over the fallen tree on the outskirts of the clearing and added the sticks to my small pile in the center of our tarps.

"Minnie, are you sure you should be exercising like that so soon after your injury?"

"How—" she started, voice catching in exertion. "How do you expect me to—to heal if I don't exercise?"

"Minnie, we've been hiking for two days straight. Trust me, you're getting plenty of exercise."

Minnie grunted, falling to her forearms. "I need to keep my core strong," she muttered to the dirt.

I rolled my eyes and crouched before my pile of sticks.

"Vera, time."

"Half-past eighteen hundred hours."

I squinted up at the near-black sky and roiling clouds, rearranging the kindling slightly before grimacing at the pile. I was no incendiary expert, and though Vera's arsonist tendencies might come in useful here, I would simply prefer to pray that the fire caught before the skies opened up on us than ask her.

"Do you think we should go ahead and radio in early? Before the storm?" Minnie asked, hovering over my shoulder like a worried mother as she did her post-workout stretches, locked on the sky above and completely oblivious to my incendiary efforts. I could tell she wasn't really asking me, using the tone of voice she reserved for when she was talking to herself.

"You don't even know that it's going to storm," mumbled Vera, arms crossed over her chest as she sat in the shadow of her tarp.

Minnie groaned, glancing over at her incredulously. "Are you kidding? Look at the sky, you bleeping idiot. Of course it's going to storm."

Vera's black eyes flickered up for the briefest of seconds before locking back on her face. "Maybe it won't. Maybe it will drizzle a bit and move on. You can't predict the weather."

I rolled my eyes in exasperation and pulled the small black lighter I'd nabbed from Vera's bag on the train out of my pocket. Tongue between my teeth, I experimentally lit a wide leaf on fire and watched it burn, twisting the glowing, crumpling warmth and tucking it beneath the little stick lean-to I'd constructed, blowing on it in the hopes it would catch. It didn't, and I frowned, poking at the smoking and charred remnants of the leaf as the buzz of radio chatter filled the clearing.

"This is Minerva Aberle checking in with the progress of Group 118's mission, over." No reply. "Tori, do you copy? This is Minerva Aberle checking in with the progress—"

A burst of static cut Minnie off, and after a few seconds of silence, an overlapping tapestry of muffled voices came through.

"...said no. But did you..."

"The captain said to close up..."

"...Oswald? I heard they're still swamped."

"...more unrest. I have orders from the queen herself to send..."

"...hear about the riots?"

"My wife said a whole group of—"

"This is the New Coranti Military Tori Headquarters Radio Reception Department. Our apologies, we're having technical difficulties due to... domestic issues. Please repeat your message."

Minnie swallowed, glancing at me over the radio still held to her lips.

"This is Minerva Aberle checking in with the progress of Group 118's mission. Over."

"Proceed. Over."

"We're well ahead of..."

A grin split my face as the pine needles burst into flames beneath the kindling, and the sticks caught fire too as the sky boomed above us. An ominous roll of thunder roared through the sky. It was bound to start pouring any second now, but I was content to watch my fledgling fire as warmth spread through both my heart and frozen hands.

"What the bleep are you doing?" hissed Minnie, transmission completed and radio abandoned. I blinked innocently up at her from where I crouched on the dirty ground by the small blaze.

"*Not* freezing to death? Enjoying what warmth I can get before the heavens open and drench us in icy rain?" I answered as innocuously as I could, slowly feeding another leaf to the fire, which rewarded me with a crackle and a puff of smoke.

Minnie whipped around to snarl at Vera, whose gleeful cackles quickly subsided. "You realize we're in enemy territory, right?" Her voice was a frantic whisper.

I shrugged, poking around the fire with a stick before adding it to the quickly disappearing pile in the flames. "We're actually on neutral ground," I corrected. "And any skirmishes are dozens of miles south."

"Do you think that means there aren't any Nillaesce patrols creeping around these woods?" Minnie gestured at my rising plume of dark, leaf-fed smoke, and I shuddered despite myself. "You've just told any hostile parties in a five-mile radius where we are."

"More like a three-point-five-mile radius, but go off," Vera chimed in, and the metaphorical smoke coming from Minnie's ears might have been a greater hazard than my little fire.

"I was rounding," Minnie spat, and I felt the heroic need to intervene before they got into another brawl.

"Everybody calm down, I'll put it out," I said, reaching for the bucket of water I'd hauled from a nearby stream.

"Ah, I wouldn't do that if I were you," tsked Vera, leaning forward in her tent to rest her chin on her hands.

Minnie gritted her teeth, her expression murderous. "She's right," she admitted, as if it pained her. Behind her, Vera grinned maniacally. "It's a lot less stealthy. You should probably smother it in dirt."

"We don't have a shovel."

"Well—"

I rolled my eyes and reached for the bucket again, drowning the fire with a hiss of steam. "If they saw the smoke already, what difference is a little steam going to make?"

Minnie groaned, snatching the empty bucket from my hands and stomping over to her tent. As I stared up as the troubled sky, clutching my jacket closer around me, the first drop of rain hit me right in the eye.

I flinched, reeling backward blind and fumbling to get beneath my tarp as the rain began to pelt the ground in earnest and lightning split the sky. It was going to storm, all right. It was going to storm big time.

I scrambled into my make-shift tent, tucking my feet in with me. Yanking my boots off with shivering fingers, I plopped them onto the ground tarp and out of the downpour before I knocked away the supports and collapsed my tarp on top of me. I could feel the large drops of water hitting the tarp resting on the bridge of my nose as I lay on my back, and though I was still dry now, I couldn't help but wonder just how waterproof these tarps were.

And the Nillaesce patrol picked that moment to attack.

# 22

*"Detective Fetz had a sixth sense, of sorts. It was often whispered, amongst his clients, that he could smell Death in the air before He struck."*

—*Tomorrow's Last Mystery, written by Roberta Tinn.*

The sound of unintelligible shouts and pounding footsteps were barely audible over the relentless torrent of rain slamming into the packed dirt of the clearing. I froze beneath my tarp, one hand resting on my pack, which I'd been checking was fully tucked away out of the rain. There was no way to know what was going on—it could be Minnie running around in circles causing a ruckus out there for all I could see.

But I knew, deep within me, that that wasn't the case.

Cursing, I shifted over and lifted the corner of my tarp to peer out at the clearing. Of course, I saw nothing through the heavy curtain of rain and the dark clouds blocking out the sun's last rays.

Then, like a gift from the heavens, a flash of lightning illuminated the clearing in brilliant detail for the briefest of seconds, painting a violent picture. As darkness fell again and the corresponding boom of thunder shook me to my bones, I dropped the tarp corner.

The Nillaesce had obviously been caught as unprepared for this unseasonal storm as our party, but I caught the click and subtle light peeking between my two tarps as they illuminated flashlights. I had a flashlight in my bag, as I was fairly certain all of us did, but I wasn't about to use it and draw even more attention to myself. We were also each given handguns and a brief lesson on gun safety, though I still wasn't exactly confident in my ability to actually shoot anything.

They shouted to each other over the downpour, and I strained to understand the words through the heavy accent of the Nillaesce dialect. Kayden had been right—all of our impersonations were so horribly off compared to the real thing. I suppressed a shudder. Living in central Coranti, there was a sense of distance from the war constantly looming over all of us. Sure, it was hard to forget it was there, but I supposed in my mind the Nillaesce soldiers had been reduced to one nameless mass of father-killing opposition. I'd never met a Nillaesce before, though I knew there were some refugee witches who braved the mountain border to move to Coranti where they could be granted amnesty. Being so close to a real Nillaesce patrol was so *real* and terrifying, and all I could think of was the countless horror stories I'd been told, even told to others, about the cruel and devoutly religious soldiers.

I wanted to hide beneath my tarp forever, but, of course, like always, Minnie had decided to play the hero.

Stupid, idiotic, foolish, dull, pig-headed, asinine, brave, heroic Minnie.

I threw off my tarp, making sure it still covered my boots and pack, and rose to my feet. I stood paralyzed for a beat too long, the biting rain drenching me in seconds. Shuddering in the cold, I charged through the rain and flashlight beams. I ignored the stinging pain in my bare feet as I stumbled over the still-cooling embers of my fire and several sharp rocks and sticks to reach Minnie's side.

"What are you doing?" I hissed at her, ducking out of the way of a flashlight beam. In typical Minnie fashion, she ignored me and continued with her moronic plan.

"Over here, you pious bleeps!" bellowed Minnie, drawing the attention of at least five flashlight-wielding Nillaesce. They shouted to each other through the trees and charged for her, and I saw the glint of light off some very sizable gun barrels. I swallowed, remembering the handgun I'd abandoned beneath my tarp in my haste. Not that it would do me much good in this rain, with my pitiable marksmanship. I could barely see in this darkness, and I was constantly wiping rain from my eyes.

Minnie, apparently, had no such misgivings about her abilities to use a firearm, and she whipped her gun out, leveling it at the approaching foes. Then she took off in the opposite direction, darting gracefully behind a tree just as the Nillaesce opened fire on her.

Apparently, the Nillaesce motto, when it came to antagonizing knuckleheads, was "shoot first, ask questions later," and, honestly, if the knucklehead in question wasn't my best friend, I couldn't exactly blame them.

At the loud crack of gunfire, I panicked, dropping to the muddy ground and squeezing my eyes shut. It was becoming increasingly clear that, unlike Minnie, I was absolutely no good in a fight.

I was paralyzed, lying in the mud, chilled to the bone, soaked in freezing water, shivering in the rain, eyes pressed shut against the rivulets of rain streaming down my face. It would be a feeling not all so different from crying, if the water wasn't so cold I thought it might freeze on my face. Someone, Nillaesce or otherwise, jumped right over me, probably mistaking me for a log of some sort.

That was just plain offensive.

I scrambled to my feet, slipping several times in the mud, and wiped the rain from my eyes. The clearing was in chaos; shapeless shadows darting in and out, flashlight beams cutting through the rain, the light appearing suspended in the constant screen. Gunfire, people shouted, people yelled, people screamed—

No.

I recognized that voice, screaming.

I cursed, loudly, and stumbled across the clearing in my socks, blundering blindly for the source of the scream.

"Minnie!" I bellowed, my already hoarse voice getting swallowed in the rain and chaos. "Minnie!"

I spotted her through the trees, thrashing against two dark figures as they dragged her away. They grabbed for her empty jacket sleeve where her right arm should have been and grasped only fabric, giving her a split second to break away. But they only snatched her back again, slamming her into a tree before hauling her away from the clearing. She was still screaming, a sound of rage and pain and pure hatred. Horrified, I realized I wasn't going to make it to her in time.

"Minnie!"

I charged toward them, through puddles and branches and howling wind, blinded by the raindrops stinging my face. As I got closer, Minnie met my eyes and started shouting at me, words tangled in the storm. One word was clear, though, and she repeated it again and again, waving at me as best she was able.

"Leave!"

I shook my head wildly, erratic breaths tearing my chest apart and mud-slicked strands of hair sticking to my face as I fought to match the Nillaesce's pace as they pushed through the undergrowth.

Then I was on the ground again, the breath stolen from my lungs and a thorned bush digging into my back. Someone was sitting on me, pressing all the air out of my body and leaving me gasping at every breath. I squinted up through the rain, trying to see the Nillaesce who had tackled me even as their gun barrel smacked into my face, breaking the skin and sending a fresh wave of pain tearing through my cheek, the warm blood quickly washed away in the rain.

I couldn't fight back. I could barely even breathe.

My vision dimmed, mouth opening and closing in silent, rasping protest as my life drained away with the rain. In my last efforts to glimpse the stone-cold face of my merciless killer, I caught a streak of bleached white hair tipped with electric blue plastered to a rain-soaked forehead.

"Edward?" I rasped.

The crushing weight on top of me toppled over in surprise, making a less-than terrifying yelp as he landed in a puddle.

"Omili, Isla, is that you?"

I let my eyes flutter shut, focusing on returning the air to my starved lungs. Edward was probably a near two hundred pounds of muscle, the dumb brute, and he'd tackled me like I was another jock in one of those sports he played.

"I'm so, so, *so* sorry, I thought you were one of those Nillaesce soldiers."

"I, I think," I wheezed out, pushing myself into a sitting position and attempting to pull the thorns from my back, "if I really was a, a Nillaesce, you'd be long dead."

I couldn't see Edward's expression in the dark, but his voice sounded sad. "What, was my tackle not good?"

A cough racked my body, and I pounded a fist on my chest as if that would undo the damage Edward had done. "No, your tackle was fine. And I suppose I should be grateful you didn't shoot me without looking clearly first." I reached a careful hand up to gingerly poke at the cut on my cheekbone where his gun had split the skin, wincing.

When my head cleared, I pulled myself to the feet, spinning in hapless circles to search the suffocating darkness.

Minnie was gone.

I could still hear distant sounds of a scuffle back at the clearing, but away from the chaos, most of the sounds were swallowed by the merciless howl of the wind.

And Minnie was gone.

"Minnie!" I screamed, my voice barely more than a hoarse and wailing whisper on the wind. Edward rested his hand on my shoulder, a gesture I supposed was meant to be comforting, but I shook it off. What could I do? I was useless. Minnie was the strong one, the brave one, the useful one. If I'd been dragged off by Nillaesce goons, Minnie would have saved me in seconds.

I didn't deserve to be her friend.

I was weak, I was powerless, I was—

Except I wasn't powerless, was I?

I pressed my eyes shut and focused on the swirling, wonderful, powerful masses of Life Energy enveloping me. I pushed past the fickle streams from the trees and huddled animals and scurrying bugs beneath the ground, feeling the energies in the clearing just out of my reach, and nothing more. The Nillaesce who'd taken Minnie were either back at clearing or long gone. I hesitated, indecision freezing me to the spot beneath the trees, where the rain was more a trickle through the branches than a full downpour.

Run in the direction I was pretty sure they'd taken Minnie when I knew there was no one close, or towards the clearing, where there were definitely people but maybe not Minnie? I spun in a circle, surveying the muffled noises and dark trees on either side, every direction identical. Did I even have a clue which direction they'd left in? I was wasting precious time, time that might cost Minnie her life.

With a curse, I spun on my heel and sprinted back towards the quickly subduing sounds of fighting.

"Minnie!" I shrieked, more a plea than a war cry. "Minnie?"

The rain intensified without the cover of the trees, and the packed-dirt clearing was one giant mud puddle, dark shapeless mounds I could only hope were tarps and packs collapsed on the ground. I caught a flash of pale skin and hair as Vera darted past, but, for the most part, the skirmish seemed to have moved out of the open area and into the cover of the trees. And I didn't see Minnie anywhere. No rain-slicked curls straightened in the downpour and clinging to her skin. No fiery dark eyes. No sign she was ever here at all.

I wanted to scream, so I did.

It felt good.

"Minnie!"

Gritting my teeth, I closed my eyes again, latching onto the strong bursts of Life Energy swirling nearby. The human energies were hard enough to distinguish from the trees around them, let alone from each other, but there were probably just less than ten.

Probably.

I didn't realize I was crying, at first, with the rain and traces of blood already sliding down my face.

I exhaled slowly, shaking like a leaf in the wind and rain, focusing on the energy, planting my metaphorical feet, pulling, pulling, pulling... The sounds around me quieted as I Drained every person fighting around the clearing, fighting to file all the energy away inside myself as I went and keep my breathing steady. I wouldn't let it overwhelm me. I wouldn't.

The power felt amazing. The strength, the clarity, the wondrous ability... I could keep pulling. I could pull and pull until I pulled too far and the Nillaesce were nothing but withering husks, life washed away in the rain. I could feel their energy, but it was tangled with the rest of Group 118.

Maybe even... Minnie?

With a grunt of effort and the slightest pang of regret, I dropped my hold on the Life Energy around me, leaving every person unconscious in the mud and a tingling awareness inside of me. So much raw energy inside me, so much power, the mere thought of tapping into it made me light-headed.

I wasn't sure what I was, but I was sure no Holder had ever felt this much power brewing in their heart of hearts, no matter how long they stored up, and any normal Drainer would have passed out or combusted or something, overwhelmed by the power they consumed.

And me?

I'd never felt so nerve-rackingly alive and yet so terrifyingly dead at the same time.

But that was life, I supposed, at its core.

I checked every unconscious form in the area, counting three Nillaesce soldiers, a patrol by the looks of it, Edward, Vera, Kayden, and Ella.

Minnie was nowhere to be seen.

I whirled, trying to find an outlet for my frustration, anger, and grief. I let the energy inside me swallow me as I ignored my sprained finger and reared back my arm to swing a clumsy, uneven, and yet very strongly intentioned punch at the tree nearest me.

Minnie would want to correct my form if she were here.

The unsuspecting tree, a giant oak, flew backward, ancient roots screaming as they were torn from the ground. Birds hiding from the rain squawked out their protest and alighted with a flutter of wings to find the nearest bush to camp in. The deafening *thump* as the tree slammed into the forest floor was only rivaled by the sound I made as I jumped out of the way of the roots rearing up to meet me with a *squelch* of mud, which flew everywhere. The still-steady stream of rain washed the mud off me almost instantly, though my clothes were more than disgusting.

I supposed that answered the question of whether a tree falling in a forest with only a broken heart to hear it made a sound.

A disbelieving sob wrenched from my throat, then another, and another, and soon I was on my knees in a puddle, forehead pressed to the trunk of the fallen tree. What was the point? Minnie wasn't here. Minnie was gone. Minnie, the witch, had been dragged off by witch hating Nillaesce to face whatever gruesome, ritualistic, "holy" death they had planned for her. My only comfort was maybe, just maybe, they wouldn't assume she was a witch.

It wasn't enough.

If I hadn't interfered, Minnie would still have over a month of training ahead of her before she had to face any real battle. If I hadn't waltzed into that recruitment office like I had any clue what I was doing, Minnie would still have a chance.

If I had pushed harder to get her to leave with me, we might have already been long gone.

Minnie was gone, and it was my fault.

But I couldn't just accept that. I refused to accept it. So that left me only one choice, then, didn't it?

# 23

*"No, darling, I can't bear another goodbye. Please won't you say you love me,*
*even if I know it's just a lie."*

*—Lyrics from the hit song "Not Goodbye" by pop artist Jean Lycro.*

A beautiful, vibrant rainbow hung in the brilliant blue sky above the clearing as I cinched the knot securing the last of the still-unconscious Nillaesce soldiers to a tree nearby—about as far as I could drag him.

He was young, eerily so. Probably a year or so younger than me, even. Here I was thinking it was inhumane for Coranti to draft sixteen-year-olds—or had this boy enlisted? Had he been so wrapped up in the Nillaesce hatred of witches that he was willing to die for this belief? Did he even know what he was risking, or had he been groomed for this by insane genocidal priests?

I sighed, pushing his head back into a more comfortable position so it rested on the tree instead of on his chest.

With the Nillaesce relatively secure, I set to work rousing the four battered and bruised Corantians lying unconscious in the mud. I had heavily debated leaving them and venturing on to find Minnie on my own, but after spending most of last night wandering barefoot through the rain and waking up half-dead in a puddle over a mile from the clearing, it was obvious I needed a plan.

And a plan I would make while hauling four ungrateful recruits after me.

"Get up, you big louts!" I bellowed, toeing Kayden's shoulder with one remarkably dry boot—my pack and boots had been preserved in a tarp sandwich throughout the chaos of last night.

With a groan, Edward stirred, rolling onto his stomach. I suspected I hadn't Drained him quite as much as the others, since he'd been farther out of my reach. If he hadn't chased after me when I returned to the clearing to search for Minnie, he might not have been hurt at all.

"You may be experiencing some mild to severe symptoms of Draining," I chirped, kicking him lightly until he rolled back over and sat up. "Side-effects may include headache, nausea, extreme fatigue, depression, loss of—"

"I've been Drained before," Edward muttered, running a hand through his mud-soaked hair. "My oldest sister, Sophia, is a pretty powerful Drainer. She graduated top of her class at the officer's academy in Lorten, married the prestigious Dr. Goulding, and now she's some fancy Lieutenant in the New Coranti Military. And I'm just the disappointment," he added sullenly.

I nodded my head sagely. "Those suffering from being extensively Drained to the point of losing consciousness are also known to be exceedingly emotionally vulnerable," I quoted from what I remembered of Ella's notes.

Edward frowned, massaging his temples and looking around the clearing, eyes landing on the tree I'd punched. "Hey, wasn't that really big tree standing up last night? What happened?"

"Oh, just the storm," I responded lightly. "Guess it had bad roots. Help me wake the others, would you?"

"Is that a fist hole in the trunk?"

I ignored him.

"Where's Minnie?" asked Kayden when we finally managed to wake them, squinting around at our little group of misfits.

I clenched my jaw, focusing on drying the tarp I'd just returned from washing at the stream. "She is... not here. But we're going to find her. She's strong. She's probably escaped already on her own, so I doubt we have to worry, and I would bet—"

"What happened?"

"Two of the Nillaesce soldiers got away, and they took her with them," answered Edward, his voice even, and I dropped the tarp to whirl on him, accusatory finger pointed in his face.

"Which is all *your* fault by the way," I spat. "I was right behind them. If you hadn't mixed me up with a Nillaesce and *tackled* me—"

"In my defense, it was dark and rainy, and you looked very similar from the back." He paused, contemplative. "Speaking of which, isn't the weather lovely this morning? There's barely a chill in the air. It's like that storm washed away all the grey skies and wind we've had the past few days."

"Don't you dare try to change the subject."

"No, it's honestly—"

"So, she's really gone," interjected Kayden glumly.

I folded my tarp as angrily as one could fold a tarp, shoving it in my pack. "Don't sound so dejected. Yes, it's bad, but we're going to get her back. So shut up and pack your bag."

"Hey, I'm mourning too, Isla. We *all* are going to miss—"

"No." I shook my head vehemently. "You're not mourning. You don't get to mourn. You barely know her, all of you. What makes you think a couple of days is equal to nearly half of your life? Minnie is my everything. My heart, my soul, my best friend, the only thing keeping me going. Sure, we fought, but we love each other. And I'm going to find her."

"She was an amazing person, and we were lucky to know her."

I felt like screaming. "No! She *is* amazing. Present tense, *is*. Not was. She's still alive, I know it."

They looked at me sadly, and I caught Ella and Edward sharing a pitying glance.

"What? It's totally possible she survived. Plausible, even. She might have gotten away, or else they have her hostage—"

Kayden's voice had lost all its soft edges. "Do you really think that's better? Have you heard what happens to Nillaesce war prisoners? Especially witches? I've heard the horror stories from a survivor, I've seen—" His voice broke. "I've seen the physical and mental scars two months in their clutches can do, and that's only if they're actually trying to keep the prisoner in one piece."

Edward rested a reassuring hand on Kayden's shoulder, and I scowled.

"But there *are* survivors, right? If there are survivors, that means there's hope—"

"Not survivors. One survivor."

The hope inside me was crumbling in my clutches, but I refused to let it go.

"Princess Daphne," whispered Ella, almost reverently.

I swallowed. I'd heard of the queen's eldest daughter, as I was sure everyone had. A talented Donor, prodigal soldier, and brilliant strategist, Princess Daphne had been a beacon of hope for a country five years into a losing war at only nineteen years old. Coranti had loved her.

Until she went off to war and didn't come home.

The Nillaesce had held her in one of their camps for two months as the queen scrambled to arrange a ransom. When they finally released her, it felt more like a message than a concession. She was broken, the rumors said.

"But she survived," I said, my voice barely more than a frail whisper.

Kayden looked like he might cry, dipping his head to busy himself with his pack while Ella gave me a death glare.

"It's alright, Kayden, we don't have to talk about it," she said.

Kayden cleared his throat and fiddled with the straps of his backpack, then met my eyes with a bleary, haunted stare. "She may have technically survived the Nillaesce, but she never really came home. She had horrible nightmares and post-traumatic stress disorder, even as her physical wounds healed. And then, one night, almost exactly three years ago, she—she—" his jaw flexed as he struggled to say the words. "Well, I'm sure rumors of what happened spread."

I raised my eyebrows. "What, that she killed herself?"

"What in the world is wrong with you?" hissed Ella, her usually soft face contorted in sympathetic rage. Giving me one last glare, she gently guided Kayden to a still-damp log, patting him on the shoulder and whispering hushed reassurances.

I shrugged, returning to my preparations.

"You're bleeding."

"Shut up, Edward," I muttered, ignoring the dried blood on my knuckles and the brighter fresh blood that spilled out when I flexed my fingers.

"You're a jerk."

"So is Vera."

"I never said she wasn't."

"Shut up, Edward." I reached for one of the bandage rolls I'd brought for Minnie and wrapped my hand. "Happy now?"

"I meant the cut on your face, but alright."

"The cut on my face *you* gave me?"

"Uh, yeah, that one. How'd you hurt your hand?"

"Seriously, you stupid oaf?" I stared flatly into his vividly blue eyes. "We were attacked," I said slowly, as if speaking to a small child, "by a Nillaesce patrol. I don't know if you were there or not, but we were quite literally fighting for our lives."

Edward didn't flinch away from my mockery. "But that's not how your knuckles got all busted up. I highly doubt *you* managed to get close enough to land a punch to the mouth of a trained fighter."

"Rude."

"And true," added Vera, slinging her pack onto her shoulder.

I scowled at her, fingers going unconsciously to the thin gold band in my pocket. "Since when do you—"

"Did you just agree with me?" asked Edward, awed.

"Don't get used to it, Eddie," she grumbled, turning towards the trail. "I just felt like piling on Islie. I still hate you."

I waved my hands wildly at her retreating back as if to exaggerate to Edward that she'd just proved my point about her moral character. "Your stupid psychological name trick doesn't work, Verrie! Give it up already!"

She made a rude gesture at me over her shoulder.

Closing my eyes, I took a long, deep breath in and exhaled slowly. I needed to focus if I wanted to save Minnie. Because I would save Minnie, because she was still alive. I could feel it, and I refused to believe otherwise.

"Alright, let's get this snail show on the road," I called, securing my pack to my back and loping off towards the remnants of the trail.

Ella frowned, adjusting her glasses, which I now noticed had gotten a small crack in the left pane. None of us had left the battle last night unscathed, apparently. "Do you have a map?"

"Not exactly, but I have a compass." I dug around in my pocket to no avail. "Actually, scratch that, I don't have a compass either. Good thing the sky is so clear, huh?"

I squinted at the sun, just beginning to crest over a nearby peak.

"And we have no idea where they could have taken Minnie?" asked Ella, lips pressed into thin slivers.

"Well, no, but this is the Nillaesce we're talking about. They think witches are devil spawn," I stage-whispered. "They aren't that bright. I'm sure they're super predictable."

"Are you using humor as a coping mechanism?"

"No one asked for a psychological analysis, Edward," I said through gritted teeth. "Plus, why would I need a coping mechanism anyway? Minnie is just fine." I sobered quickly, raising my voice to be sure Kayden and Vera could hear me too. "But she won't be fine forever. We need to find her, kick some Nillaesce butt, and get her out of wherever they're holding her."

Vera snickered. "You said butt." I glared daggers at her.

"I hate to kill the mood, but—"

"Then don't," I said, turning to Kayden. "I hate it when people say that. 'I hate to blah de dah, but…' Just stop there. If you hate to kill the mood, don't do it. The mood is just fine how it is."

Kayden, of course, ignored me. "What if she's already dead? Or shipped off to some elaborate, ritualistic murder ceremony? What then?"

I ignored his question because my brain was already too full of similar thoughts to function. Doing my best to stuff my doubts under my metaphorical bed, I raised my hand to shield my eyes from the brilliant early-morning sun as I took in the nearest peak.

"I say we get to the top of this mountain, see Nillaesce, and figure it out from there."

"Wait, I thought you actually had a plan?" drawled Vera, settling herself nonchalantly onto the nearest log.

I scowled. "And I thought maybe you knew how to shut your trap for five minutes, but I guess we're all disappointed."

Vera tsked softly. "You're slipping, Byrne. I know you can do better than that."

"We're leaving now," I spat out, jaw clenched. "Are you coming, or not?"

I stepped out of the clearing and onto the overgrown path, ignoring the pull of my sore muscles as I started carefully upwards. I didn't look back to see if they were following me, but I heard Edward's less-than-subtle whisper to Vera.

"Would you ease up on her? She's grieving."

"Doesn't mean we can excuse her being a complete pain," she said through a yawn, not even bothering to lower her voice for my sake.

I focused on placing one foot in front of the other.

As it turned out, the top of the mountain was a little harder to reach than I'd first hoped. The old hiking trail we'd been following thus far split off after about an hour of walking, winding back down into a valley and meandering south towards Split Peak.

I flattened out the trail map from Edward's pack and surveyed our options, tongue between my teeth.

"There isn't a path up this peak," Kayden helpfully informed me from where he hovered over my shoulder.

"No," I said contemplatively, eyes wandering upward. "Not on the map. But humans are curious creatures and backpacking in this part of the mountains was all the rage before the war."

"What are you saying?" asked Ella, brow furrowed.

Vera was nodding slowly. "Maybe you're right, Islie. But if there were such an abandoned trail, how would we go about finding it?"

I folded the map without care, noticing the way Edward winced when I made new, uneven creases instead of following the old ones. I tossed the partially crumpled map at him and turned to Vera.

"Which way does the raven fly? How does water decide where to go?"

"I think she's finally lost it," Edward whispered to Ella behind his hand, but Vera raised her eyebrows approvingly.

"The path of least resistance, of course."

I nodded, re-adjusting my pack and craning my neck to grin up at the peak. "Exactly."

The sun was beginning to set over Coranti just as the trees thinned out and the ground leveled. It had been a grueling day of pushing through thorns, tripping over roots, and even being swarmed by insects at one point as we traversed thin, practically nonexistent footpaths ever upward. At times, there were no switchbacks at all and we simply had to climb straight up the slope for about a dozen feet until we could rejoin the path. Our going had been slow on sore feet tired from two full days of hiking, and I was almost convinced we'd spent more time on breaks than we actually spent walking.

If Minnie were here, she would have dragged us up the mountain by sheer willpower alone. But Minnie wasn't here, and none of us had much motivation at all.

And yet, we made it. About as fast as a herd of turtles, but we made it all the same.

My legs burned with exhaustion, but we were so close now that I couldn't help but speed up. Some childish part inside of me had associated reaching the top of this mountain with finding Minnie, and though it had been the only thing to keep me moving even as my muscles screamed in opposition, now I felt a ridiculous mix of disappointment and relief when I finally pulled myself up to the highest rock.

The top of the mountain went from heavy forest, to rocky dirt, to sheer rock faces, and as I sat, sweating heavily and breathing so hard I was sure my lungs would stop working altogether, I realized I was the only one to actually climb all the way up. The others had found a small trail leading around the eastern side of my rock outcropping where they could see the glimmering lights of our enemies laid out before us.

I shuddered on my perch, drawing my knees closer to my body in the sudden chill, reaching for my jacket. I'd taken it off in the exertion of hiking, but now that I'd stopped moving and my sweat was cooling on my skin, I was shivering like a leaf. Wrapping my arms tighter around my body, I gazed out at what I could see of Nillaesce.

It was beautiful, from afar. A sunset glow painted the countryside and cities in a wash of brilliant yellows and warm oranges, all soft lines and subtle light. As the sun slipped lower in the sky, the dark and jagged shadow of the mountains began to creep across Nillaesce, until it had cast all I could see of the country into shadow. I swiveled carefully to face the sunset and the world I'd left behind.

It was off-putting, how similar the two lands looked when you sat huddled on the peak of a mountain, removed from it all. Two countries, two beliefs, and all the rest of us muddled in between. The black, the white, and a billion shades of grey.

I turned so that I sat facing the twisting range of the mountains, complete with Split Peak, instead of either country. To my left was a beautiful land steeped in shadow, a place of faith and murder and dangerous lies. To my right, my home. Where all witches were free if you could pay the price. Where riots plagued the streets and witches were being killed, whether in the war or by domestic terrorists.

We were all broken, and I just wanted to sit alone on this mountain forever, trying to put my pieces back together.

If it weren't for Minnie, I might have.

But she was one of my pieces now, like it or not, and I wasn't sure I could ever be whole again without her.

I was an idiot.

Why had I just blindly accepted her decisions? This was Minnie, renowned for her reckless and dangerous decisions. I should have demanded she ran away with me the second that Nillaesce blade cut her open.

My eyes burned, *because of the wind,* and the world was blurring before me, *because of the deepening shadow.*

I pressed my eyes shut against the tears and a sob bubbled up within me as all my suppressed doubts punched their way to the surface.

What if Minnie was being tortured right now?

What if she was lying injured in the forest somewhere?

What if she was being held in chains, awaiting a brutal, ceremonial execution?

What if she was already dead?

What would I do, if I didn't have her?

I didn't want to find out.

My fingers trailed over the golden ring in my pocket, eyes still shut against the threat of tears, head tipped back as I sat on the smooth, cold stone.

"It's not real gold, you know."

With only a huff of breath to show she'd just climbed up the jagged rock faces at the top of a mountain, Ella Bailey settled herself down beside me. I peeked open one eye to glance sideways at her, taking in her lined forehead and taut lips, the way her shoulders dipped slightly forwards as if she might curl in upon herself and disappear.

"Just sentimental value," she continued, dark eyes latching on to mine and refusing to let me go. "You know something about that, don't you, Isla Byrne?"

I broke her gaze, looking instead at the stars.

"She did have a gold ring, my mother. Her wedding ring. That was one of the first things I sold, and the money from that kept us alive and got her in a home while I tried to find a job. Didn't even begin to touch the mountain of debt from the hospital, though." She sighed. "I tried to sell that ring you have, too, but the woman at the pawnshop wouldn't give me more than ten Coran for it, so I figured I'd keep it. A memory, while the woman who used to be my mother faded beside me."

"What happened?" I asked, voice hoarse. I could see the stars so clearly from up here. They were beautiful.

Ella took so long to reply that I almost wondered if she was even still there at all. When I glanced over, her face was pinched in sorrow.

"We were in an accident," she replied finally. "My brother, my mother, and me. We were driving home from my grandma's funeral a couple of years ago—she was killed by an anti-witch mob—and the car crashed. My brother—" Ella stopped, eyes shut, to take a deep breath. I hadn't realized how fast she'd been talking until she resumed, voice slow and measured, though it still shook slightly. "My brother didn't make it, and my mother suffered a brain injury. I'm technically in the custody of my grandfather, but he's useless, and, well... here we are."

"Why are you telling me all this?"

"Because you're grieving. Because we're all grieving, from a thousand little losses." She hesitated. "And also, because I want my ring back, but I'm horrible at confrontation."

I darted a look at Ella, catching the tail end of her wry smile as she looked up at the stars.

"That would be the anxiety. But I'm here, aren't I?"

"I'm not sorry," I whispered in reply.

"For stealing my ring?"

I nodded, slowly. "I would do it again. I don't regret it. I don't regret the pain it's caused you, just like I don't regret every other little thing I've stolen to get me here. Every choice I've made, every lie I've told, every ring I've stolen, gold or not, it's all led me to this moment. And it will all be worth it if—" My voice broke, and I struggled to hold back a sob.

"If you could get her back," finished Ella gently, resting a hand on my shoulder.

"I can't lose her," I choked out through tears, throat raw. I thought I'd cried every tear I could last night, but apparently, I'd been wrong.

Ella ran a hand through my hair, such a kind gesture that it made me cry harder.

"Maybe it's time to accept that you've already lost her," she said, and I pulled violently away from her, almost sending us both toppling to our deaths.

"No!" I spat, rubbing uselessly at my tear-stained cheeks. I glanced over at where the others had begun setting up camp at the base of the peak, where the ground was relatively flatter and drier. "You don't know Minnie like I do. She's strong. She's unstoppable. She's alive. And I'm going to find her."

I dragged myself to my feet, digging in my pocket for the ring. "Take your stupid ring. We don't need it anyway." I threw it at her, not caring if she caught it or if it went skittering off the mountain face.

Painfully aware of Ella's sad stare boring into my back, I half-slid, half-climbed back down the rocks.

I would set up camp tonight.

I would sleep, really sleep, for the first time since Minnie was taken.

And then?

I was going to follow my best friend to the ends of the earth if that was what it took.

# 24

*"Goodbye, sweetheart. I'll see you on the other side. I love you."*
——*Anonymous note found near Split Peak. Author unknown.*

•• ———————— ••◉•• ———————— ••

My father's note was gone. That was my first thought when I woke, sweat soaking my back and sleeping bag twisting around me. It had slipped from its spot between my watch and my wrist at some point in the last day. I cursed my stupidity in not finding a more secure spot for it once we'd started hiking. It didn't really matter, of course; I'd memorized the notes years ago and the ink and paper were so faded you could hardly read it. But they were my father's last words to me, and I felt like I'd lost not just Minnie but my father all over again. The two most important people in my life, gone.

I was up before the sun, before even Edward, bag packed as I poured over trail maps and the map of Nillaesce and Coranti Akins had left us with. Our radio report last night had gone smoothly, facilitated through Ella and the radio she'd been carrying. Minnie's radio had been lost. Even though she hadn't answered the past few hundred times I'd tried to reach her on it, there was always a chance she still had it, which made the one we did have all the more essential.

At this point, I couldn't care less about the radio, since Minnie and I would be running off anyway as soon as I found her, but every night we gave a report was one more night the New Coranti Military wasn't hunting me down for crimes I hadn't committed. Not that they would actually expend the resources to hunt me down, but better safe than sorry, right?

My dreams had been full of rain and sobs and Minnie's screams, and I'd spent most of the night tossing and turning on the hard rock. When I finally gave up on sleep, I sat shaking beneath my tarp, sweat chilling on my skin in the cold early morning air, mind spinning in circles as I tried to formulate any semblance of a plan.

We had made it to the peak, and I still had no way to know where Minnie had been taken. I pressed my eyes shut, but my brain refused to work to create a plan.

"Good morning," yawned Edward just as the first glimmers of sunlight began to touch Nillaesce, leaving Coranti still steeped in shadow.

I didn't answer him, staring bleary-eyed at the map in hopes a magic beacon would appear, pointing to Minnie's exact location. Unfortunately, no such miracle occurred, and the lines of the map began to blur before my tired eyes.

"Did you sleep at all?" Edward asked, snatching the map from the rock I'd set it on.

"Of course I slept," I snapped, reaching in vain for the map he dangled far above me. "Stupid oaf."

Edward sighed, shaking his head in disappointment. "Omili forbid I try to express genuine concern for you."

"I don't need your concern," I replied, stifling a yawn. "Minnie does."

"Aw, Isla, I'm so sorry."

"She's not dead."

"I never said she was."

"Well, good." I faltered. "Because she's not."

Edward peered down at me in blatant pity, and with a snarl, I jumped up on the outcropping I'd been using as a table for the map. I leaped at him, grabbing the map and not caring that it tore.

"We're leaving," I muttered, stuffing the map in my bag.

"Where are we going?" asked Edward, still frowning, an odd look on him.

"To find Minnie, of course."

"I hate to break it to you, but you've got a camp full of sleeping bums."

I crossed to Vera's tarp-tent first and kicked out the supports, then, for good measure, kicked her too. I was rewarded for my efforts by a loud and rather violent string of curses.

"Up and at it, losers," I hollered, ripping away the tarps of all three and exposing them to the early morning chill. "Seriously, why have *I* had to wake you all up two days in a row?"

"Maybe," grumbled Vera, murder in her voice, "because we've been hiking for three straight days and we're all exhausted and, I don't know, some idiot Drained us all last night?"

"Night before last," I corrected, kicking her again because I could.

"Same thing."

"Not really."

"Just shut up, Byrne."

"Only if you get your lazy behind out of bed."

"First, it's not a bed. It's literally a rock slab. I spent the night on an Omili-forsaken *rock slab,* and you know what the worst part is? The rock was an *improvement* over the past two nights. An improvement, I tell you. The bar is so low that simply not having a thousand little sharp roots and rocks digging into my back is an improvement."

It was a little hard to take her seriously with her short bob of blonde hair in a wild tangle around her head, her bangs flying away from her forehead, and an errant smear of black eyeliner smudged on her face. When had she even taken the time to reapply that, in the middle of the woods? I would bet it had something to do with Ella Bailey.

The girl in question was waking up like a fairytale princess, unwrapping her sleep scarf to reveal perfectly preserved, silky black hair, which she promptly began to brush, all the while humming to herself while birds began to chirp in the background. She used some water from her pack to wash her face, the smooth, dark skin only blemished by the worry lines around her mouth and eyes.

I glanced between her and the disheveled, grumpy girl sitting at my feet and realized poor Vera didn't stand a chance. I wasn't about to tell her that, though. It was hilarious to watch her stony, bitter face crumble as she chased after an oblivious Ella.

"And second," Vera rampaged on, pushing past a yawn, "do you know how early it is? It's..." She checked her watch, and her scowl deepened. "Alright, well, it isn't actually that early, but still..."

I tuned her out, turning to check that Kayden was getting up.

"So?" Kayden asked once we were all vertical and somewhat conscious. "Which direction, fearless leader?"

"Towards Split Peak."

We had only walked for a couple of minutes when a steady buzz began to hum through the air. "Do you hear that?" I hissed, to no one in particular, head flying back and forth as I tried to locate the source.

"It sounds like a helicopter," Vera said, peering up through the trees.

I cursed, ducking my head, and scrambled to get myself fully under the cover of the trees, Vera and the others following suit.

"Can anyone get a good look?" I asked, straining to see through the foliage while keeping myself somewhat covered.

"Uh, it's definitely a helicopter," answered Edward rather loudly, squatting down behind a fern as the leaves began to sway at the passage of the helicopter close overhead. "And it's landing nearby."

"Nillaesce or Coranti?"

"How would I know? I can't see any better than you can, Isla."

"Useless oaf," I muttered, frustrated. We could wait out whoever was in that helicopter in the underbrush, but every second we were delayed from finding Minnie made me all the antsier.

I caught Vera's mouth moving as she tried to yell something over the deafening sound of the helicopter, but her words were lost. And then, as suddenly as it came, the noise whirred to a stop, leaving my ears ringing and the woods deathly quiet.

"I said," whispered Vera, "I guess there's a clearing nearby."

"Oh wow, aren't you the next Detective Fetz," I drawled.

"Who's that?"

I sighed, maybe a bit melodramatically, rummaging in my pack for the book I'd gotten on my last day in Monta, before remembering I'd left it at the inn.

"You've never read *Tomorrow's Last Mystery* by Roberta Tinn? It's a classic murder mystery, a true staple of the genre."

Vera snorted. "Alright, you stupid book nerd."

"I'm not—"

"Hush, you two," breathed Kayden, cautiously poking his head from around the stump he'd hidden behind. "They might be able to hear us."

With a painfully loud rustle of leaves, I pushed myself to my feet. "You guys stay here, I'll go take a look."

"What if they're Nillaesce and they spot you?"

"Then I'll beat those kidnapping dung-monkeys into a bloody mess until they're begging to tell me where they're keeping Minnie."

"You? You couldn't beat up a fly, let alone a group of trained soldiers."

"Watch me."

"I'd tell you not to do anything rash," muttered Vera, "but I get the feeling you're feeling particularly idiotic at the moment."

"I promise I'll get myself killed quickly so they don't torture your location out of me," I called over my shoulder, a little too loudly, as I returned to the path.

"That's not funny," hissed Ella, and was promptly shushed by Kayden.

I crept down the path, avoiding the small, brittle twigs and autumn leaves that might give me away. It was much harder than I'd anticipated, and I was sure I looked like a right fool tripping over my feet to avoid one stick and instead breaking five. Oh, to have Minnie's easy grace at this moment.

The clearing wasn't far ahead, and I pressed myself against the trunk of an ancient tree just on the outskirts. I dared a glance at the helicopter on the unnaturally smooth, packed dirt of the unnaturally large and round clearing. In bright blue, the emblem of the New Coranti Military was emblazoned on the white flank of the helicopter. I breathed a sigh of relief, though I wasn't sure why. The Coranti soldiers would just as soon kill me as the Nillaesce would, if they bought that nonsense Morren was spewing about my blood.

I returned to the cluster where my group of idiots was crouched, rather conspicuously, in the underbrush just off the path.

"It's a Coranti helicopter," I called, now knowing with some certainty that we were far enough away, and the soldiers were making enough noise disembarking, that I wouldn't be heard. Well, hopefully.

I ushered Kayden, Ella, Vera, and Edward down the path, away from the buzzing hive of activity, so we could speak freely.

"I say we put on our training shirts, the white ones, so they know whose team we're on," Edward said, slouching his pack off his shoulder to peer inside for the shirt in question.

I scoffed. "You say that like it's a game."

"Isn't it?"

"No," I snarled, yanking my own white shirt from the bottom of my bag. "This war has taken *everything* from me. This is no game. People are dying, Edward."

"I know that! I meant just like an analogy, you know, two teams of—"

"You're not the only one who has lost people, Isla," interrupted Ella, her usually calm face split into an uncharacteristic frown. "I know you and Minnie were close, but—"

I pulled the training shirt on over my head. "Just stop, Ella. We all know you don't have the mental fortitude to actually carry on a heated argument, so I'm going to stop you right there before you slip up and kill us all because of a little confrontation anxiety."

Vera was on me in an instant, pale face contorted in righteous anger. She grabbed my shirt in her fist, a gesture that might have been intimidating if she weren't several inches shorter than me. Or maybe that just made it more intimidating, I couldn't be sure.

"Stop being a bully, Byrne," Vera spat. "I can argue for her."

I put on my most patronizing grin, a monstrous knot of pain and frustration twisting inside me. "Aw, look at Verrie, showing off for her little crush. Take a hint, Roberts, she—"

My face erupted in a flash of pain as her first punch hit me, right on the cheekbone. A warm trickle of blood slid down my cheek, surprising me at first, until I realized she must have only reopened the gash from Edward's gun barrel.

I growled, pushing back at Vera with the force of Minnie. I was bigger and taller, and you could bet I was going to fight dirty.

"No one likes you," Vera said, swinging her fists wildly as I aimed a kick to her knees, one of the only things I'd picked up from Minnie's attempts to teach me basic self-defense.

"Maybe," I grunted, "if you hadn't started a useless fight with Minnie the other day, while she was still healing from a major injury, she would have had the strength to fight back and the Nillaesce wouldn't have been able to take her."

Vera gasped, though in exasperation or because I'd managed to bend one of her fingers back, I wasn't sure. Probably both.

"Stop trying to shove the blame onto other people, Isla. It's time to face the truth," she said with a growl, ramming me hard in the stomach with her elbow. I doubled over, doing my best to fend her off while fighting to get my breath back. "You're the one that started the stupid fire that brought that patrol down on us, and, honestly, you're probably the only reason Minnie was in these mountains to begin with.

"It's your fault she's gone."

I landed a weak hit to Vera's ear, but she tackled me all the same, leaning down to whisper in my ear. "It's your fault she's dead."

"She isn't dead!" I roared, grabbing a fistful of Vera's hair and yanking. But I didn't just pull her hair. I pulled what I could grasp of her Life Energy, and though she faltered slightly, she didn't crumble into a state of weakness. I frowned, struggling to pull even more, and feeling my stores of energy boil over like a pot on the stove. With a roar, I released the energy, loving the burn in my veins as the strength flooded over me. Like the night Minnie was taken, I was so powerful and yet so empty at the same time.

I shoved Vera off me with superhuman strength, the still-scabbing fist that had felled a tree bared for a fight.

She responded in turn, jumping to her feet a little too fast, a little too lithely. Edward made a grab to subdue her, and she shoved him so hard he stumbled back, without so much as breaking our stare. Edward winced, eyes wide as he shrunk away from where we circled each other on the path, two sharks set for the kill.

I spat out the blood that had dripped into my mouth, using the back of my hand to smear the steady trickle across my face.

"You wanted a fight, Byrne? I'll give you a fight."

I scoffed. "You're the one who started this fight, Roberts."

"No. You started this by being an absolute pain to everyone, twenty-four hours a day, for nearly two days. Honestly, you were a pain even before the Nillaesce jumped us, but Aberle managed to keep you relatively in check. Now, it's just plain ridiculous."

I charged Vera like a wild boar, fists flailing. She ducked my first swing easily enough and even managed to claw my bare arm with her fingernails before I tackled her, landing us both on the ground again in a mad tangle of limbs. Warm, sticky blood trailed down my hand, matting the errant strands of hair that stuck to my face, and the acrid, metallic scent of it flooded my senses, though I wasn't sure if it was mine or Vera's. Probably both.

Then someone was wrenching us apart, and shouts filled the air. I thrashed in the iron grip of whoever was holding me, assuming it was Edward, until my vision cleared and the sight unfolded around me.

A squad of Coranti soldiers, in actual combat uniforms, not the white shirts and brown pants we'd been given for training, stood in a tight circle around our little group. I counted at least ten, including whoever was currently holding my hands behind my back. They all held their guns at ready, though most looked more confused than apprehensive.

"Ed? Is that you?" A large woman with a strong jaw and dark hair pulled into a bun so tight it pulled at the edges of her scalp stepped forward. When she lowered her gun, the others followed suit, deferring to her as their leader. She helped Edward to his feet, and I could see the resemblance between the two in their warm brown skin and blue eyes.

"Hey, Sophie," he muttered, eyes locked on his feet. I'd never seen him look so demure before, and it was unsettling.

Though she was still several inches shorter than Edward, the woman, Sophie, managed to loop an arm around his neck and pull him down to her level, ruffling his hair with a grin.

"Lieutenant Goulding? What's going on?" asked one soldier, a short man probably barely out of training.

She waved a dismissive hand, still smiling widely despite Edward's obvious discomfort and the awkward air stretched between her soldiers. "At ease, all of you. This is my little brother, Ed."

Edward wrenched out of her grasp, attempting to fix his now wild strands of blue-tipped bleached hair with a wry smile. "It's good to see you, Sophie. I've missed you."

She huffed at his cold greeting, crossing massive arms over her chest. "Who are your friends?"

Edward gave the four of us an appraising look, skimming over Kayden, who was carefully slanting his face away in obvious hope that no one would recognize him, Ella, standing stiffly to the side, and finally, me and Vera, bloody, bruised, and being restrained by soldiers.

"I wouldn't exactly call them my friends." He smiled at Ella, which she returned bashfully, and amended: "Not all of them, anyway."

"What are you doing here, Ed?"

Edward frowned. "What are *you* doing here? I thought you were stationed in Tori for another month, at least."

"Stuff happens. We're in the middle of a war, little brother—"

"Stop being so patronizing. Everyone knows I'm your little brother, you don't have to keep making a big deal out of it."

"I'm just trying to be affectionate."

"Well, stop."

Sophia Goulding straightened to her full height, blue eyes glaring daggers at her brother. "Maybe you should stop being so jealous, bitter, and disrespectful. I don't appreciate you being a little brat every time I see you just because you hate how successful I am. I'm successful because I work hard, and maybe if you'd give up those stupid sports of yours you might actually do something with your life like me."

I wrenched free of the soldier holding me and stepped forward. Eight years of friendship with someone as volatile as Minnie had taught me a thing or two about defusing fights—even if maybe I, fresh from a brawl, wasn't necessarily the best suited for the job at the moment. The soldier, a thin, pale-skinned woman, was preoccupied watching the familial squabble and had loosened her grip on my arm substantially.

"Lieutenant Goulding, was it? Edward, please do introduce us."

"Omili, girl, what happened to you?" asked Goulding, her piercing gaze leaving her brother to focus on me instead. Self-consciously, I wiped at my sticky face, wincing when my fingers brushed over a patch of bruised skin that would probably turn a magnificent shade of purple later. My fingers came away dark red.

"Oh, you know," I replied, teeth gritted. "Just a little combat practice with my good friend Vera over there." I felt a slight pang in my chest at the realization that, beneath my sarcasm, I actually had begun to consider Vera a friend over the past few days. So much for that.

Goulding frowned, glancing between the two of us before focusing on my dirt and blood-streaked, formerly white shirt—and probably, the New Coranti Military emblem there. "You're all recruits, then, like Ed?"

"Yes," I answered, with my most sincere smile. It wasn't very sincere. "We're on a special mission from the queen. What are you doing here?"

"What are you doing here, *ma'am*?" she corrected.

I kept the smile at full brilliance. "Oh, there's no need to call me ma'am, Lieutenant."

I immediately regretted the smart remark—I'd always wanted to use that one, and apparently, now my inhibitions were sufficiently lowered. Goodie. To my surprise, Goulding actually laughed.

"I like you, kid. You've got spunk." She sighed, running a hand, as if through habit, over her immaculate bun, straightening phantom flyaways. "My squad and I just got flown out here as reinforcements. I probably shouldn't be telling you this, you know," she pantomimed quotation marks in the air, "'confidential' and all, but apparently, there's some big mass witch execution going on tomorrow nearby, and we're going to pop in and deal the Nillaesce a neighborly visit."

A witch execution?

Kayden and I shared a look, eyes wide.

Minnie.

# 25

*"The Battle of Split Peak, or more accurately, the Massacre of Split Peak, is easily the greatest tragedy of the Coranti-Nillaesce War thus far. Both the first and bloodiest battle of the war, the battle was initially and briefly known as the Sinea Battle, before the Sinea mountain chain became the battlefield of this war, as it has been for the last seven years."*

*—Excerpt from a historical paper published anonymously in Lilta.*

"Uh, hello? Can you hear me? Copy? Over? Roger? Right, uh, this is Ella Bailey, reporting the status of Group 118's mission. Over."

"This is the New Coranti Military Tori Headquarters Radio Reception Department. We read you loud and clear, Private. Please proceed with the update. Over."

"Alright, uh, yes. Ok. So, we've run into Lieutenant Goulding's squad, and well, if someone there wants to object, you know, that's fine, but pretty much we thought, I mean, that going with them would be best for our mission? Because it's, well, an execution thing, where we're going, and so wouldn't it kind of make sense that Darkheart is there? Since killing witches is sort of his thing? Anyways, yeah, um, over."

"Report received, Private. Captain Akins has cleared your course of action. Over."

"Right. Thank you. Group 118 signing off now. Bye. Over."

Maybe the Nillaesce deities were real after all, and if they were, they were smiling on me now. That's not what my father would say,

I knew. He was a fervent believer in luck, chance, and all the ways you could twist them to your favor.

But whether it was dumb luck or divine intervention, I finally had a lead.

I was going to save Minnie.

"Isla? Hello, anyone home up there?" Vera mocked, rapping a finger on my skull. "Oh look, all empty."

I grabbed her wrist, yanking on her with a flow of Life Energy from deep inside me. She stumbled and glared at me, wrenching her wrist away with a matching surge of strength from her stores.

"Shut up," I hissed, "or I'll give you another black eye to match the first."

Vera leered back at me, fingers flying to her bruised face before she could stop herself. "You say that like you could actually beat me in a fight."

"I was about to beat you before Goulding's crew showed up," I snarled back.

"Oh yeah? Are you willing to test that?"

"What, so eager for another fight?"

I was several inches taller than Vera, and I straightened my back fully so that I could truly look down on her.

"Alright, ladies, break it up." Edward sauntered over and pushed us apart, grinning. "I know I'm handsome, but there's no need to fight over—"

"You wish, Buck," I said.

"Shut it, Eddie," Vera growled, at the same time. I leveled her with one final glare before snorting.

"You're not worth my effort, anyway, Vera. We're going to save Minnie tomorrow, and I'm going to go to sleep so I'm well-rested."

"Good luck with that, insomniac!" jeered Vera at my retreating back. I gritted my teeth and made a rude gesture at her over my shoulder. She only laughed.

The morning of the execution dawned crisp and brittle, the skies an even, bright grey over the Sinea Mountains. Goulding and her squad packed quickly and effectively—a skill likely learned over the two-month training we should have received and perfected in years of experience. Either way, us brave souls of Group 118 were the last stragglers to leave camp, hastily and rather poorly packed bags slung over our shoulders. I straightened my magician's coat as I walked, sweeping the cape behind me so it wouldn't snag on the branches. I wasn't sure why I'd put it on.

Maybe it was the premonition in the air, the heavy feeling that something bad was coming and I would need this armor, as it was.

Maybe I was scared that I wouldn't find Minnie.

Maybe I was scared that I would.

We'd walked as far as we could from the landing site yesterday, and I'd learned that the clearing the helicopter had landed in was very commonly used by Coranti forces, as it was the closest they—we?—could quickly drop soldiers into the mountains without getting shot down by the Nillaesce.

"What's with the outfit?" asked Edward, slowing his pace to walk beside me. Probably avoiding his sister. I caught her peeking over her shoulder at Edward, eyes sad, before she returned to her straight-backed, march-like walk.

"What's going on with you and your sister?" I asked in reply.

Edward shrugged, his large feet sending rocks flying as he dragged them along the path. "You know. Sibling stuff."

"No, I don't know." I grinned drily. "Only child."

Edward frowned. "Isn't that lonely? I mean, I hate my siblings sometimes, but my childhood would have been so... quiet without them."

"How many siblings do you have?" I asked, ignoring his question once more.

"Three. One older sister, one older brother, and a little sister."

"What are their names?" I asked blankly, mouth moving on automatically to continue the small talk I couldn't be less interested in. I was grasping at straws for distraction from what was about to happen at this point.

"Obviously, you've already met Sophia, and then there's Timothy, who just turned twenty a couple of weeks ago, and Charlotte, who's fourteen."

"So you and Kayden have a lot in common, then?" I murmured, only half paying attention.

"How so?"

"I mean, you both have a witch older sister whose shadow you live in, a younger sister—"

"A witch mother, a lot of family pressure... yeah, I suppose I see the similarities. I mean, I have a brother thrown in there, my older sister is still alive, and my mom is dead, but those are all trivial details."

I nodded, not really paying attention as my eyes locked on the red-headed boy, and a fierce knot of jealousy twisted in my stomach. That stupid, baby-faced prince, that *boy*, tried to steal Minnie from me. It had almost worked. But I'd fixed things. I'd fixed things, and when I rescued Minnie from the Nillaesce, she'd see *I* was her best friend. Not Kayden, not Abby Morren, *me*. And we would run away together, to some island nation far away, and we'd never have to worry about anything ever again. Not witches, not wars, not silly crushes. Just me and Minnie, friends forever.

"You know, there is one key difference between us."

"Hm? What's that?"

"Kayden is being skipped over for a kingdom because his little sister is a witch, right? And he isn't?"

"Uh, yes. What, is the only difference between you the whole prince thing?"

"No, see, I think I'm really on to something. Kayden is still ambitious. Kayden still wants to be king. He wants to live up to his sister's memory and be the greatest prince of Coranti this nation has ever seen—which shouldn't be hard, considering it's never been a sovereign nation before Queen Isabella. That's why he's here, with us, on this mission. To prove his worth, to his mother, his country, and to himself. And, you'll notice, there was no royal uproar over his departure, not like that time Princess Alethia disappeared for about two seconds and it was on national news. The queen barely batted an eye. It's kind of sad, when you think about it." Edward sighed, kicking a pebble with his boot, sending it skittering ahead to bump against Goulding's ankle with startling accuracy. She didn't look up from her conversation.

"But me? I don't want to be a king. I've embraced my role as the family disappointment, focusing on sports and school instead of military studies like my mother wanted." He ran a hand through his bleached locks, grinning up at the electric blue tips running through his fingertips. "That's the difference between me and the prince. Ambition."

I fought down a yawn, last night's fitful sleep, my worry for Minnie, and my heavy pack all crushing my back down in an insurmountable weight. I could feel the stores of energy within me sapping as I Drained and Drained just to keep myself standing. I yawned again, squinting my eyes up at where the lieutenant and her small squad of twenty marched smoothly along the rough path. Did they *really* need all that Life Energy? Maybe if I just took a little…

"Alright, we're nearly to the execution site," called Goulding, interrupting both my train of thought and Edward's monologue, some sob story about being bullied as a child. I'd tuned him out ages ago. "We'll need to descend into the valley in plain sight of the Nillaesce, so guns up." She hesitated, glancing askance at our haggard group of five. "And, kids, stay near the back."

Minnie would've insisted on walking in the front, with the fully trained soldiers.

But she wasn't here, so we scurried to the back like the cowards we were.

My heart was thumping like the age-old washing machine at the Monta Orphanage as we crested a hill and the valley came into view, nestled between us and Split Peak. I sucked in a breath in recognition. This was where the Battle of Split Peak had started. My father had probably died near this very spot.

I shivered in the sudden chilly breeze, reminding myself that ghosts weren't real.

Forcing my eyes to focus on the small valley below us, I followed everyone's gazes down to the execution setup. It was disturbing, to say the least. Nillaesce soldiers swarmed, definitely at least fifty of them, maybe closer to a hundred, and rows of prisoners stood shackled between them. I counted maybe two dozen, and none of them easily recognizable as Minnie at first glance. We weren't that elevated from the ground level of the valley, just about as high as a two-story building, and I wrinkled my nose as the smell of the prisoners caught a breeze up to our semi-hidden perch. These were war prisoners from multiple battles throughout the mountains, all dragged through the forests for this one ceremonial execution.

They were all women, but I couldn't help but wonder which of them were actually witches.

"Excuse me, but you said *we're* the reinforcements? How many people are meeting us here?" I asked Goulding, pushing my way up to where she stood, just out of view of the Nillaesce below.

She took in my costume wordlessly before glancing at her watch. "Lieutenant Huang and her squad should be meeting us here any minute now."

I raised my eyebrows. "So, what, twenty more people? I hate to break it to you, Lieutenant, but we're still pretty outnumbered."

"You really want to question her majesty's orders? She's a tactical genius, you know."

I stood silently; arms crossed over my chest in subtle defiance. Although, honestly, what did I care if the odds were against us? I would go charging in there to save Minnie regardless.

*Unless she isn't there.*

*Unless she's already dead, or worse.*

"Seriously, don't worry about it, kid. We know what we're doing." When I still didn't look convinced, Goulding sighed, gesturing at the valley. "Look, yes, they have more soldiers than us. Yes, they have better guns than us. Yes, most of them had more training than us."

"You're really not convincing me."

"But," she replied with forced cheer. "We have magic. And that makes all the difference."

"So, we take some of their energy, give some people energy, maybe get a little energy boost?" intervened Vera, who'd appeared seemingly out of thin air behind me, making me jump. "Doesn't sound that impressive, especially in the typical small quantities of the average witch."

Goulding rolled her eyes, straightening her impeccable uniform. "Kids these days. What did they even teach you during your military strategy unit?"

"We didn't have a military strategy unit," I said. "This group operates under... special conditions. Yes, please express your horror over the assignment of a group of barely trained teenagers to the war front."

"Poor you. War is horrible. What else do you want me to say? Anyways, it's not the abilities our magic gives us that gives us our real power against the Nillaesce. It's their innate fear and hatred of magic." She turned once more to face the valley, hands lacing together behind her back, posture stiff. "What is the purpose of this whole elaborate execution ceremony, do you know?"

"Isn't it some religious thing?" I asked, feeling smart for once. "The Nillaesce have a super religious government, right?"

"A theocratic duumvirate, actually," corrected Vera.

"Yes, but that's not the point. It has more, actually, to do with the transference of magic."

"As in reproduction, or as in murder?" I chimed in.

Goulding chuckled. She was very young, only a couple of years older than Edward, I'd guess. About the same age Princess Daphne would be. It showed when she laughed, her youth.

"Murder. When you kill a witch, you get, what, like five percent of her magic?"

"Six," Vera corrected. "We estimate."

"Yeah, so the Nillaesce don't want their precious soldiers getting tainted blood. They want the magic to be gone forever when they kill a witch. They believe that killing a witch in a ceremonial process, whether by fire, drowning in blessed water, or ceremonial blade, will get rid of the magic. Obviously, we don't know if any of that actually works, and we aren't exactly about to test it. But we haven't heard any reports of super-priests hopping around the mountains, so either their ceremonial executions work, they're very good at spreading out the executions amongst soldiers, or they keep their demon magic under wraps. How hypocritical would that be, if a—"

"Goulding, shut your trap."

Goulding beamed at the woman standing before her in a matching uniform. "Olivia! Good to see you, old friend." She tossed an arm around the substantially shorter woman's shoulders with a broad grin. "Lieutenant Huang and I went to school together."

Huang grinned back, elbowing Goulding in the side. "Don't know why they gave this moron control of a squad, but here we are."

"Right back at you, bud."

Huang groaned. "You can't just say that every time I insult you. You're no fun."

"Do you always joke around right before important battles?" I asked drily.

The smiles never dropped from their faces. "Of course," answered Goulding. "You should try it sometime. Gets your energy up, helps get you on the same mental page as your team members, and, most importantly, keeps your mind off your imminent death."

"Wish I could. But my friend is down there." I nodded down at the valley.

*At least, I hope she's down there.*

Goulding and Huang exchanged a determined look, faces set. "Then let's go save her."

# 26

*"I assure you; I've only killed one Nornei in my life."*

*——The Nillaesce High Priest's response to accusations of illegal magic possession by Nillaesce purists.*

•• ———————— ••◉•• ———————— ••

The neat, orderly, and agonizingly quiet valley erupted into chaos as the first Nillaesce soldier spotted us. We descended from the slope, guns flaring, and I saw firsthand what Goulding had tried to explain to me earlier. They were hesitant to shoot at any of the women for fear of killing us and inadvertently taking our magic for themselves. I even heard what sounded like, through what I could interpret of the Nillaesce dialect, an officer yelling for them to aim to injure if they could and hold their fire if they couldn't.

And several managed, sharpshooters hitting our soldiers in the legs and even arms as we fought our way downhill. I cowered in the back of our group, holding my gun before me like a club and hoping I didn't get shot. When we reached ground level, I mainly focused on not making myself a target while I exerted a small Drain on the Nillaesce nearest me. Narrowing in on individuals was substantially harder than just pulling and pulling at anyone around me.

And it was tempting to just Drain the Coranti too.

But I refrained, if only because they were my shields and Draining them would leave me defenseless.

I noticed as several pods formed within the Coranti ranks, an obviously well-practiced formation that swelled like an ocean wave.

I watched as one pod crashed into the Nillaesce, carrying in its center a soldier with a blue patch on her uniform. If I were to guess, she would be a Drainer.

Sure enough, the Nillaesce nearest the pod crumbled to the ground, and the pod dispersed with the other soldiers falling back as the Drainer surged forward, tumbling even more Nillaesce with superhuman strength. Momentarily distracted, I spun around to take in the patches on the uniforms around me. Near the fringes of the unfolding battle, I watched a young woman with a red patch press her palms to the chest of a fallen soldier, only to fall backward, weakened, as they gasped awake. I spotted several green patches darting past, too. Holders?

I shook my head, reminding myself what I was really doing here.

I needed to find Minnie.

I pushed through the battlefield where my father had died, dodging bullets and Draining any Nillaesce who came close, filing the stolen energy away within me and loving the wonderful, warm feeling of so much power, right at my fingertips. It was comforting. It was exhilarating.

And there she was.

"Minnie!" I bellowed, losing sight of her in the chaos of the battlefield. I could barely hear my own voice over the gunshots and screams enveloping me. "Minnie!"

Where had she gone? Those dark curls, limp and tangled from the last few days, but so similar to Minnie's, were there one second and gone the next. I could have sworn she was standing right here, but now she was nowhere to be seen.

"Minnie!"

Someone grabbed me from behind in my distraction, shoving me hard off balance before yanking me back to press a knife to my throat.

"*Nornei*," they spat, the term unmistakable even to a Corantian. Witch. "Use your devil magic on me, little *nornei*, and I will slit your throat. No qualms."

I fought to keep my breaths as shallow as possible, even as panic bubbled up inside me. There were a lot of important things in my neck, things I would like to avoid being cut so I could save Minnie. I was so close. She was here, I knew it. I'd *seen* her.

At least, I was fairly sure I had.

"But—" I rasped, struggling to keep my cool as I felt a sharp prick on my trembling and horribly exposed neck. "What about your, your blood, huh? Won't it be, be tainted? My devil magic will only taint your blood if you kill me now."

The Nillaesce's breath was hot on the back of my neck. "The *Leitoi* never have to know about a little bit of *nornei* blood racing through my veins."

I shuddered.

"But I'm a good soldier," they amended. "To both the deities and the *Leitoi*. I would much rather do this the proper way, yes, and remove the stain of your *nornei* magic from this hallowed earth forever."

"Stop!" boomed a voice, and I breathed a brief sigh of relief, for some reason assuming they were saving me. It took less than a few seconds to dissuade that hope, though, as the speaker stood dozens of yards away and was yelling into a megaphone. In a Nillaesce accent. So no, definitely not trying to save me.

"We have a common enemy!" The man, clad in the smooth grey uniform of a Nillaesce officer, yelled through the megaphone, to a surprisingly attentive audience. A standstill had spread over the small battlefield, a still fire between two nearly evenly matched forces, both frozen with weapons raised, knowing one breath of movement would send them all back into a bloody battle. So, for the moment, they were still. Watching. Listening. Poised to strike.

"This is not a call to end our crusade against the hellions in the Coranti forces, nor is it a call for you to secede the rights you believe the *nornei* deserve—this is a call for a temporary alliance, for us to turn and recognize the far worse monster in our midst." The officer, as if through habit, lowered the megaphone to scan through the battlefield. I took the opportunity to attempt to dislodge the knife at my throat. No luck.

"Darkheart. He is an abomination of the worst kind, for though his actions may serve our cause, he benefits from his culling of the *nornei* population in a sinister and twisted way. He has harnessed dark *nornei* magic to a terrifying extent. The *Leitoi*, against all logic and the complaints of several high-ranking officers and priests, formed an alliance with this power-hungry sadist." Murmurs spread through the valley at the officer's open disagreement with the Nillaesce leaders. I got the feeling people didn't do that too often, at least not through a megaphone in front of a substantial number of witnesses.

"But, Aulis and Lerein bless us, I have received orders directly from the *Leitoi* to break off our alliance to this monster immediately. It has gone on too long already, and today we will rally together, two sides in opposition facing a greater threat together. Help us secure Darkheart as one unified force, and we will give him an execution benefitting a *nornei*."

That didn't exactly go over well with all the witches in the crowd.

I took advantage of the chaos by tugging hard on the energy of the soldier holding me, sending them stumbling while I yanked the blade away from my neck, cutting a gash on my chin in the process. Gritting my teeth, I whirled on the fallen woman, righteous anger flowing through my veins.

I took her energy. All of it.

I left her empty, lifeless body to be stampeded on in the bloodshed as I darted off inhumanly fast, burning up her Life Energy to find Minnie.

"Vera! No!" I heard Ella's muted cry through the chaos. Dodging behind an ancient oak near the fringes of the clearing, I saw them, sheltered by a large rock outcropping about fifty feet away. Cursing, I focused on Draining as much as I could of the Nillaesce near me and used the brief reprieve to make a bolt for the rock.

Vera was on the ground in a puddle of blood, Ella crouched protectively over her. Edward was behind a tree nearby, shooting into the battle, and Kayden was nowhere in sight. Instinctively, I found myself searching for Minnie before my brain reminded me she wasn't here.

"What happened?" I huffed, slightly out of breath.

Ella looked up at me, eyes wide, chin trembling, and cheeks already soaked with tears. "She—she—"

"I got shot," murmured Vera, her voice barely more than a hoarse whisper. She was as pale as when I first met her, but now it was from blood loss, not powder. She slowly raised a shaking hand to Ella's cheek, tucking a stray hair back into her braid with a caress so tender it made me feel like an intruder for being there. "Hey, hey, look at me."

Ella sniffled. "I'm—m—m…" She was stuttering so hard she couldn't speak.

"I'm going to be alright, you understand? I'm not dying today, and you aren't either." Vera paused, her breaths labored and shallow as pain traced lines in her face. "I need you to be strong. You can do this. I believe in you. You need to keep it together." Vera closed her eyes as she struggled to regain her breath.

My eyes roved the battle unfolding beyond the boulder as my foot tapped impatiently on the packed earth.

I was about to leave. But Vera's energy was there. I could feel it. So much energy. She must have been storing it all her life, slowly Draining herself whenever she could and saving it for when she needed it the most. Now was that time, obviously, so shouldn't she be using it right now? How badly injured was she?

She didn't think she would make it.

"Your energy…" I began, practically salivating at the raw power she possessed. What could I do with that kind of energy?

Vera reached for Ella's hand, and, to my surprise, Ella took it. Maybe what Vera felt wasn't so unrequited after all. Or maybe Ella was just mentally frail and couldn't handle a little blood. That was probably it.

That was possibly just a bit hypocritical of me, who was still avoiding looking at Vera's blood.

"I want you to Drain me."

My eyebrows rose in surprise. "Me?"

Vera sent me a death glare. "No, not you, you moron. You…" Her expression softened as she took me in, and I tried to hide whatever it was she saw in my face. "You're on a precipice, Isla. And you're just about to fall."

"Shut up, you blood-loss-fueled maniac."

"Minnie wouldn't want this," she mumbled in response, face clouded in pain.

"I said, shut up! Who are you to know what Minnie wants, anyway? You don't understand. I'm doing this *for* Minnie. She's not dead. She's here, and I'm going to find her."

"Isla," said Ella, voice laced with pity.

"She's not dead!" I shouted back. Maybe a bit too loudly. I didn't care.

Vera snorted, shaking her head. The simple action looked to take far more from her than it should have. "Ella."

"Yes?"

"I want you to Drain me."

"But she's only a Drainer, not a Drainer and a Holder. She'd have to burn up all the energy instantly, and probably wouldn't even be able to do much good with it. I'd be the far better—"

"Ella Bailey, I want you to Drain me."

"I can't—can't do that, Vera." Ella was visibly recovering from the shock of Vera being shot, and her stutter was slowly fading.

"You're going to have to."

I peered around the rock again and cursed. "If you won't do it, Ella, I will."

"Ella..." Vera was fading, eyelids fluttering as she struggled to keep them open.

It was now or never. With a deep breath, I Drained the majority of her reserves, feeling the power flood through me for an exhilarating moment before I tucked it away. That—that felt amazing. A warm, wonderful grin spread across my face. That felt spectacular.

Ella was crying so hard I hadn't thought she noticed, but when she looked up at me, her brows were drawn together in anger.

"You shouldn't have done that! She, she needed that energy—"

"Oh, shut it," I snarled, fed up with her moping. "I left her plenty. She's still breathing, isn't she?"

"Not for long," Ella muttered, lifting her glasses to wipe at her tears.

I straightened. "Then I guess we better finish this battle soon. Drag her as far from here as you can, get her all situated so she doesn't lose any more blood, and she should be fine."

Like I was the expert on blood.

"Wait! Stop! Everybody!" It was the man with the megaphone again, standing on a rock near the center of the valley. I had to resist the urge to roll my eyes. I felt… tingly. Tingly, bubbly, and buzzing all over. Not feelings I typically experienced. Was this what being drunk felt like? I needed to focus. Minnie. Minnie. I needed to find—

"Darkheart needs to be stopped, and, though it is in fact an unsavory truth, we need the aid of *nornei* to stop him. We must fight fire with fire, and in order to procure your assistance, we're willing to make some concessions we otherwise wouldn't."

I narrowed my eyes. Was this whole public ceremony fabricated to draw our forces out?

"We're listening," shouted Lieutenant Goulding, stepping out of the throng so she stood directly before the rock the Nillaesce officer stood on.

He took in a long, deep breath as if it pained him to say what he was preparing to say. I could see the smallest wrinkle between his brows, the stray hairs wrested from Goulding's bun, smell the sweat on his skin, hear the beat of her heart.

I blinked, and my senses returned to normal. Was this normal? I looked down at my trembling hands, and I couldn't see that little scar on my ring finger unless I brought my hands up to my face. I tried elevating my sight, focusing on the rampant energy bubbling up inside me until I could channel it to my eyes. The minuscule pores of the skin on my hands and the chipped black polish on my nails filled my vision and I grinned, moving my hands to take in the hair-like edges of the grass blades below.

"We are willing to release all prisoners scheduled for execution today," the officer said all in one breath as if saying it faster would make it less true.

Goulding crossed her arms over her chest, pondering the offer.

"All prisoners currently in your camps."

"This is not a time for negotiation, filthy *nornei*," the officer spat, his fragile civility fading quickly.

"Actually, I think it is," responded Goulding, voice even. "You need our help. We need you to learn to treat witches like the human beings we are. Sounds like perfect negotiating terms to me."

"We are sparing the devil's creations from the purification we planned to give them, the ceremony that would allow what fragments of souls you may possess to be released to join Aulis and Lerein in the heavens and that would cleanse our land of your wicked magic. We are making the ultimate holy sacrifice, giving up part of our righteous crusade to rid the world of a greater evil. Look me in the eyes, *nornei*, and tell me that is not already enough."

"It's not enough," Goulding said, deadpan.

"Fine," bit out the officer, fighting for the cool composure right out of his grasp. "Soldiers, ready the torches."

In the chaos, several of the Coranti prisoners had been released from their chains and secured to one of the large stakes at the far end of the valley. I breathed out a sigh of relief. None of them were Minnie.

The torches were held dangerously close to the kindling at the base of the pyres. All it would take was one sign from the man on the rock, and a dozen witches would go up in flames. The Coranti soldiers realized this too late. They were too far, the torches too close. Though some of them tried and were immediately shot down, it was obvious they couldn't make it in time to save their fellows even if there weren't guns pointed at their feet.

I could probably run fast enough to reach them, I realized idly, if I burned up all of the Life Energy Vera had spent her life saving up, plus any in my stores.

"Wait! Wait!" cried Goulding, cracking under the ultimatum. "We'll help you fight Darkheart. You're right, he is a common enemy. Just release the prisoners, and we'll help you."

The Nillaesce officer frowned, narrowing his eyes. "How do we know you won't just split the second you have what you want?"

"Because we want Darkheart dead too," replied Goulding readily.

"Lovely. I'd ask that you have the prisoners fight too if I thought they were up to it." I didn't miss the way Goulding's jaw clenched at his reference to the Nillaesce's horrific prisoner treatment Kayden had told us about.

Panic was slowly spreading its way up my spine. Where was Minnie? She hadn't been in the group at the stakes, so she must be hidden somewhere in the jostling mass of chained witches. Squinting with my new Life Energy advanced vision, I scanned the prisoners for any sight of her dark curls.

Nothing.

I pushed my way closer, shoving past Nillaesce and Coranti alike who seemed unsure how to treat each other in this temporary truce.

"How do you plan to find Darkheart, anyway?" asked Goulding, barely audible over the rising noise of Coranti soldiers fighting their way over to where the prisoners were being released to search for their comrades or friends.

"Why, I'm right here, my dear lieutenant. Whatever do you need me for?" The voice was unnaturally loud, booming out over the valley and stilling the chaos unfolding. It was taunting, terrifying, and... familiar?

"Darkheart," breathed Goulding, voice shaking slightly, and all eyes turned to where she was gawking.

And there, standing on a rock ledge overlooking the valley, was an unmistakable face I thought I'd never see again.

My father.

# 27

*"The case of Anna Byrne was one of the most unusual deaths of my medical career. After vehemently refusing any form of blood transfusions, Anna Byrne, aged thirty-six, died of childbirth complications. Her last words to me were, exactly: 'you can see my blood over my dead body.' Even this, however, was impossible, as her husband, Nicholas Byrne, confiscated her body for immediate cremation."*

—*Medical report from Dr. Luc Chiel.*

⸻ ● ⸻

"Attack him!" bellowed the Nillaesce officer from earlier, raising his fancy ceremonial sword.

Darkheart—my father?—frowned. "Are you really sure you want to attack the most powerful man in the world?"

"You aren't a man," snarled the officer. "You're a monster, twisted by *nornei* magic."

My father lifted his hand in front of his face, inspecting it. "You know, I rather like this twisted *nornei* magic." With a dramatic twist of his hand, the officer below gasped and fell to his knees. "Don't you?"

I gawked. Did he just Drain a man from fifty feet away? Most witches needed physical contact or at least close proximity to take that much Life Energy all in one pull. The sheer power he must possess... This man couldn't be the father I knew and loved. But all it took was one zoomed-in look at the lines of his face, the stormy grey of his eyes, and the slope of his nose to see it was the man who had raised me. Had he always had this kind of power, and had only hidden it from me? He must have, of course, because Darkheart had been an urban legend since before I was born.

Who was my father?

"Anyone else willing to try that? No? Didn't think so." Darkheart continued looking at his hand, speaking in an even, conversational tone as the officer lay slumped on the ground. Was he dead? "Power is a beautiful thing. People love to talk about power, love to theorize and philosophize and guess and poke. They'll say that knowledge is power, that with great power comes great responsibility, that power corrupts, that there must be a balance of power—but whatever you want to say about power, the truth remains. And you know what that truth is? *I* have the power." He grinned. "I have the power to bring every single one of you to your knees, but because I have that power, I won't have to use it. You'll all get on your knees anyway. Isn't that right?"

Tears pricked at the corners of my vision, and I wiped them away angrily with the back of my hand. I didn't have time to deal with my father—no, not my father. He was Darkheart, and I had to find Minnie.

But with the still-welling tears rose the fears I'd squashed down so deep inside it took the reappearance of my long-lost father to awaken them.

There was a very real possibility that Minnie was dead.

More than a possibility. A plausibility.

Dread coiled in my stomach, and I buckled over, bile rising in my throat as my vision swam.

Minnie might be dead.

Darkheart's grin turned sinister. "Bow down to me, witches and soldiers and faithful alike. Bow down to me!"

As some of Nillaesce and even Coranti soldiers began to fall to their knees, Goulding stood even higher. "We don't bow to terrorists!" she shouted, raising her gun in a mirror to the Nillaesce officer's actions. But unlike with him, her soldiers reacted immediately, charging the slope Darkheart stood on with a myriad of battle cries. In the ensuing chaos, I shook off my temporary paralysis, shoving those fears back where they belonged and darting for the half-freed prisoners.

Minnie had to be alive, and I had to find her.

I shoved past chained witches in various stages of terror and bafflement, my gaze barely skimming each face. Not Minnie. Not Minnie. Still not Minnie. Where was she? She'd probably already escaped on her own.

That was it.

She'd escaped on her own and was off eating chocolate somewhere, scheming to break me free of my commitment to the New Coranti Military. She was dancing on the graves of the foolish Nillaesce who'd tried to capture her.

My pace increased until I was racing down the lines of prisoners, frantically searching for that dimpled smile, those determined eyes.

She wasn't a pile of ashes, burned in some obscure execution in the middle of the woods. She wasn't locked in a cold dungeon somewhere, slowly starving to death. She wasn't being tortured, she wasn't being drowned, she wasn't being beheaded by a ceremonial blade, she wasn't-

A raucous cheer broke out, almost deafening as it spread across the forces of intermingled Nillaesce and Coranti soldiers, all bunched around a single point: Darkheart, on his knees, with Goulding's gun pressed to his skull and that Nillaesce officer, who apparently wasn't dead after all, with his blade to his throat. It might have been symbolic, to someone else; perhaps a sign of peace; perhaps a beacon of hope for the little girl I used to be, the girl who sat and prayed to imaginary deities for this war to end.

I reached the last prisoner.

Her wild brown curls were a frazzled mess, matted with blood to her forehead in one spot. She was probably in her late twenties, but the look in her eyes was a hundred years old. Her dark skin was streaked with blood and dirt, lines cut through where tears fell in steady streams. There was a mole, right above her upper lip, and her jaw was round and cherub-like.

But none of that was relevant. All that mattered was that she wasn't Minnie.

I had the strongest urge to punch her, to kick her, to scream and rage and cry as she sniffled before me, raising her bowed head just the slightest bit in hope. She thought I was here to free her.

I turned away, one warm tear burning a trail down my wind-numbed face.

"You're not going to kill me," said Darkheart, and I didn't have the mental energy to even try to reconcile this man with my beloved father, the ex-soldier who just wanted to be a cobbler. His voice, still unnaturally magnified, was so calm I wouldn't believe the multitude of weapons poised to kill him if I was staring right at them. "Not here, not now."

A click echoed in the quiet valley as Goulding removed the safety of her handgun, still pressed to Darkheart's skull. "You want to bet?"

I knew that smile, the one creeping up his face. It was the smile he made when he knew he was about to win a game of Wild Knight and couldn't be bothered to hide it. My father had never had a great bluff face.

"You're not going to kill me..." His eyes flitted to her name patch. "Lieutenant Goulding. Do you want to know how I know that?"

"Not particularly," ground out Goulding, teeth gritted.

"You're not going to kill me," he continued, as if she'd never spoken, "because the second you do, you're going to feel the most wonderful rush of power flowing through your veins. Power like you've never imagined. The power to take the energy from anyone with a flick of your hand." Darkheart flicked his hand, and though nothing happened, Goulding flinched. "It's intoxicating, to be frank."

"I wouldn't get all your power, just six percent," corrected Goulding.

Darkheart tsked his tongue. "And, see, that's where you're wrong. When you kill a natural witch, you get six percent of her power. That power is converted, diluted, into a new type of magic. The kind that turns your blood black." He shifted his head slightly, revealing the inky black droplet running down his neck from where the Nillaesce officer still rested his ceremonial sword. "And when you kill me? You get all of that magic. Pure and unfiltered.

"And I suppose you could guess what happens then." Darkheart cocked his head to the horde of soldiers below his rock where the three of them stood, all with guns pointed at him. "You become the new Darkheart, for about two minutes. The Nillaesce charge you, intent on giving you a proper execution to get rid of my magic forever. "

"Then I suppose we are in agreement," said the Nillaesce officer, a bit feebly, and I noticed now how severely his whole body was shaking, like a leaf caught in a gust of wind. "We must give this monster a proper execution, through fire, holy water, or sacred blade."

Darkheart hummed softly under his breath. "But are you really so sure about that? What science backs up these magic three methods of destroying magic, other than the alleged words of your deities? It is hard to truly measure in small amounts, when only six percent of the magic is passed on. Since the Nillaesce don't have the blood analysis technology available to the Coranti, and the Corantians aren't exactly in the business of killing their precious witches for experimentation purposes, can you really ever know what method of murder stops the passing along of magic?"

"He's stalling," spat the Nillaesce officer.

Goulding narrowed her eyes at Darkheart, chewing her lip in thought. "But he has a point, doesn't he? This is a precarious situation. We need to kill him as soon as possible so he can't escape, but I'm not about to risk killing him through one of your stupid religious ceremonies. If we can't find a way to get rid of all that power, it'll just keep getting passed around and around. Kill the person who killed Darkheart, and then kill the person who killed the person who killed Darkheart, and then—"

"I get the point," said the Nillaesce. "But what exactly are we supposed to do about it?"

"You know," murmured Darkheart contemplatively, as if thinking out loud. "I suppose that's why you Nillaesce have your one-*nornei* rule, huh?" The Nillaesce officer visibly stiffened. "It's supposed to be all religious and meaningful and stuff, but really it's because, deep down, you aren't that sure if your trusted methods work or not."

"Ridiculous," growled the Nillaesce officer. "This monster speaks nonsense. He knows nothing of our culture."

Goulding snorted. "Your culture? That's rich. You Nillaesce prance around on your high horses, like you aren't just a society of genocidal freaks."

"And you are a heretical, half-formed nation based on ambition and demon-magic and ridiculous ideals."

Tensions were rising between the two parties on the ground, some weapons shifting away from Darkheart and towards each other as a rift formed, shattering the fragile truce.

"Well, this has been fun, but oh, would you look at the time, I really should be going." Darkheart gave his captors an apologetic look, to which they responded with tired annoyance and bafflement.

"He really is insane, isn't he?"

Like a veil dropping on the valley, Nillaesce soldiers and most of the Coranti crumpled to the ground. I stumbled, feeling the Drain eating away at my Life Energy even where I stood at the fringes of the fray, but I quickly matched the pull on my energy with the energy I'd taken from Vera. It wouldn't last forever, but for now, I was relatively unaffected.

I spotted nearly twenty soldiers in the crowd, who I assumed to be Holders, doing the same thing to varying degrees of success. There were some, the more powerful Drainers in the mix, who turned to the Nillaesce nearest them, pulling on the dregs of their Life Energy. But since normal Drainers couldn't store what they took, they had to constantly have a source of energy to combat Darkheart's Drain. They fell second, after the non-witches and Donors.

"Are you really trying to Drain me, Lieutenant?" Darkheart's magnified voice drew my gaze back to the outcropping, where the Nillaesce officer lay crumpled and Darkheart and Goulding stood eye-to-eye. "It was a nice try, I suppose, but I don't think you want to get in a Drain-off with the likes of me." His lip twisted down into a familiar frown, like when I played a card he hadn't expected in our almost-nightly game of Wild Knight.

They stared at each other for a tense few seconds, locked in a fatal staring contest in the true test of who was the stronger Drainer, as

Holders fought their way past slumped forms, numbers dwindling as they succumbed to the Drain.

Goulding never stood a chance.

"I *did* say I had unimaginable power, right?" jibed Darkheart, grinning down at the weakened valley as he kicked Goulding's lifeless form away with the toe of his boot.

Maybe it was just my imagination, but I could have sworn I heard Edward's weak cry as his sister slid down the mountainside.

I gritted my teeth, increasing my Drain on the energy inside me to a staggering pace as I strode briskly across the valley, stepping over the barely moving bodies of soldiers being slowly Drained of their energy. This had gone on too long.

I needed answers, and if anyone here had them, it would be my father.

He didn't look surprised to see me when I heaved myself up the slope to his outcropping with a sizable burst of energy. When I stood in front of him, surprised to see I was nearly his height now, I felt the drop of his veil from my shoulders as he released the Drain on me.

"Isla," he said, voice startlingly soft without the magnification. Or maybe he just genuinely loved me.

I wanted to break down.

I wanted to cry and jump into his arms like I was eight years old again, and he could pat my hair and console me.

I wanted to go back in time, to when we were together and happy and unworried.

But I needed to find Minnie, and I needed the truth.

I nodded numbly, not looking at his face. "So," I muttered, "You're Darkheart. Thanks for telling me, Dad."

"Well, yes, I suppose so," he replied idly, straightening his ominous and ridiculously costume-like black coat. "Not the original, of course."

I scowled. "What's that supposed to mean?"

"Your mother was the most dangerous, violent woman I knew." His stormy grey eyes, creased and lined at the edges, looked haunted even as a wistful smile played across his lips. "Be careful with love,

Isla dear, it will rip you apart and tear you down if you aren't careful with it."

"Stop being dramatic," I spat, fed up. "You don't get to abandon me for half my life and then toss a nonsensical half-witted proverb about love at me when I inadvertently find you again."

My father sighed, leaning forward to rest his hands on my shoulders in a familiar, comforting gesture. "It wasn't exactly my choice, sweetheart. I didn't want to leave you, and I didn't want to get sent off to the front." There was an agony painted in the lines of his face I didn't want to recognize. "Of course I didn't want to abandon you, but I knew you were strong, like your mother. I knew, after the things I've had to do, you'd do better without me in your life."

"What, then, you just killed hundreds of witches after you left?" I bit back, refusing to crumble at his soft words. He was my father. He was supposed to be there for me. He was supposed to tell me the truth.

"No," he sighed, massaging his temples. "I killed the original Darkheart."

I gaped. "No offense, oh great master cobbler, but how in the world did you manage that?" He used to laugh at my jokes. He used to smile whenever he could. He used to grab me in his arms and swing me around until we both fell into a giggling pile on the floor. He used to tell me I got his sense of humor and my mother's wit.

He smiled now, but there was no mirth behind it. Just sadness. So much sadness, it made him almost unrecognizable.

"How'd I manage it?" he echoed, voice breaking slightly. "She asked me to do it, when she was laying in her hospital bed, the monitor beside her ticking down the moments until she died. That's how I killed Darkheart. That's how I became Darkheart. And that's how I lost the love of my life."

"Oh," I said, finding myself temporarily at a loss for words. My eyes drifted away from the broken man before me, watching as if from some great distance the chaos sprawled out beneath us. Suddenly, it all felt so inconsequential. Like drugged ants, soldiers from both sides lay sprawled across the valley, either still or moving sluggishly. And we stood above them, two shards of broken glass so worn down by time that they no longer fit back together.

"She would be proud of you, you know."

My eyes refocused on my father, and I cleared my throat. "My mother, the witch-killer?" I replied drily, distantly. "Great."

My father only smiled at me. "I got most of her power, but you got some too, didn't you?"

I blinked at him, understanding trickling through the haze of anger and confusion. "That's why my blood is a little too dark," I said slowly. "That's why I can use different types of magic. That's why I'm a witch at all when my mother's family was one long line of historical non-witches."

"Yes—"

"Why didn't you tell me?" I demanded, rage flooding my veins. "I've been in the dark my whole life. I've been living in fear of my power, of what it can do. I've had to make my own path, my own choices, my own realizations. I've had nothing but terror and hate and grit and..." And Minnie. Minnie, the only reason I was here today at all. Minnie, who kept me sane. Minnie, who was both a shoulder to cry on and an arm to lean on. Minnie, who lifted me up when I was at my worst. Minnie, who had been there when my father wasn't.

My father was speaking, but I wasn't listening. He'd wanted to tell me, he'd planned to tell me, the circumstances hadn't worked out, excuses and more excuses.

"I didn't come here for you," I interrupted him, jaw set. "I came here for my friend. She's a witch, taken prisoner by the Nillaesce."

"Oh, sweetheart, I'm so sorry—"

"You had them in your pocket until today," I said coldly, and he followed my gaze across the slumped forms below us. "If anyone knows where she is, it should be you. Where is she? Where is she?"

My father looked hesitant. "Well, there are a few camps nearby she could have been taken to if she was captured in the last few days, but I don't know—"

"Minerva Lilianne Aberle. She's short. Dark brown hair, curly, goes down to her waist. Dark brown eyes." I paused. "She only has one arm."

Recognition flashed in his eyes, even as his face fell in sympathy. No.

No, no, no.

"Isla," he said, voice painfully pitying. I'd never known my father to speak to me with such pity in his voice. "Isla, sweetheart, I'm sorry. She's gone."

"Gone?" I asked, hating the way my voice shook. "Gone, as in they took her to the capital for an execution?" I'd heard they did that for high-priority witches and important officers. It wasn't ideal, but maybe I could—

"No, Isla, they didn't." He cleared his throat. "They burned her. Yesterday. Near this very valley, actually. They made a big deal about it, because of her... disability. They said it was a sign from their deities that she was the devil's work, unfit to walk this earth." He put his hand back on my shoulder, pulling me in for a comforting hug. I pressed my eyes shut against the furious tears welling up. "I know it's hard, sweetheart."

"Those monsters," I spat, shaking uncontrollably in my father's steadying embrace.

"We'll make them pay," he murmured into my hair, rubbing my back.

I gritted my teeth, unable to control the way my lips curled into a snarl as I buried my head into his chest.

"We'll make them all pay," I agreed, pulling away from my father to face the unconscious forms of the scattered Nillaesce and Coranti soldiers. The Coranti, who forced her into this fight—her and my father both. And the Nillaesce, who killed her in the end.

"We'll make them pay," I repeated, standing on the ledge with my father beside me. I raised my arm, and he seemed to understand. I reached out with my magic, easily grabbing onto the Drained dregs of Life Energy left in the soldiers below.

I only hesitated for a second, the sudden wind whipping strands of filthy, blood-caked hair into my eyes.

Was this the right thing to do?

Was this what Minnie would have wanted?

I gritted my teeth. Of course, it wasn't what Minnie would have wanted, but Minnie was gone now, and it was all their fault.

*I will avenge her.*

My voice cracked slightly as I whispered one final time, my voice almost lost in the wind, "We'll make them pay."

And with my father's help, I pulled.

I pulled until there was nothing left.

"Starting here."

# EPILOGUE

*"The Second Massacre of Split Peak has taken the world by storm. Far more chilling and mysterious than the original, without a doubt. And with no known survivors of the battle, no one can quite be sure what happened that day."*

—*Darkheart's Largest Mass Killing Yet—And He Didn't Just Kill Witches This Time, an article by Liltan journalist Becky Starr.*

•• ———————— ••●•• ———————— ••

Nicholas Byrne's boots thumped dully on the stone floor. He wished the floors were tiled, and the acoustics were better, so his steps would sound more ominous. Shouldn't the entrance of the most powerful man—no, even the most powerful *person*—in the world be preceded by the noise of his boots? He'd designed and made these shoes himself, with a slight platform to make him taller and heavy, spiked metal soles to grip the mountainside and sound impressive when he walked.

But the walls and floors of the Nillaesce war prison nearest his stronghold had the audacity to swallow the sound of his boots.

"Mr. D-darkheart, sir," stuttered a young guard, barely able to stand he was shaking so hard. He was blocking Byrne's path. Byrne had gotten used to the way the Nillaesce spoke, even begun to emulate it, but he still missed the familiar sound of a Corantian accent. Maybe with his daughter around, he'd hear it more. The thought brought a brief smile to his face, which immediately fell when the guard spoke again. "Sir, my, my commanding officer said t-that our alliance has, uh, it has f-fallen through?"

Byrne shook his head at the lack of taste these spineless Nillaesce officers had, who sent guards barely old enough to grow facial hair to kick the most dangerous person in the world out of their prison? The world would really be better off once he was in charge—the Nillaesce would be the next to go after the witches. It was an honorable goal, he consoled himself. And if his sweet, kind Isla could see the end too, didn't that justify the means? They would end this war. They would crush both sides and come out on top.

And Nicholas Byrne? He would be more than the most powerful person in the world.

He would be a god.

With an annoyed sigh, he swept aside the young guard with little more than a tug on his energy and a push of his boot.

He didn't like using force, not when he didn't have to. He'd never had the same bloodlust as Anna. No, Byrne was a more pragmatic sort. He wanted the power. And he'd get the power. Whether he had to lie, cheat, scheme, or blackmail to get it, he would get what he wanted. Even if he had to occasionally use force, to fill the bloody footprints Anna had left him.

Byrne shoved the next guard who stood in his way into the wall, lifting them off the ground a few inches with a burst of energy from his stores, newly replenished from yesterday's events at Split Peak. The place he'd nearly died, and the place he'd made his debut as the new Darkheart.

"I'm looking for someone," he growled, using the most menacing voice he could. Anna had mocked him for his high-pitched voice when they were younger, and he'd responded by pitching it as low as he could until she was laughing uncontrollably at how ridiculous he sounded.

But Anna was gone. It was harder, he supposed, because it felt like she was with him always. Maybe if he could forget her, forget how much he'd loved her, it would all make sense. It was some menial comfort, in a way, that Isla didn't look much like her at all. She had his light brown hair, his grey eyes, though a bit lighter, and she even spoke a bit like him. But every now and then, he'd catch a glance of her smile out of the corner of his eye and see not Isla, but short black hair, mesmerizing blue eyes, and a smile that could sell hell to an angel.

But Anna was gone.

He was Darkheart now.

And he loved it.

He'd loved the theatre, once, before he'd started making shoes— it had been a passing hobby, not a true passion. But he'd loved it all the same, until he'd loved Anna, until he'd loved his cobbling, until he'd loved his daughter. And he'd been content for a bit after Anna was gone. When the power had lain dormant. When it was just him and Isla, like a glimpse at a happy family life he'd never had before.

"Wh-who?" stuttered out the guard, no more eloquent under pressure than the scrawny kid he'd first encountered. "Who are you looking for, sir?"

"The one-armed witch," he replied, loosening his grip on the guard slightly. "The one scheduled to be executed tomorrow."

The guard's eyes widened slightly in recognition, and Byrne lowered him back down to the ground.

"Excuse my asking, sir, but what do you need with the *nornei*?" the guard ventured, straightening his uniform.

"Does it matter?" asked Byrne, knowing his reputation alone was enough to make the guard cave in.

The guard hesitated, torn between the right answer and the answer that would let him live a few minutes longer. "N-no, sir, I suppose it doesn't."

The guard led Byrne down several winding staircases and through poorly lit, quickly constructed tunnels. In the corner of his brain, Byrne wondered if this was a trap. But, of course, with the sort of power he had, it wouldn't be too hard to escape.

"We aren't quite sure what sort of *nornei* it is, sir, so no one is particularly eager to go near it," the guard explained, voice unconsciously lower, when they stood before a single, isolated cell door. Unlike several others they'd passed throughout the prison, there were no screams, moans, or pleas wailing from this cell. No one banged on the door, no one rattled their chains, no one let out choked sobs.

Just silence.

It occurred to Byrne that maybe the witch was dead. That would be annoying, if he'd gone through all this fuss after his inconvenient split with the Nillaesce, doubtlessly spreading rumors all throughout the Nillaesce ranks, and the witch was dead.

"You aren't sure what type of magic the witch has?" Darkheart asked, one eyebrow raised. "You mean to say, you aren't sure if she's a witch at all?"

The guard looked confused. "Well, it hasn't exactly done any magic that we've seen, sir, but would you look at that arm? Of course, it's a *nornei*. The priests took one look and said as much."

"She could be an amputee," argued Byrne, though he knew it wouldn't matter. These Nillaesce were all a bunch of brainwashed religious freaks, and it was so unimaginably… boring. He was glad to have his daughter back. Glad to get to know her again. A flash of grief flashed through him—not the familiar, bittersweet grief that surfaced every time something reminded him of Anna, but the heartbreaking loss of the years he'd spent away from Isla. A part of him regretted the situation, but seeing Isla alive and well had been like a divine eraser for his guilt. It would be worth it, in time. When they fixed this broken corner of the world, together.

"The Holy Ones wouldn't inflict such a demonic marking on an *Eirhenn*," replied the guard with such innocent confidence that Byrne almost pitied him.

Almost.

His lip twisted in disgust. Anna had hated unnecessary death with a passion and would only kill a confirmed witch. It was a waste, to end a life with no corresponding magic transferal. What had happened yesterday, with Isla… That was an exception. It was just a bit too far. He promised himself, then, that he wouldn't let another massacre like that happen. Isla had been grieving. He understood, of course he did, but it had really been out of hand. Maybe, just the slightest bit, he felt guilty for the part he'd played.

Maybe.

Byrne let out a long-suffering sigh. "Alright, open the door."

The guard hesitated, and Byrne leveled his most intimidating look on the man, though even with his boots he was still a bit shorter than the guard.

"Open the door," he repeated, voice dangerous, "and I might let you live."

With an audible gulp, the guard fumbled through his keyring with shaking fingers, removing a small black key, which Byrne immediately plucked from his grasp. He left the guard with one last sugar-sweet smile before he pulled just enough energy to send the guard into unconsciousness. Byrne grinned at the familiar rush of power in his veins. That feeling never got old.

"Thank you," he said, giving the fallen guard a mocking salute before turning to the cell door and fitting the key in the lock. It was time to get his leverage.

He hadn't seen his daughter in a long time, after all, and it was clear she still harbored some resentment towards him for that.

It simply wouldn't do to have someone so important to her, someone capable of unleashing such powerful grief, to burn on a Nillaesce stake.

He'd much rather have such a powerful bargaining chip in his possession.

"Jonsson," crackled the radio at the guard's hip, the words hard for Byrne to make out through the heavy Nillaesce accent. "Jonsson? Why are you not at your post? Jonsson, report. Jonsson, where are you?"

Byrne sighed.

Well, that was inconvenient.

He wrenched open the cell door with a god-awful screech, surveying the small yet pungent room within. At first glance, he thought it was empty, but as his eyes adjusted, he took in the form before him. Only her back was visible as she hung askew from the ceiling, limp curls of dark hair swaying as she pulled herself higher, lowered herself, and pulled up again.

She must have known he was here, unless she was deaf or extremely stupid.

But she didn't stop, grunting as she finished yet another successful pull-up.

One-armed.

From a broken pipe in the ceiling.

"Stop." He didn't have time for this.

The girl froze, mid-pull, at the sound of his voice. For a second Byrne wondered if she could recognize his voice, and from what? Had he met her before? Then, of course, he realized. It was his accent. She was wondering what a Corantian was doing in her cell, across the border, in Nillaesce territory. Perhaps, she was hoping he was here to save her.

The one-armed witch dropped from the ceiling with a hiss of pain, and he wondered how she'd even managed to get up there in the first place. But, he supposed, it was like his mother always said. *Idiocy finds a way.*

Her face was a bloody mess, streaked with dirt, traced in jagged cuts caked with dried blood, and shining with sweat from her exercise. She heavily favored her right side, wincing around the blood-soaked patch in her formerly white shirt. It was a miracle she was walking at all, let alone doing one-armed pull-ups.

Feeling a headache forming, Byrne rubbed the spot between his eyes as he turned away from the cell, stepping gingerly over the guard. He knew she would follow. Whether through hope, curiosity, idiocy, or all three, she would follow.

"Follow me, one-armed witch. We're leaving."

# THE END

G. N. Solomon

Made in the USA
Middletown, DE
23 September 2021